"I have taken care of her," Martha said in her defense.

"And very well, I might add."

"What did Remy think was so strange?" Martha asked.

"Why don't you ask her?" Zelda replied. Picking up her clothes from the kitchen floor, she walked out naked, with a sassy swing to her hips.

"Slut," Martha murmured to herself under her breath, though she had every intention of giving in to the woman's wish to be tied. Perhaps she'd just leave her bound to a post in the basement, naked, with the rats running around her feet. The thought was perfectly divine, though she should be ashamed of herself for having such wicked thoughts. There was too much wickedness about, too much. That's probably what made for the whole murderous mess.

Also by ELIZABETH OLIVER:

Pagan Dreams

THE SM MURDER:
MURDER AT ROMAN HILL

ELIZABETH OLIVER

ROSEBUD

The SM Murder
Copyright © 1995 by Elizabeth Oliver
All Rights Reserved

No part of this book may be reproduced, stored in a retrieval system, or transmitted in any form, by any means, including mechanical, electronic, photocopying, recording or otherwise, without prior written permission of the publishers.

First Rosebud Edition 1995

First Printing December 1995

ISBN 1-56333-353-8

Cover Photograph © 1995 by Trevor Watson

Cover Design by Dayna Navaro

Manufactured in the United States of America
Published by Masquerade Books, Inc.
801 Second Avenue
New York, N.Y. 10017

CHAPTER ONE

Leslie ran her hand along Rosalie's thigh, moving it in between her lover's legs to where she was soft and very wet. Rosalie moved against Leslie's hand, her body rising and falling to the crescendo of her inner drummer beating.

"More, love, fuck me hard," Rosalie gasped in a husky voice. Leslie's hand slapped each pulsing thigh to part them wide. She wanted the interior, right in the middle where the purple-pink cunt throbbed. One finger after another slipped inside as Leslie's mouth came down to cover Rosalie's clit and suck.

"That's right, little bitch," Leslie said, pausing for a moment to egg her on. She slapped Rosalie's thighs between laps at the growing pool of juice in her hand.

She watched the broad rear buck, her full breasts bouncing against her chest. Leslie squeezed one of Rosalie's nipples and listened for the sound of feigned protest to follow. She let the nipple go to see it remain a tight bud, a fine little knot she'd soon bite one more time, until it really hurt. She wanted to hear Rosalie's gasp of pain.

"Do me harder!" Rosalie cried. The sweating girl squeezed her cunt against Leslie's hand. Squeezed hard, and then released, her whole torso relaxing, only to tighten one more time. She did a strange orgasmic shimmy while she spouted some Spanish words that Leslie didn't understand, and then she collapsed in the bed's soft cotton sheets. A hot afternoon sun bathed them both, and their sweat made the two women cling to each other in a sticky soft pool of sensation.

"*Ah, si*, I'm in love," Rosalie murmured.

"*Ah, si*, my love, in love with your body," Leslie replied, as she drifted into her own world lying back in the pile of rumpled sheets. She was thinking of Rosalie, but she was also thinking of other lovers, the ones that weren't available to her now.

"Why not be in love with my body?" Rosalie answered, smiling broadly. She moved around to recline on her side and stroke Leslie's naked belly. She ran her long red nails down the surface of her partner's skin, making red lines.

With her bright sunshine face, Rosalie had claimed nearly three months of Leslie's time. It was much more than she thought she'd give the sweet, honey-brown girl. Then again, Rosalie was hardly a girl, somewhere between twenty-five and thirty, though her Latin form, long black hair, and wide black eyes made her look so innocent—as if she were still a child. But Rosalie wasn't sweet at all. She was a fucking hellion in bed, and she did what she damned well pleased—which was okay with Leslie, since she had never wanted anything permanent with this woman.

Rosalie was convenient, however. She gave Leslie a good excuse to stay home at night, avoid bars and prickly intimate moments with women she really didn't want to go to bed with. She could enjoy Rosalie's voracious appetite for sex, and her delicious body. Even the Spanish the woman sprinkled into their lovemaking had an exotic quality that Leslie relished. They were two grown, freethinking women who had come together because it was easy and fun and without strings or regrets.

The phone jangled noisily and Leslie reached out to answer it, knocking the whole thing onto the floor.

"Leslie, Leslie!" She heard a man's anxious voice on the other end.

"Yeah, Yeah, I'm here," she answered, sitting up as she pulled the phone back up from the floor by its cord.

"I tried to find you at the office, but you weren't there. What are you doing in bed at this hour?" he asked.

Leslie recognized John Longcore's voice. There was that unmistakable soft, low pitch he must have developed as a teacher. She feared it was likely monotonous to listen to for any length of time, poor students.

"What do you usually do in bed at three in the afternoon?" Leslie replied. "I'm certainly not sick."

"Good, then you'll be able to help me right way."

"Is it better than making love?" Leslie asked.

"Of course not, but it's an emergency."

"What's up?" Leslie asked, trying to sound interested, though at the moment the idea of going to work wasn't greeted favorably by either body or mind.

"It's Betsy," John said, as if that should explain it all. He sounded worried.

"Yeah?" Leslie recalled John's brunette sister with a good deal of regret. She was about the only woman she knew who hadn't slept with Betsy Longcore. The luscious little thing looked as innocent as a child—like Rosalie, she supposed, without the Spanish—but she had a reputation for sucking pussy that reached all around the city.

"She's been arrested," John said, with voice cracking.

"What!"

"Felicia Roman was murdered yesterday, or this morning or something."

"Betsy killed Felicia?" Leslie gasped, astonished. She always thought it would be the other way around. The rude Felicia was a holy terror.

"No, damn it, no!" John started to shout.

"Hey, calm down," Leslie said, realizing that her good friend was about to come unglued.

"The police think they have enough circumstantial evidence to charge her. She's been in custody since early this morning."

"And you'd like me to investigate?"

"Yes." She could sense the tears she couldn't see in John's soft blue eyes. He had a perpetual sadness about him, which was likely all the worse now. "I don't know what to do, but I know she didn't do it," John assured her.

"Have you seen her?"

"She called from the jail—they took her in right away. I got her a lawyer. But I think this calls for more than just a good defense. There are a bunch of women living up on the Hill, any one of whom could have killed Felicia. Betsy says she's innocent, and I believe her."

Lots of people are innocent, Leslie thought to herself. "I'll look into this, see what I can do John. You just stay calm."

"You know I can't." His voice was practically cracking.

"Yeah, I know. Maybe have a stiff drink," she said sympathetically, as she hung up the phone.

She knew John Longcore from the marches a few years back. He was a sweet gay man with lots of charm, but not much backbone in a crisis. And damn it, what a crisis. Felicia Roman murdered—that wasn't as hard to believe as the idea that the woman was gone, dead. Leslie hadn't even bothered to ask how it happened. Likely it was very messy—Felicia would fight like a tiger. Who would have the guts, the audacity to do it? My god, Leslie figured anyone that murdered Felicia would likely be haunted into eternity by the woman's ghost.

And Betsy Longcore, she mused to herself. Sweet, generous little hussy that she was, did she have it in her?

"What's wrong?" Rosalie asked, dropping her arm around Leslie's shoulder. She felt so seductively warm Leslie would have liked to have fallen back into bed with her.

"Gotta go, murder in the wind," she said.

"Oh, not again!" Rosalie said despondently. Leslie had just finished a murder case.

"It's the job, hon," Leslie answered.

"You be careful. I don't need my lover murdered," Rosalie said, concerned. She wasn't used to Leslie's PI job, and for that matter, Leslie had never gotten used to murder.

"Don't worry, Rosa, the murdering is done, and the body's cold in the morgue," Leslie reminded her.

"Maybe so, but what's to prevent the murderer from striking again?" She was hot already and ready to argue.

"You're letting TV miniseries get to you, Rosalie," Leslie replied dryly. "Besides I don't die—that's not in my plans, at least not at a murder scene."

Leslie pulled herself off the bed and searched the floor for her clothes which had been ripped from her by her pawing lover much earlier. There were just jeans and a denim shirt left. Her underwear had been ripped in the foray—a nice touch that always excited her because it meant that Rosalie was so smitten that she couldn't help herself. Buttoning her shirt, she stopped halfway so her cleavage showed. "You approve?" Leslie asked. Rosalie liked the show of flesh, being a flagrant exhibitionist herself.

"Yeah, you push them at me much more, I'll ruin your shirt, too," she replied, with a sweet, seductive smile.

Leslie smiled back. "Maybe you should worry. I might attract another woman," she teased.

"Then let her join us," Rosalie said, her eyes lit up like a Spanish dancer's.

"By the way, where are *you* going?" Leslie asked her lover. "Didn't you have some meeting scheduled?"

"New York. I have to nurse this client through the

next few days. I've got some commercials lined up, should be a breeze, but old Helen needs to have me there." She looked sweet, pouty, and downcast, all just to make Leslie feel better.

Leslie nodded, thinking it was probably not a bad thing that her lover was leaving for a few days. She could spare Rosalie all the gory details, and spare herself Rosalie's unnecessary concern. "You gonna be screwing around?" Leslie asked her. "I want to know how much latitude I have while you're gone. Isn't Helen a *special* friend?"

"Ah, I don't know what she'll want to do. But you know me. Have fun, I always say," Rosalie replied with a lusty grin.

That meant Rosalie would be having the time of her life with someone, if not Helen, in New York. Leslie breathed deeply, thinking it was satisfactory enough. No strings, no obligations. She turned to watch Rosalie's nicely rounded backside disappear into the bathroom. Then, picking up the phone, she dialed her partner Robin Penny.

"Hey, where you been?" Robin blurted out when she heard Leslie's voice. "I can't run this damned business by myself, or have you decided being a private eye just isn't exciting enough for you, you have to find your little tramps to fuck with?..."

"What are you so pissed about?" Leslie charged back.

"I've been sitting here in this hot, stuffy office all day, while you're taking the day off. You know how monotonous it is going over books while this ceiling fan drones on all day. God! Have I got a headache. If I weren't on the first floor, I'd just jump out the window and end it all."

"Hey that could look kinda cute, you offing yourself that way and screwing it up," Leslie suggested, trying to lighten her frustrated former lover and business partner's mood.

"Sorta typical for me, screwing up? Is that what you're saying?" Robin replied sarcastically.

"I never said that. I can't do this work without you, you know that," Leslie said.

"Just don't go leaving me on a day like this and with the books in such a mess. You should be whipped for leaving the accounts like this."

"Listen, don't you go complaining about all your hard labor. You weren't in the office all day," Leslie charged. "I got a call, said no one answered the office number."

"I have to eat sometime," Robin replied, still obviously irritated with her partner.

It was clear there was little Leslie was going to say to appease her. "Well, not to change the subject and disturb your snit, but we've got a new case."

"Well, that's refreshing," Robin said. "What's up?"

"Felicia Roman is dead." Boy, did that sound crass coming out so quickly, Leslie realized, but she didn't know how else to break the news.

"What?"

"Felicia was murdered."

"My god, when?"

"Last night, yesterday, I guess." Leslie could imagine the blood draining from Robin's already pale face. She suspected tears were forming in her partner's blue eyes.

"How?"

"Don't know all the details. John Longcore called. They've arrested Betsy, and he's a basket case. He needs us to snoop around and see what really happened. You want to meet me at police headquarters in, say, a half hour?"

"Yeah, sure," Robin replied, without an ounce of enthusiasm. Murder was never her favorite kind of work, and this one was likely to affect her more than usual.

"You going to be okay?" Leslie asked.

"Felicia's dead—that's pretty strange, huh?" Robin said softly.

"That's what I thought," Leslie agreed. "Say, why don't I do the preliminaries at police headquarters, and we'll get together later and discuss it?"

"No, I'll go. I have to," Robin replied.

Leslie knew the first hot-fired emotions in Robin would be subsiding now, as the sensuous blonde stuffed another loss into her heart and became the model detective. Robin had been Felicia's lover ten years ago, and it shouldn't affect her now, but Robin would still feel the loss very dearly, even if the feelings didn't show on the outside.

Robin was efficient, responsible, and steady, even though she really had the temperament to break down at the drop of a hat. Leslie feared that her partner just might lose it this time. She often thought that the detective business was too rough for the woman. Yet Robin had always loved the puzzle of investigations, putting disparate pieces together in her own curious way. She had the knack for coming up with the right answers, using some mysterious intuitive process that Leslie didn't understand. This case would shake her more than normal—Leslie almost wished she hadn't called her, but then Robin would have been very upset when she found out.

CHAPTER TWO

"Can you tell us what you have on Betsy Longcore?" Leslie asked, politely addressing the rotund detective behind the metal desk. She and Robin felt as if they had been shoehorned into the cramped office where there was hardly a breath of air to be had. Robin coughed while she and her partner tried to see through the cloud of smoke surrounding them. The blustery detective was exactly the kind of man that they abhorred—reason enough to enjoy the company of women.

"A knife, Betsy Longcore's knife, complete with her fingerprints. She and the Roman lady were into this bondage stuff. Figure she got a little too into it and she stabbed her. There are enough reported arguments between the two to suggest a decent motive."

"Betsy found the body?"

"Betsy Longcore killed her. She had the knife in her hand. Didn't let go of it until the police came on the scene and took it from her."

"There're a lot of explanations for the knife," Leslie charged.

"Yeah, and one good one—she murdered the dyke."

Leslie sighed "Is that all you have?"

"Aw, ladies, there's a whole lot more," he said, leaning back in his chair and blowing more smoke in their faces. "We got pictures of Felicia Roman with all sorts of women. Real, what do you call it, 'dom.'" He just had to snicker as he said it. "Your Betsy Longcore was jealous. Had every reason to be. The way I see it, she'd had enough of her lover lady running around on her. Plus, she was in the house all night, she admits that. With everything else we have, we don't need a whole lot more. We got some bags of evidence to comb through, but I don't think it's gonna change a thing." The detective ground his jaw against the cigar, a little spittle running from the corner of his mouth.

Leslie waved the cloud of smoke out of her face, then tried to catch a fresh breath. "There were three other women in the house that night, too. Have you considered them?" Leslie asked.

"Let's see," the detective looked at his reports. "There were three, yeah, all living in that fleabag of an old house. There's this Martha Quigley, Remy...ah something or other, real long name, and some chick, Zelda, from New Orleans. They tell me they were playing their own parlor games that night, and that they were all fast asleep in their bedrooms at the time of the murder."

"You assume they're not lying?" Leslie said in disbelief.

"We're considering their stories, Ms. Patrick. But you can leave that for us to sift through."

"It seems to me that you really have a lot of possibilities that you're not seriously considering. How about Jane Hugh?" Leslie asked.

"Yeah, I got something on her too. She was in a lesbo bar with a bunch of dyke friends of hers. Her story checks out." The detective looked up at them with a case-closed attitude and a silly smirk. "You two play their games?" he asked, motioning to Robin and Leslie with a perverse, insinuating gleam in his eye.

Leslie had to bite her tongue.

"You're out of order, Detective," Robin said, with a degree of purpose that Leslie rarely saw from her partner.

There didn't seem to be much point in continuing the conversation. There was obviously plenty of evidence to indict Betsy, but there were also enough loose ends to tie knots all around Roman Hill Estate.

"How about some dinner?" Leslie asked, when she and Robin were out on the street again, breathing the fresh air.

"I don't know whether I want to eat after that," Robin answered.

"I know what you mean," Leslie replied. "But I'm still famished. A little food might settle me down."

They found a small diner near the station and sat down opposite each other in a booth, both ordering soup and crackers.

"My stomach is doing flip-flops," Robin said, staring into Leslie's green eyes. "Pictures were pretty horrible. Not a lot of blood, just that small wound." Her voice trailed off.

"You had trouble looking at them, didn't you?" Leslie said. "You didn't have to, you know."

"It was okay. They didn't really look like her. Her face especially, twisted so strangely. By the way, did you notice the knots on those bindings?" Robin added, suddenly having gathered her senses and returning to business.

"Sort of. Why?" Leslie replied.

"Tied by an expert; they were all the same," Robin said. "I don't think Betsy could have done it. She's not a top—never has been, that I can tell."

"Someone else could have done the ropes," Leslie suggested.

"An accomplice, yes, but it doesn't feel like that." There was a faraway look in Robin's eye, as if she'd gone someplace else in her mind, just to find the answers.

"Suppose we ought to go to Roman Hill tomorrow," Leslie suggested.

Robin nodded. "Those women up there are holding back, if that's all they told the police. Little enclave they have there, they're probably all trying to protect each other. I mean they all might have wanted Felicia dead."

Leslie smiled. "That could very well be. I think we need to look at motives here. It would appear, except for Jane, that they all had opportunity."

"No airtight alibis," Robin agreed. "But then again, I'm afraid that every woman who has ever known Felicia would have some kind of motive for murder."

"You too?"

"God, yes, cantankerous hellion that she was. Until

I decided that she was certifiably crazy, I wanted to ring her neck a dozen times."

Leslie tried not to laugh, though she was glad to see Robin lighten, even if it was just a little. She would love to have had her in bed that night, just to hold her again. Unfortunately, she couldn't think of a way to get her there. The rule about their platonic business relationship was firm from Leslie's, as well as Robin's, point of view, and had been for several years. Though this was one day that Leslie wished she could break it.

"Suppose we meet at the Hill, ten o'clock?" Leslie suggested.

"Sounds good. I need a long night's sleep," Robin replied.

"You get one. You do look awfully tired."

After the soup, crackers, a little more stilted talk, and a tender good-bye, Robin watched Leslie walk toward her truck. Her brunette friend then stopped to look back at her, until Robin was at her own car and getting in. That little protective gesture was rather sweet, Robin thought. But then that was Leslie's way, even if Robin hated the idea that her partner thought she needed protection right now.

After watching Leslie drive away, Robin drove uptown, to a seedier side of the city where there were dank apartments, empty office buildings, and a smattering of light industrial factories on their last legs. There were papers fluttering in the streets, turned-over trash cans, and an eerie, lonesome feeling about this part of town; even drug dealers and hookers steered clear, simply because there was no one with money to buy what they offered. A few sad people wandered about, on their way from one lonely moment of their lives to another, somewhere in one of the squalid flats above ground level.

The little flat that Robin sought was up three flights of stairs, and taking those stairs was like walking into another world, away from the menial world on the street and far away from the life that she led most of the time. Robin saw from the street that the light was on—Britta was home. She breathed a sigh of relief and began the long trek.

Robin's knock on the door produced a vague reply, which was enough encouragement to walk on in, even though she wasn't quite sure what the woman had said. It didn't really matter—Robin would go in regardless. Inside, she looked around the expansive apartment searching for what she wanted. She was prickly all over, heat rushing into her thighs the moment she smelled the incense burning. It was a conditioned response after so many times in Britta's den.

"You look like shit," the woman said from the fog of smoke around her.

Robin looked up to see the object of her search reclining on a daybed in one corner of the room. "You'll take me tonight, please?" Robin asked cautiously.

The woman stared at her, as if she were reading a page from the book Robin wrote inside her heart.

"Of course, my little Robbie," she answered, noting Robin's thinly disguised distress. "You need it especially hard tonight, perhaps?"

Robin nodded. The incense was so thick it was beginning to burn her nostrils. She breathed it deeply, thinking there was a trace of cigarette smoke in the vapors, along with the scent of some mystical Eastern herbal concoction. She breathed deeply again, letting the smoke soothe her into the other side of her life. The heat between her legs burned hotter yet.

"You should have called first, but I'll take you. You can sit on the stool," Britta said.

Robin spied the familiar piece resting innocently between her and the woman on the bed. It was a little round thing, the needlepoint cushion on top the only comfortable part of it. Barely a foot off the ground, when Robin sat down on it, her legs were above her bottom, and naturally spread wide apart. Of course this was part of Britta's design. The position was submissive.

Sitting on it now, though, in jeans and not a revealing skirt—or nothing at all—didn't have quite the same effect. Her cunt would be spread out and exposed if she was dressed properly for a meeting with Britta.

"Working?" Britta asked, seeing the way Robin was attired.

"Yes."

"Too much for you?"

"I just need to forget everything for awhile. An old friend of mine's dead."

The dom almost broke out in a tender smile, but like so many things with her, it was too subtle to know if it really was there. The woman remained reclined on her couch, looking like some queen bee. Her strawberry-blonde hair, piled on top of her head, was half falling down, as if it were time for bed and it didn't matter how it looked anymore. Still, her lips were red like a musty old brick, and she gave off an ancient scent even though she wasn't very old. She could be haughty or kind, depending on the need. The look she flashed now was disgust.

"You'll take off your clothes and find something I'd like to see you wear," she said, waving Robin to a corner of the room where a massive wardrobe stood with its doors open and garments spilling out around the floor.

Robin rose, walked to the wardrobe, and disrobed. There was just her blouse, bra, jeans, and panties to shed, and of course her shoes and socks. Naked, she felt a chill in the air that gave her goose bumps. A slender woman with gentle curves, Robin's best assets were her shapely legs, and her perky breasts that, though not large, stood out full and round with large nipples. They were frequently so hard that they poked shamelessly through almost any garment. Robin knew Britta would admire her, even though the dom wouldn't say a word about her lust. But Robin liked pleasing the mistress this way.

Reaching inside the mass of clothes, she pulled out a red leather bustier, thinking Britta would be pleased. She let the mistress see what she'd chosen, her eyes submissively lowered while she waited for the woman to respond.

"That'll be enough," Britta said as she watched, her eyes intently focused on every move Robin made.

In front of the mirror, Robin pulled the two sides of the bustier around her middle so that they nearly met; then she laced them as tightly as she could, feeling a swell inside her loins as the self-imposed bondage began to play with her mind.

"Pull it tighter, Robbie, will you?" the woman said.

Robin tugged harder, pulling at her breasts so that they were pushed up to the top, having nowhere else to go. Her nipples sat just over the edge of the leather. Below, the bustier stopped just past her waist. The soft swell of her hips and her triangle cunt radiated an aura of the erotic need rumbling through her.

"You can sit now," she was instructed.

"You will have my ass, won't you?" Robin asked anxiously, as she returned to the needlepoint submissive's stool.

"I'll have what I want," Britta answered. "And then maybe I'll give you what you need. You are unscheduled tonight. You know how intrusions piss me off."

On the stool again, with her legs spread wide, Robin's cunt was the way the mistress wanted it—unprotected. Her labia were naturally parted so that Britta could see the deep purple folds of skin and the dark cunthole. The wisps of blonde hair around the pretty spread-out pussy glistened with wet female dew.

"Put your arms behind you," the mistress said. "Wrists together."

Rising from the lounge, Britta gathered her cuffs and rope from a shelf beside her. She was a large, firm woman, her massive breasts swinging loosely in front of her as her hips swayed and her cunt moved before Robin's watchful gaze. She could see the dark cunt through the filmy purple caftan Britta wore. She had dark, thick pussy curls which Robin might end up feasting on as she had before, that massive cunt pressed in her face for her mouth to service. It would please her if she did it again this night, though she hoped that other things, things that she had come for and needed most, would prevail first.

The mistress jerked Robin's arms, holding them tightly together as she clamped the cuffs on her wrists and bound her arms together with ropes. Robin sat on the needlepoint stool with thrust-out breasts, her flesh softly jiggling above the corset. The awkward position hurt, but it was a good hurt because it served its intended purpose—to make the submissive mindful of her position in the scheme of things inside this flat.

"This is for me," Britta said, taking a crop from the wall. The long black riding crop ended with a loose leather tip of thin tied leather cords. Britta used the crop to whack at Robins tits with at least a dozen fierce cuts. It was horrid, and Robin was instantly near tears. She said nothing, but a bit of a groan escaped her lips, which was more than Britta wanted. She always demanded quiet, just the sounds of leather and skin during correction—at least at the beginning. Sound when the session ended didn't matter that much.

"Don't make me gag you, little Robbie," the mistress purred. "I want to hear the leather when it hits your tits." She ran the crop along the red lines that had appeared where the skin was once flawless, digging the thing into the other woman's breasts so that she winced. They were marked enough to last for a few days. The poking and prodding hurt as much as the striking. She struck them each one more time, and Robin didn't utter a sound, though she again winced with pain.

Putting the crop under her arm, the mistress bent down and took each exposed nipple and rolled it between her thumb and index fingers, squeezing it hard, and using her fingernails to pierce the flesh. Robin finally squealed when the pain was too much to bear in silence. Britta let them go, and the throbbing sensation that followed was as acute as the squeezing. The submissive breathed a heavy sigh of relief.

"You're feeling like a poor, pitiful baby tonight, aren't you, little one?" Britta purred. "Stand up." She stepped back to watch her submissive struggle to rise. It was almost impossible for Robin to stand from a crouch with her arms and hands bound as they were. When she was finally on her feet, Britta shoved her toward an apparatus at the far end of the room; a waist-high beam covered in leather with a half-dozen places at the bottom and down the sides to fasten a submissive to the structure.

"Bend over," the mistress said, poking Robin with the riding crop. Britta secured her, bottoms up, her rear cleft exposed. Robin couldn't move for fear of falling if she did. She wished the mistress would untie her arms, but she would never protest or suggest.

Britta used the same crop she'd used on her tits, initially flailing her with a dozen strokes and then a dozen more. Robin's bottom began to burn, and she squirmed as much as she dared. But as much as it hurt, she knew it wasn't enough. She wanted more, and Britta would give it to her.

Britta now chose a heavier implement, with at least two-dozen shreds of eighteen-inch-long leather, bundled together, woven at one end into a handle. This whip could be ruthless or affectionate, but it was always capricious.

"You want this in the worst way, don't you?" Britta said, as she ran the cool leather against her submissive's skin. Robin felt it on her back, along her already red ass and down her thighs. The mistress turned the thing around and pressed the thick stalk against her submissive's pussy as if she were trying to force it inside. It wasn't likely to fit, though the way it moved against her netherlips, it massaged them. Robin was aroused, and her hips began to shift back and forth to maximize the feeling.

Standing back, Britta observed the view critically, thinking Robin was certainly a well-built submissive, with physical assets perfect for her needs. Her bottom was round, the cheeks perfectly shaped; her cunt seemed larger than some, the cleft full so that it beckoned to be punished, just as the other sensuous places of Robin's body cried out to be abused.

Britta landed several blows of her whip of thongs against Robin's back. A dozen there first, and then she lowered her arm to cover the red ass with another dozen.

Robin felt the instrument, soft at first and then biting when it cut into her skin. The feeling went right inside her as a caress might. She wanted to be knocked out of her thoughts, driven to a never-never land on the wings of this leather instrument. If it flailed her for hours, she'd be happy. She was looking for a long, hard session.

In a stream of fire, the whip cascaded at her shoulders again, then found her bottom once more. The mistress made it sing each time, the sounds welcome relief to Robin's ears, just as the piercing pain was welcome to her soul. When the mistress found her rear cleft with some thin thongs, Robin shrieked for just an instant.

After a time, Britta removed the ropes and shackles from Robin's arms and wrists, then retied her hands to the bottom of the wooden structure. It was easier for Robin this way, even though it meant a more brutal chastisement. Mistress Britta wanted Robin's whole back available; and letting loose, she delivered her blows repeatedly, rhythmically, in the tempo of a march, with a beat as steady as feet that keep in measured cadence.

With each blow, Robin was losing a piece of herself, flinging her ego back to its source where she didn't have to think of anything at all. This was the bliss. Nothingness. Pure, sweet fiery pain, then nothingness. Like spiraling down to the bottom of everything with nothing to get in the way of her surrender. Just selflessness remaining, rushing over her like an embracing shroud, protecting her, loving her with its sweet abuse.

When the mistress finished one series of blows and paused, Robin wanted more. She churned her forgotten rear to remind the mistress that she was waiting. Britta started again, and a peak followed, then she paused again. The stops and starts were as rhythmical as the blows. A lovely agony.

When the whip began again, Robin wanted it harder, and the mistress obliged till her subject's backside was red top to bottom, and little lines appeared everywhere that might break the skin, though they did not. Not a drop of blood. She was a very good mistress for prudent whippings.

When Britta stopped, it was as though a clear window shone inside Robin's soul. Her mind was empty. Not a thought or idea or notion captured her brain—just quiet and a cool thereafter.

Pressed against her cunt, Britta's hand massaged her with such gentleness that she was prepared to scream as loudly as she had when the whip had cut into her so viciously at the end. But then the mistress spanked her, alternating tenderness with vicious slaps to tender cuntlips. She drove the end of her whip into Robin's cunt, and the submissive's body climaxed on the second thrust, tightening her muscles around the violating handle, trying to grasp every sensation and hold it forever.

Then it was over. The first thought on returning was that the incense was too thick around her, the smoke too harsh to let her breathe easily. It burned her throat the way hash might, if she inhaled. It didn't soothe her the way it had earlier.

She remained tied for some time while watched by Britta, who liked to see the red fade away and the backside pale again. The mistress knew what marks would remain the next day. There were many small red spots that would take days to fade, that might bruise underneath the skin and leave Robbie thinking of her.

Britta had orgasmed before she'd let Robbie have hers. She'd felt the rush inside her body, in the middle of her last cadence of blows—the ones that were aimed right on the center of Robbie's asscheeks. She'd heard her submissive scream when she laid the whip on hard, and that made her own orgasm begin, letting her feel her private agony in the midst of Robbie's. It came in a wave that passed through her, as psychological as it was physical—Robbie was good for that. Britta liked giving punishment, as the satisfaction was her personal treasure.

This was a good whipping, the mistress thought, as good for Robbie as it was for her. She could almost be glad the little one had interrupted her evening. She could punish her again for not making an appointment ahead of time, but she wouldn't be that nasty. Besides, she was tired.

"So Felicia's dead," Britta said, having heard about it on the news earlier that day.

Robin murmured something the mistress assumed was a yes.

"So sad," she mused. "I once let her be a slave to

me, but she was impossible to train. Sometimes she'd give herself to me so fully, there was no way I could satisfy her need for punishment. I'd have to back away because I couldn't hurt her, not really, no more than I could hurt you. Then sometimes Felicia would bark at me, the little bitch, and her eyes would flash like she had demons coming from them, as if the sky had turned to flames, and then to ash. She'd die on me, act like a baby. I loved her when she was with me, but I could never do anything with her extremes." Britta's voice drifted off. "Can you imagine that, a woman too extreme for me?" The question was rhetorical. The mistress came to her senses and eyed her submissive, still tied to the whipping bar.

"You know, if you came to me more often, Robbie, I could do more for you. You could make a fine full-time servant."

That was something Robin would never do. She heard Britta shuffle around her. Remaining upside down was becoming painful in her thighs, and her head was pounding, the blood racing to it. Robin remained there for perhaps another hour—she wasn't sure of the time. She *was* sure her mistress climaxed again hearing the familiar groans.

Robin shrank back into herself wondering what it would be like to be the woman's slave, twenty-four hours a day, every day. Once when she had had enough of her life, Robin had taken three days off, landing in Britta's den. She was made to bow, then ignored for hours, and then abused, becoming so self-less that she had a hard time returning to her life, as she realized how easy it would be to give herself away to the hard pleasures of servitude. Britta had talked about her staying many times since; but even though she let Robin stay that one time, she wouldn't let her stay now.

The mistress finally undid the bonds on her arms, and, grabbing Robin's hair, pulled her to her feet, which remained spread wide. Now Robin could rest her cunt against the leather-covered bar to keep her balance.

"Put your hands behind your head," Britta ordered.

Robin laced her fingers at the base of her neck and opened her elbows the way the mistress wanted. Her tits had almost completely popped out of the corset. The nipples were rock hard. Robin didn't bother to look down at the white flesh that was still marked with red where the crop had hit her. In a minute there would be more to join the other marks. It was Britta's trademark, something to put up with in order to have the rest of her needed treatment. Actually, Robin didn't mind the marks. The next day she would look in the mirror at them and remember this moment, remember being submissively degraded. It would make her masturbate just thinking of it. She would open her blouse during the day and think of this, knowing that as bad as life was on the other side, these uncommon moments were her private indulgence. She wished she had someone to show these to who would appreciate them. She wanted it to be Leslie, but that would never happen.

Britta took the thin crop again and flailed the fair flesh so that it burned, so that there were as many new cuts as old. Robin cringed with each one, hoping each was the last, though when it wasn't, she welcomed the next with a wince and a tiny screech. The pain that traversed her would tingle down to her cunt, so much that she knew she'd masturbate soon.

There was a final blow and the mistress announced, "You can go now."

Freed, Robin removed the leather bustier and returned it to the wardrobe, neatly hanging it inside while dozens of Britta's things were still strewn about in one wild mess. Taking her own clothes, she then dressed. She felt a comforting tightness in her body: the soreness where the whip had struck ached though her pleasantly. She didn't say a word while she restored the respectability of her clothes. They never talked. By some already established agreement with Britta, Robin was always submissively silent. In truth, she had nothing to say to the woman, actions speaking much louder than words.

It was midnight in the real world.

The street was hazy with fog and an orange light that was uncomfortable to Robin's eyes. But her mind was clear, and her body was at peace. She'd be able to sleep, and then meet Leslie in the morning.

CHAPTER THREE

Robin drove to the Hill as if she were going home. She had to shake that feeling from her that this was a homecoming—it was all too familiar. It was a mystery how could she remember it so well after ten years. But then Felicia's face would often cross her mind, distinct and very clear. That had to be the impression everyone had of Miss Felicia Roman; good or bad, it was always distinct.

The house stood as a monument to Victorian bric-a-brac, turrets, front porches, and dank, musty smells. As she got out of her car, Robin looked up at the tower room, imagining what Felicia had looked like lying dead in her room. It was only appropriate that the woman die there on top of her satin covers between the four posters of her massive antique mahogany bed. Even the bondage wasn't so strange.

Robin could almost smell Felicia still, as if her Tea Rose perfume were making its way down to her on a breeze, beckoning her back inside. The two years she'd spent in this house seemed like they were yesterday, when she was much too young to be playing around with the likes of Felicia Roman. Felicia was younger then, too, though it always seemed as if the woman were ageless, born at a certain plateau of enlightenment, never to go beyond that point, but never to be less than she was, and never to fall into disrepair the way old ladies sometimes do. Thinking back, Robin figured that she must have been well over forty when she died.

Felicia always seemed so fully intelligent and poised on first meeting. She had a way of putting people at ease with her gentle ways, her bright eyes, and her affectionate smile. But after a time, like everyone else that knew her, Robin came to believe that Felicia was either crazy or too complex to be handled with any real understanding.

Though it had been years since Robin had been up the hill, the grounds about the estate looked the same as they'd always looked. Felicia kept it sensuously wild, letting the gardens get overgrown, the vines intertwining erotically. The whole place was one pulsing, breathing organ of vegetation, each plant dependent on the others for survival, a little like the very jungle of Felicia's thoughts, and the intimate jungle of the world that surrounded her. It was a haven away, a lesbian enclave. In the center of a city that had treated her ruthlessly, Felicia triumphed because she spat in the face of the people that mocked her.

The remarkable woman was a capricious charmer with an innocent face; she was a dark-eyed bitch with rope and whip, a 1940s movie queen in platform shoes and satin dress, a dominatrix, a femme fatale, a withering lily, a fairy, a fox, and a monster. She was a natural-born blonde, but it wasn't a pretty blonde, so she changed the color of her hair with the seasons and her mood; she changed her manner of dress as easily, and she changed her heart a dozen times a day.

That she was indescribable made her intriguing and, ultimately, dangerous.

Dead now, how sad, all that charm lost forever. It was an empty, wasted feeling looking at the mansion through the eyes of a survivor. Robin half expected the place to fall into the ground, swallowed up by the earth, taken back by the elements, since what gave it life had vanished.

"You been inside yet?"

Robin turned upon hearing Leslie's voice. She watched her partner approach.

"No, just remembering back." They stared up at the house. It was the kind of place that led the eye to the top, to the turret and steep gabled roof, the widow's walk around one side and all the intricate filigree that decorated it. Part of it was freshly painted, while in other places the paint was peeling from the wood siding. A remarkable structure for a remarkable woman.

"Good memories?" Leslie asked.

"Bittersweet at best," Robin replied.

Leslie gave her a friendly hug, then pulled away, though remaining close enough to keep Robin surrounded by one arm. Leslie thought she had to show some affection, some regard for what her partner must be feeling.

"I'm okay really, much better than last night."

"I thought you were going to have a problem looking at those pictures of her yesterday."

"Well, I managed."

"I suppose it was all a little cleaner murder than it should have been—a very neat killer."

"Got her right where it mattered," Robin agreed.

"Not some crazy person: I'd say they were in control of themselves. Likely not as much passion of the moment as deliberate intent."

"The ropes would tell you that too," Robin offered.

"You know a lot about bondage?" Leslie asked, knowing Robin knew more than she did.

"Some."

"Felicia was really into it."

"It's not so strange," Robin replied. "S&M was one of Felicia's many fetishes."

"Like what else?" Leslie asked.

"Anything really—leather, manacles, rope, enemas, spanking, playing roles."

"Did you ever tie her up?" Leslie asked.

"No. It was the other way around."

"Oh," Leslie replied. She'd known for years that Robin had these inclinations. They'd mulled the whole S&M scene over in great detail at one time; but with Leslie not interested in pursing this kinkier sex, it became one of those touchy relationship issues that they mutually agreed not to discuss.

"I'm not unlike Betsy, if you think about it. That's why I'm so sure she didn't kill her."

"You would never have killed her?"

"Not like that. Submissives work in a different way."

"But wouldn't that be a good way to throw someone off track?"

"I just don't think she has it in her for this kind of murder. Poison maybe, but a knife in the chest? She looks too squeamish to me. And the knots—they were perfect, every one of them the same, as if the assailant had done them a thousand times. A submissive turning dom for a night wouldn't do that, unless she was very calculating. I don't think Betsy could be that calculating, or that thorough."

"Let's hope you're right for her sake," Leslie said. "And John's. He's already called me this morning wanting to know when I'm going to find the real killer and get Betsy out of jail. I didn't have much to tell him. But he's sent a retainer, so at least we're being paid for this one. Unfortunately, he's going to be one of those who thinks that we can ask a few questions and be done with it."

"Why don't we go inside and meet these women?" Robin suggested. "They're a curious bunch but pretty much what you'd expect to have around Felicia."

"Were there lots of women around when you were with Felicia?" Leslie asked.

"Always. She was insatiable. She had to have people to play off of."

"Well, these women were pretty mum with the police. I hope we can find out more than they did."

"We'd better," Robin said dryly. "But then, why would they want to talk once Betsy was arrested? If Betsy didn't kill Felicia, the murderer would be perfectly happy to keep things exactly as they are."

"Maybe there was more than one murderer," Leslie suggested.

"Yes. You'd think the police would have waited a little longer before making their conclusion. It's quite a delicious puzzle."

"Thanks for recuperating your detective mentality," Leslie said, grateful to see Robin's classic cool and eagerness for the investigation return.

"It never goes away, sweetie," Robin said. "Just my pleasant disposition."

The two walked side by side to the mansion, climbing the impressive steps that led to the front porch. The old brick walk was breaking up in places, though it showed signs of being repaired in some spots.

"Quite a place, isn't it?" Leslie exclaimed, admiring the massive posts on either side of the steps.

"Yes it is," a voice replied unexpectedly.

They turned to see a redheaded woman sitting in a Kennedy rocker, with a glass of iced tea in one hand and a cigarette in the other. A soft haze of smoke surrounded her pleasant face.

"You the police again?" she said, peering out of wire-rimmed glasses with thick lenses, between locks of curly hair that fell over her eyes. Her plump body rocked unconsciously in the chair, keeping it going with a little push of her foot now and again.

"We're private detectives," Robin answered.

"Leslie Patrick and Robin Penny," Leslie said by way of introduction.

"Penny and Patrick, or is it Patrick and Penny?" the redhead asked.

"Patrick Penny Investigations," Leslie replied.

The woman nodded and smiled. "I suppose people think you're a man with that name. Aren't they a little surprised by two lesbian women? You are lesbians, aren't you?"

"You're very astute: we don't really advertise that fact," Leslie answered.

"Oh, but we all have a way of knowing," the woman said.

"The name takes people by surprise," Robin said, as if she owed the redhead further explanation. "Since neither one of us is into conventional thinking, we kind of like the idea. Do you mind if we ask you a few questions about Felicia Roman's murder?"

The woman shrank back in her chair for an instant at the mention of Felicia's name. "God, it was horrible, wasn't it?"

"Most certainly," Robin replied.

"Are you Remy or Martha?" Leslie asked.

"Neither. Zelda Wing," she answered. She tucked one foot up under her and continued to rock in the chair. When she leaned forward to put her empty glass on the floor, the two investigators could see down the front of her cotton blouse to a pair of smooth alabaster white breasts. The gesture seemed very deliberate.

Robin noted the pink ribbon at her neck that matched her pink shorts.

"You were here the night of the murder?"

"Sleeping like a baby in the room next to Remy and Martha. I do sleep very soundly. I take a little sleeping pill most nights because I sometimes have trouble drifting off, but when I finally do fall asleep it takes six alarm clocks and lots of sun to wake me. Of course I told the police all that. So why are you asking questions?" She blew smoke from her nostrils and mouth.

"We represent Betsy Longcore."

"Too bad. She's guilty as sin. Anyone here for a minute could see it coming. Ole Felicia changed her affections like her underwear, and she was about to dump Betsy for Martha. Not that Martha was going to jump at the chance. But that's how Felicia works. She gets her hooks in you and you can't get away." Zelda sounded very sure of her facts. "I mean, I feel a little sorry for Betsy. She should have known how the woman operates after two years together, but to kill her? Little extreme, don't you think?"

"You seem to know a lot about Felicia. You are just a guest here, Felicia's guest? Did you know her personally?" Robin asked.

"Know her personally? No. But I've been here long enough. You see things being an observer. But then, I shouldn't have to tell you that in your line of work. I sized up the situation the moment I arrived and met those two. It was a relationship on the rocks. You should have seen the daggers in Betsy's eyes, nasty darts they were. Of course with Felicia wandering all over hell and back trying to keep her cunt satisfied, I wouldn't blame Betsy for being pissed."

"Betsy says she spent the night on the back porch. Can you confirm that?" Leslie asked, interrupting what appeared to be a long, rambling monologue.

"Yeah, I suppose so. She'd slept on the back porch half the time I was here. I'm not sure why. Probably because Felicia was entertaining god knows who in her room and didn't want her there. Then again, I couldn't tell you for sure because, as I said, once I'm sleeping I don't wake up. But you know, that's no alibi anyway. She could have drifted upstairs anytime and run that knife into Felicia's heart. And besides, who else would want to kill Felicia?" Zelda asked innocently.

"That's what we're here to find out," Robin said. "Felicia knew lots of people. And by the way, tell us, what brought you to Roman Hill?"

"I've been visiting Remy and Martha. Martha and I are old friends from college."

"And where was that?" Leslie asked.

"State U., up north," Zelda said, while she nodded in the appropriate direction.

"Are Martha and Remy inside?" Robin asked.

"Yeah, go on in," Zelda told them. Her cigarette had burned down to the filter, and she dropped it to the floor and crushed it with her foot. She reached down to pick up her flip-top pack, showing her breasts again. The two detectives opened the screen and let themselves inside as Zelda lit another cigarette and restored the cloud of smoke around her.

"She's a bit too glib," Robin murmured.

"But that succulent flesh," Leslie whispered.

"You need sex that bad?..." Robin whispered back.

"Only the right kind," Leslie said, letting the thought drop. Yeah, it would be good to have Robin in her arms again, but now was hardly the time to seduce her.

Making their way through the house, Leslie noticed an old smell right off, the way most old houses smell—of dust too deep to find, and furniture polish, and the scent of flowers that lingers long in the air. Leslie was immediately transported back in time to her childhood. The feeling was very strange, especially since she was investigating a murder.

"This place could give me the spooks," she said to Robin.

"Isn't it terrific? I'm just glad I don't live here anymore. Just walking through these rooms, I keep thinking I'll see Felicia swooning around some corner."

With Robin knowing exactly where to go, they

quickly found Martha and Remy in the kitchen, the two immediately looking up at them with surprised faces.

"We're Robin and Leslie, Patrick Penny Investigations. We're looking into Felicia's death for Betsy Longcore's brother."

Remy's eyes were puffy from crying.

"Do you mind if we ask a few questions?" Leslie continued.

"Not at all. I'm Martha," a bustling plump woman replied as she stood at the kitchen counter, efficiently making sandwiches while Remy sat on a stool and watched. "We thought a picnic later today might get us out of this place for a while," she explained herself. "This is a miserable, miserable affair. The shock. Well, you can never tell. You live with people for awhile and don't realize the things they will do." The industrious Martha was a voluptuous woman with a heavy chest and a broad bottom, which she moved with a sensuous grace.

Remy was younger than Martha, with a pretty face and a trim body. Her feet dangled over the edge of the stool, not reaching the floor. Her round face and curly brown hair made her look heavier than she really was. Her eyes would twinkle under other circumstances, though not now. As she leaned against the counter, she ran her hands through her hair and found a lock to twist in her finger. "It was horrible," Remy said, biting her lip like a little child. "I hate blood." She shuddered, raising her shoulders, frightened as if she'd just seen a ghost. Tears welled in her already red eyes.

"Please understand, this is quite stressful for us all," Martha explained. "Felicia was a very prominent woman, highly thought of. Her death is quite a shock, particularly under the circumstances. We've all been thoroughly wounded by this messy business." She shook her head and sighed deeply.

"I'm sure that's true," Leslie agreed thoughtfully.

"And Betsy—well, that almost seems impossible to believe. Poor woman must have had some mental problem, I'd say," Martha continued.

"Did you hear anything suspicious in the house that night?" Leslie asked.

"Well, let's see. Remy and I were in bed together. We are lovers you understand. We went to bed at the normal hour—I guess it was nearly eleven. Then we had some music on. We like to fall asleep with gently soothing melodies. It's very restorative," Martha replied. "However, it was difficult to hear anything but ourselves." She had a habit of smiling quickly between sentences as if to punctuate them.

"I see," Robin replied. "And Zelda? You can account for her whereabouts?"

"We said goodnight to her before we closed the door. She seemed quite tired to me. I think she uses drugs to sleep. But then, at the time of the murder, we were asleep with the music still on," she reminded them.

"Zelda just told us that Felicia had her eyes on you, Martha. That she was changing her affections." Robin went to the heart of the matter to witness her reaction.

The question didn't faze Martha as she methodically spread mayonnaise on six slices of brown bread. She smiled again, that brief reflex. "Felicia set her sights on a new woman all the time. We'd had a few brief moments, but I'm in love with Remy. Felicia knew that and so did Betsy. And so did Remy," she hastened to add, looking at the woman at the other end of the counter. Remy shrugged and nervously grabbed a piece of cheese, which immediately went to her mouth.

"How did you come to live in this house?" Leslie asked.

"We've lived with Felicia for three years, off and on at first. Before Betsy came. Felicia brought her home one night from some party, and she's stayed ever since. Until now, of course. Let me tell you, that girl came here with Felicia showing her off as some little submissive, you know with collar and all, but she certainly hasn't acted very submissive lately."

"How's that?" Robin asked.

"Oh, I'm not into this much, all the SM stuff that Felicia and these other women get so excited about. But Betsy certainly had a mind of her own. Oh, she deferred to Felicia at first, but then she got wise, I suppose. Realized what the woman was—a little crazy we all think," Martha said in hushed tones as if the dead woman might have heard her from her grave. "Betsy acted like Felicia's habits didn't bother her, but I'm not so sure. How can you love someone and have your eyes on so many other women all the time? It's not really natural now, is it?"

"You think that Betsy killed Felicia?" Robin asked.

"That very well may be. That girl's got a nasty dark side. She and Felicia were having some very fiery confrontations recently, and everyone knew that. Betsy seemed determined to change the woman. Everyone should know that a woman like Felicia would never change, never. Crazy and wild from the word go, she went to her death that way, and I don't know a soul who knew Felicia that thought it would be any different. I can't tell you that Betsy killed her, but I'd say she's a pretty good bet.

"But then, you might also want to talk to Jane Hugh. She had one asskicker of a fight with Felicia a few days ago. And the two of them were constantly bitching—neither one of them liked the other and they made no bones about it. For the life of me, I don't know why Felicia put up with the woman. She's so, so…" she couldn't find the right word.

"And tell me, where are you from originally?" Leslie asked.

"Maine, but I've lived in the area for years. I'm the librarian at the university. You can check that out."

"And Remy?" Robin turned to the quiet woman on the stool. She had popped a cherry tomato in her mouth.

"She's from Maine too," Martha answered for her. "She's been working in the lab at the university."

Remy smiled and cocked her head as if to confirm what Martha said. She still looked like she might cry at any minute.

"By the way," Leslie asked, "who gets this estate with Felicia gone?"

"Why, I don't know," Martha said. "Felicia had all kinds of crazy business deals, like everything else. I suppose Betsy stands to inherit some of this, but I'm sure there are other hands waiting to open."

"What will the two of you do?" Robin asked.

"I'm not sure," Martha said. "But Felicia always assured me that we'd have a home here. I suppose we'll have to wait until the will is read and we know for sure who owns this place. Then, well, we'll all get on with our lives eventually, won't we?"

Robin nodded.

"Thank you both for your help. We may need to ask a few more questions at another time. I hope that it won't pose any problem, but I think this should be good for now," Leslie said.

"We're happy to help," Martha replied. "Having nothing to hide, we don't have anything to worry about," she assured them. "If you want to talk to Jane Hugh, I think she's at her cottage. I haven't seen that old jalopy she drives leave today."

"I don't believe her," Robin said, as the two slipped out the back door and down the stairs.

"You don't believe Martha? About what? She seems awfully straightforward to me," Leslie replied.

"I'm going to do some checking on her. She was too pat, and the way she answered for Remy, not letting the woman get a word in edgewise—she acted as if she had to get all her little tidbits in so we'd be satisfied. I think those two have another story to tell. And you notice she didn't really tell us why she was living here in the first place. Of course it's pretty typical of Felicia, picking up people like stray cats. She never liked living here without a bunch of other people around. You know, that's what I hate about cases like this. No really clear-cut evidence. Any of the three of them could have done it, as well as Betsy."

"You're right there," Leslie agreed, though she knew that rather than hating the enigma, Robin thrived on it. Too many suspects made the joy of unraveling the solution that much more interesting for her partner.

A brick path through the garden led to the back of the property and the caretaker's cottage. Well hidden from the house, it was small, likely just one room, made of brick, with huge windows in the front.

"Quaint place," Leslie observed.

"Yeah, those windows are new. They kind of modernize the place, I suppose," Robin suggested, looking at it carefully. She stared intently for awhile, trying to recall what it had looked like ten years before. The biggest difference she noticed was that the gardens surrounding the small place were more manicured than the rest of Felicia's gardens. The well cared for beds of flowers and the neatly trimmed hedges made this part of the estate stand out from the rest, almost like a small corner of civilization that stands out boldly next to the savage wilds. "You should know what Felicia used this for when I lived here," Robin said.

"Do I want to?"

"She had a dungeon years ago, before there were any big clubs, when lesbians, let alone lesbian SM, was inside the closet so far that it was hard to find it."

"Is that why you were with her?" Leslie asked, turning to her partner. The personal question stuck out from the rest of Leslie's *informational* questions, making Robin instantly bristle.

"I told you a long time ago that I don't want to discuss my life with Felicia with you." Robin reminded her of an old edict.

"I know that, and I'm not trying to pry. But we were together then, and we're not now. And this is a case. The more I understand about this woman—a woman I might add you knew better than you know most victims—the more I know, and the more likely we'll get to the bottom of things."

"I realize that, but let's just keep the questions to general things," Robin retorted.

The wall raised around her was not likely to be

penetrated—Leslie knew that from many previous tries. "Damn, when you want to be closed-lipped you sure are," Leslie remarked. "So Felicia? She was a dom?"

"She was whatever suited her fancy," Robin replied.

The two detectives reached the cottage, and as they rounded the end of a massive hedge, they turned to see a woman pruning the dense foliage that ran along the pathway. The broad-shouldered, slim-hipped woman wore a man's sleeveless undershirt, so that when she leaned over or even raised her arm, her breasts were exposed. Her hair was shaved on the back and sides of her head and spiked on the top. Her large hands looked manly and her posture stern, though there was a surprisingly pleasant look in her eyes that suggested a softer woman underneath the obvious dyke surface.

"We're investigating Felicia's murder, working for the Longcore family," Leslie announced. "You're Jane Hugh?"

"I am." The woman held out her hand to shake theirs.

"We have a few questions," Leslie continued.

"So ask away," she said, unconcerned, as she returned to the hedge.

"We heard about some altercation between you and Felicia on the day of her death. Suppose you tell us about your relationship with your employer," Leslie said.

"I wasn't her employee. I work around the place because it's half mine, and if I didn't take care of it, it would go to hell in six weeks. Felicia wasn't very good at taking care of anything."

"Half the place?" Robin asked. "That's not common knowledge, is it?"

"It wouldn't be. Felicia would never tell anyone that, but I have a fifty-percent share of this estate. She owed me money and was only willing to deed half the place to me. She was paying off the rest from her trust fund. I've stayed around here to make sure I get my money back. She could have given me the whole house to pay me off, but she had to live here. One of those family things," Jane said sarcastically. "She was a 'Roman' and would live at Roman Hill till the day of her death. Of course now that's happened."

"And now the entire house is yours."

"I suppose," she shrugged. A curious faraway look appeared in her eyes as she deftly used the hefty pair of garden trimmers to shape the hedge.

Even as Jane was privately musing, Leslie noted how the woman stared at her chest, where her blouse opened to show the deep cleavage. "You have a reputation," Leslie prodded gently.

"As a dom? Is that what you're referring to? I don't hide that. Part of my life, but I play my games in a local club, not here."

"Felicia was tied to her bed when she was murdered. Signs of a 'scene'—that's what you call it— whip marks on her body. The ropes, the knots, it all looked very professional."

"Like I did it?" Jane said smirking. "Hell, I could have killed her in a second, but I didn't. You know, I'll likely lose in this deal with her dead. Probate lawyers will eat up half my money. So why would I kill her?"

"You fought with her all the time," Leslie said.

"If you didn't like Felicia, you fought with her— there wasn't much in between. We didn't like each other. Besides, ladies...," there was a mocking tone in her voice, a look in her eye as if she was imagining the two detectives in bondage, "...I was at the club the night she died. You check that with the crowd there, they know me well. Even the police, as inefficient as they are, have already figured that out."

"The club?" Robin asked.

"Sapphos In Chains," Jane replied.

She'd heard of it.

"And those ropes," Jane continued. "Anyone can tie expert knots in minutes. It's hardly an art."

"If you didn't commit the crime, who do you think did?" Robin asked.

"Any of those dames in the big house—who's to say? Probably Betsy. She may look like an innocent little thing, but she's a hellion at heart."

"You know firsthand?" Robin asked.

"Wish I did, but no. I could have really given that wench a good time, better than Felicia. Miss High Horse always pressed people too hard: she didn't understand tact and timing and how to use a little gentleness with her obsessions. Then again, that's likely what killed her. The obsession made her loose her judgment, not that she ever had really good judgment, she'd just run out of lives. You know, like a cat—she was on her ninth." A trace of melancholy remained in her voice, even as she spoke of Felicia with a healthy degree of scorn.

"Thank you for your help," Leslie said, with a hasty grin.

The woman nodded and returned to her work.

Leslie and Robin meandered toward the garden on their way to their cars. Stopping in a small patio at the center of the wild vegetation, Leslie eyed an attractive stone fountain, unused and now filled with dark, dead, shiny leaves floating with algae on top of the stagnant water. Rising from the center of the decaying piece was Venus, naked, standing in an alluring pose of beckoning with downcast eyes and a facial expression that betrayed her lust.

"Felicia posed for it," Robin told her.

"Why does that not surprise me?" Leslie said, admiring the simplicity of the well-carved stone.

"I watched her for two weeks, standing stock still in the middle of this garden, exactly where the fountain stands now. There was some cosmic reason for that which escapes me now," Robin said. "She was quite stimulating, shivering here with nothing on. It was fall, just before the bad weather when the days were still warm. I remember the leaves, like they are now, beginning to fall, the red and orange and brown making the picture look as sad as any autumn day. She insisted on posing nude like that even when it was getting too cold. She had to have the work finished by spring. She was really mad that she couldn't find a female stonecutter, and all her secrets were carved by a man. Just goes to show that Felicia didn't always get everything she wanted."

"What did she want?" Leslie asked. "I mean, for all her wild lifestyle, what was she looking for?"

"I'm not really sure. I certainly don't think she knew. I suppose if you asked her, she'd tell you what she wanted for that instant. But whether she got what she really needed? I doubt it."

"So what do you think?" Leslie asked, changing direction. "Give me the answer—will we have this wrapped up by the end of the week?"

"No," Robin replied. "This one is going to take some time. If everybody has their airtight story, we're going to have the find the flaws, and that's going to take some searching. One of us needs to check on Jane, the other on the ladies from Maine and that little tart from New Orleans. If she's spent two weeks in New Orleans I'd be surprised," Robin added with a caustic twist.

"I'll check the club," Leslie volunteered.

"Really?" Robin looked at her in surprise. "I thought you'd give that to me."

"No, not on this one. I'll be more objective," Leslie said. "You might end up the being the entertainment, rather than getting the information we need."

"Yeah, sure, that's not my style. I don't play around in public clubs. But you go ahead and check the place out, it will do you good."

"What's that supposed to mean? I've been to places like Sapphos before."

"This time maybe you'll appreciate the games, get into them a little. It might help you understand Felicia and this case and her killer."

Leslie considered for a moment her feelings about the SM scene, one she'd viewed with a good deal of distaste and a dash of judgment, even though she always tried to have a live-and-let-live point of view.

"You might understand me better, too," Robin added sardonically.

"I'll keep that in mind," Leslie replied. "So what do you have in mind for those three inside?"

"I have a few hunches on the others that I want to follow. And I'll need to talk to Betsy. I haven't really gotten the flavor of things between all these women yet. There was obviously a lot of fucking around going on, but we've got to get behind that to what's not so apparent between them." They began to move out of the garden, Robin giving the statue in the center one last longing glance. "Just be sure you get a good look at Jane in action," she reminded Leslie.

"Like, what am I supposed to see?" Leslie asked.

"Get your information, but watch Jane's style, see what kind of dom she is. Might tell you a few things we need to know."

Leslie nodded, not sure exactly what Robin meant, but was certain that she'd soon find out.

CHAPTER FOUR

"Remy's sleeping peacefully. This has really rocked her," Martha said as she returned to the kitchen from upstairs. Zelda was wiping the countertops and putting away their picnic basket. "I gave her a sedative. I hope it will knock her out for awhile. She really needs the rest: she hardly slept last night for all her crying."

Zelda looked up at Martha, smiling generously.

"I should have known something like this would happen," Martha continued. "I knew it was much too frenetic for us, even if this house seems like such a stable place, up here out of the way. The stress on Remy is really too much. She shouldn't have had to live through it. I blame myself. I mean, does it hurt to have a little something extra for yourself?" She looked at the bright-faced redhead with a quizzical expression.

"You can't blame yourself," Zelda assured her. "Who could have predicted that this would happen? I mean, I hardly knew her at all, but it seemed like Felicia created the chaos around her and had done so for a number of years. That was part of the fun it, at least until now." She was trying hard to be sympathetic.

Martha tried a smile. "Thank you. I'm not sure what I would have done with Remy if you hadn't been here to help."

Zelda put the sponge back on the sink and deposited the cleaning things underneath the counter, then turned back to Martha, a soothing, soft expression on her face. "You're afraid Remy killed her, aren't you?" Zelda said.

Martha bristled. "I think Betsy killed Felicia. Remy is just remembering her past," Martha stated flatly.

"Let's hope you're right," the redhead replied, moving closer to the woman at the other end of the counter. "Perhaps her trauma *is* just from remembering her past," Zelda offered. Her lips curled into a tiny smirk. "So, she's sleeping, huh?"

"Yes," Martha sighed.

Zelda leaned forward on the counter, picking grapes from a bowl and popping them in her mouth. The way her lips curled about them, the way she smiled, the way her eyes lit with a lush glow reminded Martha of Felicia, just for a second, though she was nothing like Felicia—a far warmer, less disturbed aura surrounded her.

"Tell me," Zelda said, "what *did* you do with Felicia?"

Martha chuckled darkly, remembering. "Felicia had

voracious appetites for every kinky thing. Well, you can guess she liked all manner of B&D and SM, and, good heavens, I'm not sure what else. She liked the spontaneous most, I think. I don't doubt she had great sex with Betsy, but no one woman would satisfy her completely," Martha advised the redhead. "And you know, she wasn't as much of a dom as everyone thinks she was." Martha's eyes glimmered knowingly in a gossipy way.

"Oh?"

"She asked me to spank her ass one day when I was making dinner."

"Really? Right here in the kitchen?" Zelda's eyes flashed.

"Yes. I was chopping stew beef with a meat cleaver, and she sidled up to me like you're doing now." Martha paused to appraise Zelda's look, realizing she was being seduced into something. "She said 'I've got to be spanked real hard, would you bend me over?' She had that big, flat butter paddle in her hand." Martha pointed to the utensil hanging on the wall with a half-dozen other spoons and spatulas.

"This one?" Zelda asked, grabbing the wooden implement from its place.

"Yeah."

Zelda ran her hand along the smooth surface of the paddle. "So what did you do to her?"

"I spanked her, just like she asked."

"How?" Zelda's breasts gleamed in the heat. They seemed to be spilling out of her low-cut blouse. She pulled herself from the counter and moved closer to Martha, her eyes communicating desire.

"You want me to tell you exactly what I did?" Martha asked, a little embarrassed.

"No," Zelda replied with a gay smile. "I want you to show me."

Martha's eyes flared brightly, then dimmed as she considered the woman's proposal. "You're serious about this, aren't you?"

"Why, yes," Zelda replied, as if Martha should understand completely.

Martha took the butter paddle from her, inspecting the redheaded vamp with a careful eye. They didn't know each other well, having Remy in common but little else. Even she could be the murderer. But it still didn't detract from the delicious woman's allure. She wanted Zelda's hands on her breasts. She wanted to kiss the woman's neck and run her nails down her torso. It wouldn't hurt to start her with a red ass. A sudden explosion of unfulfilled needs raced through her. She missed this kind of thing. Remy only wanted her sex soft and gentle. "Drop your shorts," she said.

Zelda smiled happily as she backed away from the counter and reached for the waistband of her shorts.

"You know it's not quite the same," Martha said. "Felicia was wearing a red flowered sundress. I remember it so well."

"But an ass is an ass," Zelda said sweetly, as she unzipped the pink shorts and let them fall to the floor.

It was a sweet cunt that gazed back at Martha, a luscious little triangle with soft red curls that were already dewy wet.

"Felicia bent over the table and pulled up her dress. I didn't even have to ask her," Martha continued.

Zelda turned around with a pleased snicker, then bent over the heavy butcher-block table.

"She spread her ass for me with her hands, digging

her nails into her bottom till it was turning red," Martha added.

Zelda reached around and planted a hand on each asscheek, squeezing her bottom roughly and pulling the cheeks apart the way Felicia had done.

Martha viewed the alabaster white bottom, now turning red, with mounting lust, and it spurred her memories of Felicia. It had only been weeks ago that their games had begun. Always out of the blue, moments of stolen lust when Remy and Betsy weren't around. This ass was whiter than Felicia's, and broader. A pleasant kind of plump: Zelda, like her name, was a woman from another time—not unlike Felicia, Martha was beginning to think. Though she was likely more of a dabbler than Felicia, with her infinite lusts.

"She wanted it to hurt," Martha said approaching the fine, round, offered bottom.

"Hummm, yes, make it hurt," the redhead murmured, taking her hands from her bottom and grabbing the far edge of the table.

Martha waited until the red scratches faded away before beginning. Then drawing back her arm, she brought the paddle down on Zelda's naked bottom. Martha watched the woman's body jerk, her flesh jiggle, and the red rise in the imprint of the paddle's oval end, right at the center of the round asscheek. She smacked her a dozen times more, hearing a low, sensuous growl erupt from Zelda's lips.

Then Martha dropped the paddle, wanting to feel the rising red with her hands. She slapped the surface again and again with the palm of her hand, and the whimpering woman wanted more. She pelted her with one vicious blow after another, then picked up the paddle and began another ferocious excursion around the bright red flesh.

"Oh, yes, please, make it hurt more, damn yes!"

Martha felt a burning between her own thighs. The heat was delightful, just the way it had been with the sultry sorceress of this house. Dropping the paddle again, Martha's hand reached into Zelda's cunt to find a wet stream of female juice flowing.

"Have you come yet?" she asked.

"No, but spank me more."

"More still?" Martha questioned.

"Yes, I want to cry," Zelda purred. For a moment she'd reached back and played with her own red ass, but anticipating another round of blows from the paddle, she brought her hands forward to hold on to the table edge once more.

Picking up the paddle again, Martha slapped the woman harder still, with no mercy. The rain of blows didn't cease until she heard the woman cry, a flood of tears finally spilling from her eyes. Even so, Zelda wasn't protesting this—she loved every minute of it. But her need for punishment changed to a need for release.

"Please suck me," she wailed loudly. The paddle stopped its vicious excursion, and Zelda provocatively pushed her red ass toward Martha.

"You little slut," Martha said, slapping the offered butt. "Get on the table and show me your tits."

Zelda pulled her blouse away, and her voluptuous body was sticky with sweat. She pressed against Martha. "I need you now: let's go upstairs."

"Not upstairs, on the porch," Martha countered, taking the redhead by her hand and leading her to the back porch, where Felicia's pink floral chaise lounge lay empty.

Martha stripped while Zelda lay back looking at the woman's naked tits and cunt. Martha's soft body would be a mellow pleasure to enjoy, the redhead decided. There were wispy black hairs covering her cunt, but they were glistening with obvious sexual arousal.

"You like your body spanked?" Martha asked, as she descended on the reclining Zelda.

"Yes, I do. I like sex rough."

"You like leather and whips too?"

Not hearing an answer, Martha put her head between Zelda's tits and kissed her there. She squeezed the fleshy mounds with hands that pinched her so hard that the other woman squealed. It hurt her, though she obviously enjoyed the hurt.

"Oh, God, please more," Zelda moaned.

Martha nibbled at the nipples, then bit the white skin with her teeth. She sucked hard, and when she backed away there was a quarter-sized red mark against the pale background. Martha smacked her more, on her thighs, her breasts, her raw ass, making her way about the eager body with equally eager intent. She pulled the red pussy hair and Zelda squealed. She pulled it again until there were more tears forming in the slut's eyes. Three of Martha's fingers slipped inside the wet, sloshy cunt as her mouth descended on a bright pink swollen clit.

Zelda gasped loudly. Her body tensed, released and tensed again, so that Martha could feel the pulsing against her penetrating fingers.

"Oooo, my, yes, more," Zelda's quiet whimper continued as her belly churned and her hips bucked.

Then she went limp.

"You're a fine dom," Zelda murmured, opening her

eyes to see Martha staring at her from between her still-open legs. "You want yours now, don't you?"

"I'll have mine now, little bitch, or I'll really whip you," Martha said.

"What a choice," Zelda replied, smiling broadly. She pulled Martha down to her body, and they exchanged places on the chaise. Then, with Martha's legs spread wide, Zelda made a feast on the succulent flesh, running her tongue along the wet hole, sucking at the hard bud clit, and pulling gently at Martha's soft labia. The redhead listened for the response, a welcome groaning sound greeting her ears, so melodic and intensely private a sound, until Martha's coming noises deepened and a soft orgasm moved through her body. Then she let out a vibrant "ah, yes."

The two remained pressed against each other on the small space of the chaise lounge, quietly recouping. Intertwined, it almost seemed that they had been lovers for years, not just an hour. They heard the birds, the pleasant afternoon chirping, the hum of insects, the sounds of a city in the far distance.

"Maybe this was a way to repair ourselves after the death," Martha suggested, as much to herself as to Zelda. It had been a good release.

"Maybe. I guess for you perhaps," Zelda suggested. "But I hardly knew her." She sounded cold and detached.

"I suppose you're right," Martha agreed.

Zelda propped herself up on one elbow and looked at the naked body next to her. "Felicia let you make love to her?" the redhead asked curiously.

"I wouldn't call it making love. Love was never the feeling I had. Felicia liked to play with me, and she liked me on top," Martha replied.

"You were her dom?"

"Not really. I always had the feeling that she had someone who that took her places I'd never even think of going."

"You mean the really nasty stuff? Why didn't you?" Zelda asked.

"I do what pleases me. This pleased me, it pleases me now. It was the same sort of thing that I did with Felicia," Martha answered pleasantly, though she wasn't planning to answer any more questions from this woman.

Zelda nodded.

"Ah, what do we have here?" The reclining women looked up to see Jane Hugh standing on the other side of the screen door. Her shadow loomed over them, clouding the sunshine that had warmed them so well. "A little ode to the dead?" Jane suggested

"And you haven't made love since she died?" Zelda said with a touch of mockery.

"Not in Felicia's bed," Jane said.

"Oh, so you *are* in mourning for the woman. You sound so respectful, now that she'd dead," Zelda answered, maintaining a slightly caustic attitude. No one expected Jane to be mourning Felicia's death, not the way they'd fought.

"I don't give a shit what you two do, but I need the keys to Felicia's car. I have to move it to get some equipment from behind it."

"They're hanging where they always do," Martha said, pulling away from the voluptuous little nymph beside her.

"The bitch redhead needs a trip to the club. You should bring her," Jane suggested as she walked with Martha into the house.

"I don't think we have that kind of relationship," Martha advised her. "But she does like it nasty. Why don't you take her? I think, for all her talk, she was admiring you."

"I don't like her," Jane remarked.

"Well, she doesn't like you either, but that's all the more reason, don't you think?" Martha replied, smiling.

While Martha dressed, Jane plucked the keys from the hook and walked to the door.

"I really do like the women I top. It makes the scene much more appealing. You know, you could come for yourself," Jane offered, "if you really need some good stuff to take your mind off this mess here."

"Thanks, but I have enough sex here to keep me busy," Martha replied.

"Suit yourself," Jane said, and she walked out.

When the screen door banged again, it was Zelda returning to the kitchen. While Martha put a teapot on the stove, she admired the red blotches that still marred Zelda's alabaster skin.

"Next time you'll tie me," Zelda suggested.

"I could. But where? In the basement? Perhaps you're looking for dungeons? We don't really have one here."

"I'm looking for fun," Zelda said, her eyes twinkling even more than they had earlier.

"Anywhere you can get it?" Martha asked.

"You think I'm loose, don't you?"

"I don't know you: I don't really know why you're here." It was a question that had been burning at Martha for days. Perhaps the sex between the two of them had made her bold. But there was something suspicious about Zelda's presence, and about her relationship with the sleeping Remy.

"She wanted me here, Remy did," Zelda said.

"Oh?"

"Yes, she called me two weeks ago to tell me that things were kind of strange here. She invited me for a visit. Haven't you asked her?"

"No, not really. She was glad to see you. I suppose it was just something she knew about and I didn't," Martha answered.

"And that's odd because you know everything that Remy does," Zelda said.

"I have taken care of her," Martha said in her defense.

"And very well, I might add."

"What did Remy think was so strange?" Martha asked.

"Why don't you ask her?" Zelda replied. Picking up her clothes from the kitchen floor, she walked out naked, with a sassy swing to her hips.

"Slut," Martha murmured to herself under her breath, though she had every intention of giving in to the woman's wish to be tied. Perhaps she'd just leave her bound to a post in the basement, naked, with the rats running around her feet. The thought was perfectly divine, though she should be ashamed of herself for having such wicked thoughts. There was too much wickedness about, too much. That's probably what made for the whole murderous mess.

CHAPTER FIVE

The sound of jail cells clanging shut always sent a strange shiver through Robin. Not a sound that anyone should ever get used to, she thought. For a cell, this one wasn't bad, and at least Betsy had it to herself. There was not likely any other prisoner in this facility that Betsy would find good company. At least being a murder suspect gave her some privileges.

Betsy sat on her bunk giving Robin a slightly hopeful look on seeing a friendly face. She looked up at the detective, looking lost in her blue prison dress in this jail cell, with nothing but a bed and wash-basin for company.

"How are things for you?" Robin asked.

"What can I expect?" Betsy replied with a bashful blush.

If she wasn't innocent, she sure looked it, Robin thought.

"Leslie and I have done some preliminary work. We believe you're innocent, but we're going to have to do some real digging to find the real murderer. We need more information," Robin explained.

"I'll do anything I can to help you, if you can just get me out of here," Betsy said.

"Well then, let's talk about that night, see if you know something we don't know." She looked down at the police's prime suspect, thinking their conversation seemed particularly awkward with the detective standing and the suspect looking up at her. "Do you mind if I sit?" she asked.

"Oh, sure," Betsy said, moving over on the bed. "Not much for socializing, is it?"

Robin smiled kindly. "Tell me now, you were sleeping downstairs that night. Why was that?"

"Maybe half my nights I spent on the sleeping porch," Betsy explained.

"Was Felicia expecting someone else, perhaps?"

"No. But we'd been fighting a lot, and I wanted to be by myself. Besides, Felicia would often stay up late and read, or do whatever she did by herself, and I was very tired."

"So you heard nothing until you discovered her the next morning."

"I got up about seven and couldn't go back to sleep, so I went upstairs, just planning to get some clothes, and I found her." Her face looked a little ashen remembering the moment.

"You took the knife and held on to it?" Robin continued.

"I thought she might be alive, that I could revive

her. I had to pull it out. I think I must have screamed, because Martha came running, and, well, you know the rest."

Robin listened carefully to the story, mostly to the sadness that seemed overwhelming. "Tell me a little more about your housemates," the detective continued.

"Remy and Martha?"

"And Zelda."

"Well, she wasn't really a housemate," Betsy replied.

"Yes, I know, but she was there the night that Felicia was murdered. Which makes her a suspect, as much as anyone."

"Well, let me see," Betsy said thoughtfully. "Remy and Martha came from Maine, I know that."

"They were living with Felicia before you and she got together?"

"Yes. They were always friendly with me, really pleasant."

"Do you know how they met?"

"I think they were in college together somewhere. The name Brightwood comes to mind, but that's not a college, is it?" The small woman looked uncertain, as if a cloud surrounded her. "They never really talked about their pasts. I guess you could say there was always this assumption that things had been kind of bad for Remy, and she was happier just not thinking or talking about it."

"Did they go anywhere, out of town? Have any friends they talked about?"

"I don't remember that they took any trips," Betsy said, trying to remember. "They went to movies together and talked about work, but I can't recall anything else. They were very quiet women most of the time."

Robin knew that there were likely a dozen clues Betsy could bring up, but the woman just didn't know where in her memory to look.

"To your knowledge were they into SM?"

"Oh, I don't think so. I can't, even in my wildest imaginings, see Remy doing any sort of scene like that. She's much too fragile."

"And what about Zelda?"

"We were told she was a friend of Remy's. I kind of figured that she knew Zelda from college maybe, certainly before she came here. It wasn't really explained, but it was pretty clear that the two hadn't seen each other in some time."

"Why do you say that?" Robin probed.

"Oh, you know that kind of odd recognition when you haven't seen each other in some time."

"They were close then, at one time?"

"I think so."

"Martha suggested that she and Zelda were college friends?" Robin probed.

"They never mentioned that to me. I assumed the connection between those two is Remy. Besides, when Zelda arrived at the house, you could see that Martha had never laid eyes on the woman."

"I wonder why Martha would say that?" Robin mused aloud.

"She probably thought she had to say that to protect Remy. In case you haven't noticed, Martha dotes on the woman. Of course she dotes on everyone, but especially Remy. You can really see the affection in her eyes. And worry. She's always worried about Remy, though Remy hates that. Of course I'd hate that too, being fawned over all the time. Remy was really very pleasant with me. I liked her. Not as a lover—she's not my type—but she might have become a friend, we just never had much time together. Remy's working at the lab a lot, and then Martha spirits her away when she gets home."

"Did you find anything suspicious about Zelda?" Robin asked.

Betsy considered the question for some moments. "No, not really. She's kind of fun in a way. But we didn't have much time together."

Robin eyed Betsy for some moments, trying to get a real fix on the woman and her now dead lover.

"Was Felicia leaving you for Martha?" Robin asked.

"No," Betsy answered immediately, shaking her head emphatically.

"Yet she was having sex with her?"

"But that was expected. You had allow to Felicia her liberty. You couldn't keep her from having sex with other women; it would frustrate the hell out of you, and it would be completely impossible for Felicia. Yeah, the police are making a big deal of the way we argued, but it wasn't about sex. I knew that I couldn't satisfy her completely."

"Then what did you argue about?" Robin asked.

Betsy took a deep breath. "It's hard to explain my relationship with Felicia. She was a very odd woman."

"I knew Felicia personally: I think I can understand some of what you're saying."

"You did?"

"Yes, it was a long time ago, but I know enough about what she's like."

Betsy nodded, looking relieved by the information, grateful that she didn't have to explain more. "I let Felicia sort of have me when we first got together, and she was very good at taking. She was very generous, lavish, with her home and sex and just about everything. But she wanted me to be a certain way. I was wanting a more equal, independent relationship these last few months. What I really wanted was more from her. I loved the sex we had, but I wanted to give to her more. She had a problem with that. I guess you could say she had me in this compartment, and that's where I belonged. She didn't want it any other way."

"And you fought about this?"

"I didn't really believe that I could make her change. But I had to try."

"Were you planning to leave Felicia?" Robin asked on a hunch.

"Funny, I hardly admitted it to myself, but I knew I couldn't stay with things the way they were. In the back of my mind I thought about leaving, but I never really discussed it with Felicia. I considered it the last resort."

"Had you threatened her in any way, particularly the day of her death?"

"No, not at all. I tried talking with her, reasoning with her, suggesting things that we could do differently. She was just stuck on things being her way. In that respect she wasn't unlike other lovers I've had. And if I left, I left. Hell, I've left a half-dozen lovers, and the thought of leaving Felicia was almost as good as the idea of staying."

"But you loved her?" Robin asked.

"Yes, I loved her very much. There was a lot there to love, even though there was a lot to detest."

Robin could easily agree with that. "I've had the same dilemma myself," Robin admitted, without indicating why it was so familiar to her. "The police say Felicia left you a substantial sum in her will."

"I guess so, but I never really thought much about that. I don't need much money—not that I have a lot, I just don't require it. I certainly don't need Felicia's money."

"I heard, too, that you were trying to encourage Felicia to turn Roman Hill into a bed and breakfast?"

"Yes. She needed the money. She always needed more money: she was far too extravagant. She had debts all over the place."

"Did you know that Jane owns half the house?"

The look of shock on Betsy's face was genuine.

"Did you?" Robin repeated.

"No." She paused. "But it makes sense, lots of sense. Do you think Jane killed her?"

"It's a possibility; so are the other three women. You don't remember anything else about them, about their lives before they came to Roman Hill?"

"Oh, god, I don't know," Betsy replied, seeming distressed. "Just too much to consider all at once."

"Listen, you've been very helpful, and if you think of anything, anything at all that might help us out…you are talking to John every day, aren't you?"

"Yes."

"If you can't get to Leslie or me, tell him, and he'll pass it along to us."

"I will," Betsy replied with that same hopeful look on her face that she had when Robin arrived. She was certainly a seductive little thing, even in prison blues.

"And don't give up hope. We've just started."

CHAPTER SIX

Jane's club was downtown, on the fringe of the commercial district. It was a good five miles away from Roman Hill, though it could easily be reached in ten minutes, since freeway on and off ramps were near both places. Leslie checked, starting out that night at the base of Roman Hill, timing the trip downtown.

Sapphos In Chains was located in an old warehouse building, something perfectly suited to the activity that went on there. Expecting a certain clientele and a certain manner of dress, Leslie wore a pair of brown leather pants she'd bought years before when one lover had a motorcycle and she had consented to ride along behind her. The lovely vibrating feeling in her cunt as she rode the cycle was enough to keep her in the relationship for awhile, though she was a little scared of being so "out there" and vulnerable on the bike. In addition to the pants, she found a vest of Rosalie's that worked pretty well by itself as a leather halter, just barely covering her breasts, showing lots of cleavage without looking too feminine.

Seeing herself in the mirror, she figured she struck a dominant persona. The submissive thing never really felt quite right, but then the dom stuff just wasn't her either. Wielding whips and tying lovers down was not her idea of fun. She much preferred luscious warm bodies and hands exploring her flesh. She didn't mind a few good spanks on the butt, or even on the thighs, pinched nipples, rough grabbing; but she liked to be equal with her partners. She likely lost Robin because of this, but you can't make people into something they are not, she believed.

Pulling more things from Rosalie's vast wardrobe, she donned a pair of leather boots that looked perfect for her attire and found some large silver cross earrings—a style she'd never wear on her own. She thought she might add a collar at her neck, but that didn't quite fit. She added some touches of makeup that she wasn't used to wearing, though she did take some pleasure in a tube of bright red lipstick she found in Rosalie's things. Finishing off her look, she combed her long brunette hair into a tight bun at the back of her head, giving her face a more severe look than she was used to. But it was a stunning transformation. She could almost feel it excite her, though she had no idea what to do with the feelings generated inside her. It was certainly appropriate for the club, which she'd heard was one of the most creatively nasty places anywhere around.

She pulled up in front of the club, and a leather-clad woman motioned her to a parking lot next door. Leslie was thankful that it was well lit: something about this whole scene was a little precarious, especially the chances these women took for their nightlife. She guessed that most simply weren't worried about their safety—too tough for anyone, man or woman, to tangle with. Even as a PI, however, Leslie was always respectful of her safety. Certainly there was safety in numbers here, and the street wasn't empty. Several other nightclubs dotted the area, one for a straight yuppie crowd of singles and a dank-looking gay men's bar a few blocks down the street.

Entering Sapphos In Chains took Leslie into a world that she was not unfamiliar with. She'd been to a half-dozen lesbian clubs over the years that were not unlike this place, mostly for investigations. However, she'd never been quite so interested in blending in with the crowd. Finding out about Jane's activities with as much subtlety as possible was her intention. The police had already checked the woman's alibi for the night of the murder. Leslie was more interested in seeing if there were any holes in it. A thirty-minute drive to Roman Hill and back wasn't impossible— little more than a bathroom break. It would be easy to fall into the cracks in a place like this, people not being really certain when you came, when you left, or how long you were gone.

The nightclub was a busy, sensuous place, the costumes pretty much predictable with lots of leather and chains, and a little lace adorning some submissives. There were doms that looked like men and those with lipstick and wild hair that had a real flair for being feminine: there were submissives of every persuasion. It was a rather eclectic gathering on the whole.

As Leslie made her way about the club, it appeared to have at least a dozen rooms on two levels, connected by a broad metal stairway. The predominant color was black, though the variety of light and dark that greeted her eyes surprised her. In some places there was blinding light and white walls. In other areas it was dark and so smoky she could hardly see in front of her face. The music changed with the rooms, though it all seemed to blend in a gentle cacophony, not some heavy metal harshness that would have made her head pound in seconds.

It was the sensuality of Sapphos In Chains that impressed her the most. She could not ignore the lesbian bonding, the open expression of female/female sensuality that was often so difficult on the outside. In that respect the place was no different than other lesbian bars with softer themes. It was not uncommon to see tender gestures between tops and bottoms, and subtle love songs being sung between women whose proclivities were hard to pinpoint.

No one was aggressive with her, which Leslie liked. Perhaps the sign at the door actually stated the rules: NO ONE'S FORCED TO DO ANYTHING INSIDE THIS PLACE, DON'T FORGET IT! She almost snickered upon seeing it.

There were plenty of winsome smiles from unattached women, eyes that beckoned her, and a few mild physical gestures that warmed her, though she didn't respond to them overtly.

Leslie sat down at the bar and ordered a Coke as she looked around, trying to feel her way into the playground around her. The scenes were so fascinating, each one so different, that she could have stared at the little soap operas for hours, mesmerized by the relationships between these women. No wonder Robin liked this world—her former lover was a real student of the drama of life and its personal relationships. She might often loose her perspective when it was a relationship of her own—Robin had some really bad ones—but she'd become a master of discernment when it came to other people, no doubt because she was willing to walk into most any situation and just sit down and study it for hours. Leslie thought that was rather boring, wanting more action in her life: but here, this place did provide some special features you couldn't find elsewhere that made observing more stimulating. She tried to take it as slow and easy as Robin would. She could always ask her questions later.

Leslie looked around at the different ways people used their clothing to express their positions. She especially liked the "chain" look. One submissive wearing an extended collar of a dozen chains over her naked torso made Leslie grind her cunt against the stool she was sitting on. The youngish looking blonde was led on a leash to a table where she was ordered to sit. Her hands were instantly tied behind her so that her breasts were about as blatantly displayed as she ever seen two feminine mounds. It didn't hurt that these were at least C-cup tits, natural ones at that, with large brown aureoles and very tiny hard nipples. Leslie was close enough to see little goose bumps appear on the surface of the submissive's skin. Since it wasn't cold in the place—in fact it was rather warm— she assumed the blonde woman was aroused. Her butch top left her at the table, a stern order spoken directly in her face that Leslie couldn't hear. But she saw the little shiver that ran through the blonde and the look of fear in eyes that had been circled heavily in eyeliner.

"You planning some fun, a scene perhaps?" a tall black woman asked her. She was dressed in a short skirt, boots, and a leather bustier. She must have been nearly six-feet tall in stocking feet, much more in her high-heeled boots.

"I'm just looking around: it's my first time here," Leslie explained.

The woman looked down Leslie's vest, admiring the deep cleavage and the little jiggle of her breasts as she moved.

"You submissive or dominant?"

"I'd likely switch," Leslie said, though she didn't know why.

The woman looked at her with an air of approval.

"I switch myself. I like to top most of the time, but I do like my ass beat on occasion. Not more than once a month, mind you." The black woman's thick lips were gilded with the most amazing lipstick—red and gold hues seemed to glisten as she moved her mouth. Leslie would have liked to have kissed her on the mouth, felt those lips surround her own much smaller ones.

"Leta," the woman announced her name as she sat down.

"I'm Leslie." It felt a little more comforting having someone sit next to her, a little safer, perhaps, too. This woman was not nearly as forbidding as some in the crowd. Leslie especially liked her eyes. They were made up beautifully, with great care, but her makeup didn't detract from a gentle quality that flowed from them.

"May I?" Leta asked, as she deliberately gazed into Leslie's gaping vest.

"Sure," Leslie answered, thinking that it wouldn't bother her at all if she and this woman found a private room where they could explore each other all night, though that wasn't her purpose for coming to this place. Hadn't she joked with Robin that she was going to the club so that Robin wouldn't be distracted?

Leta reached inside Leslie's vest and found her nipple. She squeezed it harshly as she pulled it out, and Leslie jerked, wincing just slightly with the pain, though it wasn't without its pleasure. She could feel the effect all the way to her cunt. In fact, this small act made her realize how hot she really was. Even if it was just the voyeuring that turned her on, she was turned on.

"Such a pretty pink," Leta said, seeing the exposed nipple. "I'd like to clamp them both," she suggested. "Later, maybe, after you get accustomed to things, we could find a room and I'd give you a wonderful introduction to B&D."

Leslie smiled, thinking that Leta would be a perfect partner for a first time. "I'll see what happens tonight," she replied.

Leta slid off her stool and pressed her lips against Leslie's neck, then smiled and walked away. She had a graceful gait, so slow and easy: it was hard not to be seduced by her. After she left, Leslie remembered with some regret that she didn't even think of asking Leta about her suspect.

About an hour after she arrived, Leslie noticed Jane Hugh walk in the door. The butch woman hardly looked different than she had that afternoon when the two PI's had interviewed her. Just her clothes had changed: she was wearing pants, and a leather shirt that laced up the front. Her breasts pressing against the leather were larger looking that Leslie remembered them. She wore cowboy boots and had her hands were stuffed into her pockets.

A soft, uncompelling submissive instantly landed on her arm, whispering something in her ear. Jane put her hand on the woman's cheek, gently, but with an unmistakable authority that could have easily slapped the woman in the face. The submissive kissed her. Leslie could hear the other woman call her "sir." The term fit, easily describing Jane's position.

Leslie turned on her stool just enough so that Jane wouldn't see her. This wasn't exactly a stakeout; it was much more a subjective fact-finding mission. And though she didn't intend to remain incognito all night, she hoped she could remained unrecognized for a while longer.

After the submissive's quick greeting was over, Jane made her way past the bar, not seeing Leslie, disappearing into the back of the club.

"You like her?" a voice asked.

Leslie turned around, a little startled to find that her watchfulness had been observed.

"She fascinates me," Leslie said truthfully.

"You haven't been here before, have you?" the woman asked. She wore a black T-shirt and skirt. Fairly unremarkable. But her head was shaved bald and she had a half-dozen earrings piercing each ear. On the left side an earring at the bottom hung almost to her shoulder.

"No."

"Sometimes she runs things here, Jane does. She's

like an electrical current. You really should see what she's going to do with Dagne tonight."

"Who's Dagne?" Leslie asked. "The blonde that was kissing her?"

"Oh, no! Dag's a real bitch, and Jane's gonna beat her ass tonight. Getting uppity."

"Oh?"

"Yeah, Dagne usually tops, but every once and awhile we all think she needs to be taken down a peg."

"So tonight's the night?" Leslie said. This was one conversation she needed to keep going. The loquacious woman might tell her everything she needed to know.

"I think so, but fireworks won't start for awhile—Jane's into Chris a lot now, so they're probably getting it on privately."

"How long do they stay in there?"

"Who knows," the woman shrugged. "Sometimes hours, if they're really into something."

"A lot lately you say? Chris her girlfriend?"

"Yeah, but not really. Jane's been kinda messed up since her lady was murdered."

"You mean Felicia?" Leslie guessed.

"Yeah, you knew her?"

"A friend of mine used to live with her."

"Really? She was a strange one, but I think Jane really had something for her. Brought her here a couple of times. Once she made her really sweat on the pulleys back there. I don't think I've ever seen anything so wild as those two. That Felicia woman looked like she could go on forever."

"What were they like?" Leslie asked, her eyes brightening in admiration so that her talkative friend would keep talking.

"They were in here a month ago, I think. Jane had the dame crawling on the floor. I've never seen anyone lick boots the way she did. I'm told she was a dom most of the time, but the way she acted, you'd never believe it. The brand on her ass? They say Jane did that, but no one can really say."

"A brand?"

"Yeah, there's lots of woman doing that now. I guess it's not as painful as it would seem. I mean if you're into pain, how much worse could it be? That bitch? She had one right in the middle of her pretty ass. Some weird something, musta meant something to them."

"Did you see them in a scene together?"

"Kinda, part of one anyway, when she had her on the pulleys, but you see I'm getting awfully hot while it's going on, and this little thing comes in and leans on my arm, and I couldn't wait any longer so I took out my stuff on her butt. We were both really roaring." She remembered the delicious moment with a lusty grin. "Anyway, by the time I'm done, Jane closes the door on the audience. Damn that lady screamed like holy hell. But she was the most peaceful bitch I'd ever seen when she left. I think she must have looked like that when she was dead, that peaceful. They say she was tied up and all when she died. I'm surprised they didn't arrest Jane, though you know we don't talk to police much here, and we never use last names. Keeps things pretty clean. I figure most people aren't using real names anyway, not at first."

"You think Jane might have killed her?" Leslie asked in her best gossipy, nondetective tone of voice.

"Wouldn't that be a hoot!" she exclaimed. "But nah, Jane's not like that. I think she really liked the bitch even though she treated her like dirt."

"You saw them together a lot?"

"No, just a couple of times. The other times I don't really remember any other scenes together. But I think the Felicia lady liked to show herself off. Seems like one night she was masturbating in the middle of the orgy room with everyone watching. Yeah, I remember that," the woman's memory was suddenly revitalized. "She was just really getting herself off. That's probably the first time I seen her here. Her hand's in her crotch, some flimsy dress all messed up all over the place around her. Yeah, she was a real nasty whore that night too. She was whipping herself while Jane stared at her, barking commands at her in this weird whisper. You couldn't quite hear, but you could feel the stuff between them. Damn insane if you ask me."

"She was whipping herself?" Leslie asked.

"Little leather thong whip. Real little, like maybe she carried the thing around all the time. This vacant face she had. I remember that the most—the vacant face that would suddenly light up with a new picture all over it. She was a real chameleon. When she was flailing herself, she did it all over. I was thinking that the whip really had to hurt her cunt, but she seemed real happy about it, all red and raw like it was."

"I never knew the woman. I guess it was my loss," Leslie said. She was finding it difficult not to be aroused by the way the woman talked, by the stories of Felicia, though it seemed a little crass to be getting off on someone who was now dead and not yet in her grave.

"You ever see Betsy, the woman they arrested?" Leslie asked.

"No, at least I don't think so. God, her picture has

been plastered all over the place. Cute thing. I'd guess she was submissive, so I'm not sure how they're putting this murder on her, but if you're in the scene, I think you can really go either way depending on your mood. Except doms like Jane. They never switch."

"You played with her?"

"Naw, but maybe sometime. I've never come on to her. I like my doms more feminine, kinda like you." Her eyes suddenly gleamed with interest. Finished talking, she was ready for a change.

"Sorry, I'm waiting for someone," Leslie said.

"Sure, I know," the woman replied, smiling, not at all hurt by rejection. For the second time that night, a woman slipped off the seat next to Leslie, moving on to something she needed that Leslie wasn't ready to provide.

At least she was getting somewhere, Leslie thought. Perhaps if she remained in her seat, she'd eventually find out everything that she needed to know.

In her apartment, Robin went through the pieces of the puzzle so far uncovered. Felicia, Betsy, the three women, Jane Hugh. She wondered at these five that had been so close to Felicia the night of her death, as if they'd been appointed to the position. Was there some cosmic force that had brought them together this way? Even more important, was there some connection between them? Had they all conspired to murder? She remembered an Agatha Christie, *Murder on the Orient Express*, with Poirot discovering this band of travelers had each sunk a knife into the old victim's body. Was this the case here? Certainly these women might all have wanted Felicia dead. But the wounds didn't suggest multiple murderers. The knife wound was clean, deep, and very steady, by someone very clear about their motive at that instant.

Up till this time, Robin had thought about the murder in the abstract, not yet ready to think about the woman who had tied up Felicia Roman one night, only to stab her in the chest. Now the questions came freely, some answers clear, others as obvious as mud.

She thought that if she could imagine it clearly enough in her head, the picture of the killer's face might just miraculously appear.

Had it been an impulse or something carefully planned? Had a B&D scene gone awry? Was there a woman who placed Felicia in bondage only to have another stab her in the chest? Did one women tie her up, another use a whip, while others watched? Or was it, as everyone assumed, the act of a solo assailant?

And what was Felicia thinking at the moment of her death? Did she even know that it was about to happen? Did she have any idea that there was a knife poised and ready to strike? Would her expression not have been more surprised at the moment of death? Would there not have been more signs of struggle, more tugging against the bonds that held her fast? There were no signs of a struggle. She seemed as peaceful as a lamb in death.

How many times, Robin wondered to herself, had her own eyes been closed to the outside world when she traversed the inner realms in a moment of masochistic frenzy. She could never imagine opening her eyes at the moment when a whip struck unless she was ordered to. Britta had done that before; made Robin look into her face while she whipped her. It was another kind of submission that was almost impossible for Robin to agree to. Too intimate, too fucking intimate. Maybe she needed to love someone for that. But she'd endured it anyway—submissives do that.

She'd rather be blindfolded, though, or remain with her eyes closed. She assumed that most submissives preferred that, too, and how easy it would be to kill a bound submissive when their eyes were closed.

The very fact that Felicia enjoyed the bondage, had likely asked for it, was a surprise. Perhaps she was more of a bottom than anyone knew. Certainly it seemed she trusted someone more than she had a right to.

But the three women were Robin's concern now. It was clear that Remy and Martha were hiding their past, one that was obviously troubling. And Zelda—a wild card, there to commit murder? Or just there on a fluke? Robin didn't know when she'd had a more fascinating set of suspects.

At least she had a place to start. She picked up the phone and dialed a friend at State U.

"Diane," she said, hearing her friend's voice answer.

"That you, Rob?"

"Yeah, how are you?"

The two exchanged greetings, then Robin got down to business.

"I need you to check on something for me, two students you had, say mid to late seventies."

"What are the names?"

"Martha Quigley and Zelda Wing."

"I'll check in the morning."

"And another possibility, Remy Thurston-Moore."

"Got them. This a case?" Diane asked.

"Yeah, Felicia Roman's murder."

"My god, I heard about it, isn't it terrible? And you, Rob, how are you doing with this? Investigating it too? Isn't that kinda tough?" As usual, Diane was rambling on, not letting Robin get a word in edgewise.

"I'm fine. Felicia made an impact on me ten years ago, certainly not one I'll forget, but I can't say I have enough feeling left to really mourn her death. It's just a little weird digging into all this stuff now."

"I think the murderer had to have had a really unique reason," Diane said. "Not something you'd expect. That would fit Felicia, don't you think?"

"That's what I figure," Robin said. "Every lover she ever had wanted her dead at one time or another, but no one would kill her for the way she loved them. She was obsessive about everyone. That was part of the magic."

"Exactly. I'm kinda pissed I never had a chance at her," Diane said.

"I bet you are," Robin replied, thinking of Diane's kinkier side. She was not a bar scene woman, but rather the kind of woman that Felicia loved the most—the one-on-one kind who had fun with a good drama. Diane's love affairs were always whirlwind romances that "would last forever," always happily dying a week after they began.

"Listen, I have someone here," Diane said. "I'll get back to you tomorrow about these three. Anything particular you want me to look up?"

"Everything—when they were here, how they might know each other, where they lived, if you have that. The classes they took, anything."

"I'll see what I can find. You know I love this part of my job, all this investigative stuff. Just don't be telling anyone what I'm up to. I don't want to get in trouble."

"I promise Di, now get back to your sex," Robin replied.

She listened for the little chuckle on the other end of the phone, knowing that Diane had a lover in bed with her right then. It was part of the joy of calling her at this hour—she could have a little vicarious thrill thinking of the two women making love right now.

Leslie, feeling a little light-headed and achy, pulled herself off the safety of the bar stool and made her way to the toilet. Three Cokes had gone through her and she had to pee. The bathroom was a little eerie, the yellow bulb making it glow with a strange light. From what she could see, the place was spotless. There were five stalls, but one was locked—Leslie could hear the sound of two women inside. It seemed a little ridiculous that, when every imaginable kind of behavior was allowed out in the club, why would two women hide themselves in a bathroom stall? Fantasy is a strange thing.

There was a small crack in the stall through which Leslie could see the two woman groping each other in a typical moment of lesbian passion. When one dropped to the floor and began to suck the other's cunt, Leslie chose a stall at the far end of the bathroom and did her business.

Returning to the outer rooms, Leslie took stock of the situation. Seeing Leta standing by the door to one room, she ambled slowly to her side. She smiled when the woman turned to her.

"Jane has Dagne on the pillory," Leta said, explaining the scene simply.

Looking inside the room, it took Leslie some seconds to get used to the darkness that surrounded the two women in the center. Standing on a raised platform in the center of the room was a leather-clad woman who indeed looked far more dom that her submissive pose. She was locked into an apparatus, her hands and head in stocks, her bottom thrust out lewdly, her legs spread wide. Jane held a dildo in her hand and was in the process of greasing it with some slick cream. At just the right angle it gleamed in the strange light that shone from a dim bulb in one corner.

"Getting too bitchy for your own good; we'll put you in your place, whore," said Jane, seething quietly at her captive. She wasn't performing, even though there was an audience of nearly twenty scattered around the room and in two doorways. This seemed as if it were something personal between the two.

Jane smacked her hand hard against one of Dagne's asscheeks, then against the other one. She pried the submissive's ass wide, exposing a puckering anus. From where Leslie stood she couldn't see it all clearly, but there was enough of a view to keep her happy. She watched as Jane pressed the enormous dildo against Dagne's ass. She assumed it was her ass by the way Jane was more careful than if it had been a cunt she was violating.

Once Jane made the initial penetration, Leslie watched as she shoved the thing deeper still, her powerful arm pushing it forcefully, all to the tune of Dagne's plaintive protests. The grunts were deep, but she wasn't screaming; and somehow Leslie didn't think she would. This might be punishment well earned, some revenge on the pecking order of this place, but it was consensual.

"You like this in you, don't you?" Jane said, as she moved the dildo in and out of the stretched channel.

"My God, please," Dagne gasped, the expression on her face sheer agony.

"You want it harder, don't you?"

"No!" she mounted a vibrant challenge.

But it wasn't Dagne's place to control this one. Jane prodded the submissive rear with a force that scared Leslie, but that didn't seem at all unusual to the crowd of watchers. When she was finally finished with the rape, Jane reached for straps which she used to tie the dildo inside the woman's ass. She worked carefully, with expert attention to the details of the knots she tied. Leslie was instantly reminded of the knots on Felicia's bonds and Robin's assertion that it took an expert to craft those so easily.

Once the dildo was fixed in Dagne's ass, Jane stood back and took a set of clamps which she attached to the woman's dangling breasts. After attaching a chain between the two, all Jane had to do was pull on it to have the woman crying out in pain, trying to pull away from the torture—a circumstance that would only make the agony worse. But, since getting away was impossible, why would a submissive think that pulling back would help the pain? Maybe it was all unconscious, Leslie thought.

When Jane pulled a strap from the wall, Leslie jumped back horrified.

"It's not as bad as it looks," Leta, whispered in her ear, noticing the pained expression on Leslie's face.

"But..."

"Just watch," Leta told her.

A comforting hand appeared on Leslie's back. Leta's. Leslie snuggled into the warmth that began to flood her.

The strap was two feet long, three inches wide,

with a heavy handle that seemed perfectly suited to Jane's broad hands and powerful arms. She started in on Dagne's butt with a series of soft snaps of the strap. When it landed there was a sharp smacking sound, followed by a blush rising on the surface of the woman's skin. It wasn't easy to see the color since the room was dark, but Leslie could imagine that, before long, Dagne's ass and thighs, her flanks, and everywhere Jane peppered the nasty strap, would be a wild shade of crimson.

As she proceeded, Jane's smacks became harder. The efficient dom settled into a steady, even tempo, one that Dagne could count on, one in which a submissive might find some sexual arousal. It started that way, with Dagne beginning to grunt and groan as if her loins were burning, the pain beginning to create an edge to shoot for. But Jane was not about to let her have her way so easily. Changing tempos, starting and stopping, she kept the woman in suspended sexual agony, unable to predict what was coming next.

During one brief pause, Jane dropped the strap to her side and gently petted the woman's thighs. She purred some inaudible sounds into Dagne's ear, some sweet nothings that made the woman shrink away—as much as she could, considering her bondage.

Wanting her ass higher and tighter, Jane removed ankle straps and shoved a box under her feet. Dagne was made to stand on the box so that her ass end was higher than her head and shoulders. Her legs were tied together at the ankles so she couldn't move them. The dildo remained in her ass, making the position look incredibly uncomfortable to Leslie's watchful eyes.

Appraising her submissive's pose and finding it to

her liking, Jane took the strap in hand and let it fly nastily, stroke after stroke landing on Dagne's asscheeks, until the woman was crying and in such agony that Leslie feared she'd pass out. Jane stopped at the very moment that the breathless room finally seemed to change sides in this battle of women, when the audience wanted an end to the vicious punishment, or at least a necessary pause.

It was a pause—Jane was hardly finished. She taunted her submissive with a spate of nasty gestures— pulling on the nipple clamps, tugging on Dagne's mane of red-dyed hair, and smacking her with her hand.

Then, taking a thin cane that was hanging on the wall, Jane swished the nasty implement through the air. It hissed, striking Dagne's bottom at the center of her asscheeks.

Dagne's howl filled the room, and the audience collectively cringed.

The deliberate dom waltzed around the punished, thrust-out bottom, making Dagne wait for the next cut. She pulled the nipple chain, and the woman howled again.

"You'll remember who's boss here, won't you, bitch?"

When Dagne didn't answer, Jane jerked the chain again.

"Yes, sir," Dagne blared.

"And you'll take another six cuts, won't you?" Jane said.

"Yes, sir."

Jane jerked the chain.

"You have quite an audience, my dearest Dagne. Tell them how much you want it, bitch! Tell them!" Jane's voice was haughty, but her look was filled with concern. A strange kind of nurturing this was; like nothing Leslie had ever seen.

"Please, sir, give me more." Desire and fear made Dagne's voice tremble.

With one last jerk on the chain, Jane returned to Dagne's ass and ripped off four nasty cuts in a row. Another two followed closely, each accompanied by an agonizing scream.

It was silent afterwards, except for the sound of Jane returning the cane to a hook on the wall.

"She doesn't want it unless there's a little blood. She's never been afraid to go that deep," Leta said. "And Dagne will be happy for it tomorrow when she looks at it."

"Happy?" Leslie whispered softly.

"Very," Leta assured her.

Jane became ever so gentle. Her large hands stroked the bound woman with a most tender touch. "You stay here for awhile so everyone sees you," Jane said, without an ounce of the haughtiness that had accompanied her earlier comments. "Dorie will take care of your bottom." She continued to stroke Dagne's back with the same gentleness that was present in her soothing tone of voice. Jane put her fingers to Dagne's mouth, the submissive licking them with delirious abandon.

"You own me, darlin' Dagne," Jane said. "I'm not always so sweet."

"Yes, sir."

Jane moved away, nodding to a woman on the side of the room; then walking to the doorway, she passed by Leslie and the crowd of others that had watched the remarkable scene.

Just steps beyond Leslie, Jane suddenly turned around and confronted the investigator.

"My, you look stunning tonight," Jane said, looking down at the leather vest and Leslie's cleavage. "A new line of work, or are you here on old business?"

"I was intrigued," Leslie answered, not too sure how Jane would greet her appearance at *her* club.

"You find out everything you wanted to know about me from my friends?" Jane asked.

"More than I expected," Leslie replied.

"Really? Ready to indict me?"

Leslie confronted a woman who was terribly sure of herself. Her look of amusement impressed the investigator. "When I'm ready, you'll know," Leslie answered, without making a commitment. She respected Sir Jane in a way she hadn't expected.

Then, changing gears altogether, Jane inspected Leslie from head to toe, as if she were preparing to place her in bondage. "I'm sure there's some sassy submissive that would like to serve you here. Don't miss the opportunity. Unless, of course, you'd rather submit. Then I'd take you right now."

Leslie was startled by the surge of energy that suddenly raced through her on hearing Jane's suggestion. "I'm sure I'll have exactly what I need here tonight," Leslie replied, trying not to give away her feelings.

Jane flashed a strangely charming grin—charming only because it came from Jane whose whole persona was exceedingly hard and cold most of the time.

To the detective's surprise, she felt a gnawing in her loins: some relief was necessary. And once Jane sauntered off, Leslie became aware of Leta's hand resting casually on her bottom, her long fingers beginning to fondle her there.

"Should we take care of this?" the woman asked,

when Leslie looked back at the tempting black woman.

Leslie nodded, still unsure what she was getting herself into: but she was so horny she was ready for anything. Leta led her by the hand through the crowd of dispersing guests, to a room at the back of the club. Though it was small, just an eight by eight cell, it was complete with all the SM paraphernalia necessary to contrive most any scene.

Inside the room, Leta began to undo the buttons of Leslie's vest. "What perfect breasts," she said, when they were exposed for her inspection. "So white." Leslie was thinking similar things about the black woman, watching Leta's chocolate brown tits move seductively up and down in her bustier.

Taking Leslie's nipples between her fingers, Leta squeezed them lightly. "Have you ever had these clamped?" the woman asked.

"No," Leslie replied.

From the pocket of her skirt, the woman pulled out nipple clamps, dangling them before Leslie's eyes. Despite Leslie's dominant attire, apparently Leta thought of herself as the dominant in this scene and Leslie her untrained submissive. For some reason, Leslie didn't mind that, even though there was a little fear of the pain that might follow.

"We'll start really slowly," Leta assured her with loving tones. Taking each nipple in her slender black hands, she attached the biting clamps to them. Since the buds of Leslie's breasts were already erect it was that much easier. "Such enormous nipples, you should have them pierced." The thought made Leslie shudder, even though she probably would have consented to just about anything at that moment. Little rings? She wondered what they would look like pierced through her flesh.

The sensations that followed were exquisite, and a soft burning feeling moved through her body, settling in her cunt. The heavy chain that joined the two nipples dangled between her breasts and gave her a constant stimulation she couldn't ignore. Even though her submission had just begun, she was starting to comprehend the reasons for this kind of sex.

Backing away, Leta admired Leslie's leather-clad bottom. She reached out and ran her hand along the polished surface of her pants.

"Humm, yes," Leslie groaned, feeling the gesture all the way to her cunt.

When Leta smacked her with her hand, a satisfying warmth spreading through Leslie's rear. A dozen smacks and the lovely sensation just mounted.

"On your hands and knees," Leta ordered—even though there was hardly a demand in her voice.

Anxious for the sensations to continue, Leslie readily complied, while Leta drew a riding crop from the wall. The woman walked around her submissive, taunting her as she whisked the implement through the air, its sound as noxious as Sir Jane's cane. Unlike the cane, however, this instrument had a wide, flat end that would make a far different impression on a yielding ass. At first just taunting her, Leta made a sudden change, quickly rapping Leslie's bottom with a half-dozen sharp snaps. The sound was ferocious, each strike to Leslie's upturned bottom seemingly ruthless, though it only added another measure of delight. Leslie tried to forget the way she'd so abruptly consented to this, and how in the past she'd believed that being submissive was contrary to her nature. All her former objections didn't seem to matter in light of what she was feeling. Her squirms and moans were just pleas for more raps from the riding crop. She was not the least bit upset when the smacks became harder still.

"You ready for this?" the gentle dominant purred as she bent down, reaching around Leslie's waist to find the button on her leather jeans. She had them off Leslie's ass seconds later, before the submissive could reply. Seeing Leslie's bare butt wiggling expectantly was all the answer she needed. "My, I've hardly made it red," Leta noticed. "Your pants have protected you too well. You'll have to learn to take a whole lot more before we'll call you a submissive." She said it sweetly, but she meant it.

This time when the crop landed, it sent sharp jolts through Leslie's rear, though they were still no less welcome. There was no way she would stop, even as she felt a steady burn rising on her bottom, a burn that was quickly turning to pain. What she needed thereafter was a climax. She could feel it roaring inside her so strongly, she thought she would explode. She ached in ways she'd never even imagined before.

When Leta collapsed at her side, the smooth black hand found its way between Leslie's legs where she was sopping wet. The two tumbled together, arms around each other, Leslie welcoming the sensuous kisses that covered her face and neck. It was only seconds and Leslie came, her hips jolting wildly, the fire in her body going on and on and on.

"Come here, slut, and please me," Leta demanded. Without giving her time to recoup, she was pulling Leslie to a glistening pussy that was raw and ready for its own pleasure. She came with little whimpers after just a moment of Leslie's attention to her throbbing clit.

"You like this more than you thought? Perhaps?" Leta suggested, as Leslie snuggled against the woman's smooth, dark legs. Indeed, she loved it more than she ever imagined she would. She was taken by Leta's nurturing style, though making love to her was not so very different from ways she might have made love to other lovers—to Rosalie, and at one time to Robin. She would never have called it SM—she thought of SM as savage and cruel, but there was nothing brutal about this at all.

What fascinated her even more than this was Jane and her heavy-handed ruthlessness. The cunning darkness, mixed with a little trace of tenderness; a remarkable desire was born in her, seeing the way Jane brutally ravaged Dagne. Leslie hungered to call that woman "sir," to bow at her feet, to give up her body for the same mean, yet tender discipline.

CHAPTER SEVEN

"You what!" Robin exclaimed.

"I had sex with a black woman at the club. She used a riding crop on my ass." For some inexplicable reason, Leslie had to tell Robin about the sex before she even mentioned her discoveries at Sapphos. It was the next morning, and the two were eating cheese Danish, getting crumbs all over the desk in the small office they shared.

"And you were worried about me getting distracted? Do I have to go back and ask the questions?" Robin said wiping her face and taking a long drink of coffee.

"No, I found out plenty," Leslie replied.

"Like what?" Robin wanted proof.

"Like Jane dominating Felicia," Leslie said, rather proud of the revelation.

"What?"

"They were heavy into SM games at Sapphos. Jane brought her there several times, and apparently Felicia was having the time of her life bowing to Sir Jane. Does that surprise you?" Leslie asked, looking at Robin's surprised expression.

"I don't really know. But it certainly complicates things. Not one of the other four women suggested the possibility. Apparently the two kept it very quiet," Robin surmised.

"Not only that, but one woman I talked to thought that Jane was really in love with Felicia."

"In love?" Robin wanted more.

"Felicia was apparently very special to our suspect, and their intimate moments were not any secret to the women at the club."

"How interesting," Robin said. "I'd never have guessed that Felicia would want a woman as tough as Jane."

"She may not be as tough as you think. Despite her hard-ass butch dyke manner, she has a really sweet side, as if there's a tender old dame under the surface."

"Is this what people said of her, or what you saw?"

"What I saw? I watched her top one of the club's doms. She was terrifying every second, though there was this undercurrent of care. It was really quite amazing."

"It doesn't really surprise me; the really good tops are like that, at least the ones I've been with." Robin readily thought of Britta, the sad woman who was so lovingly mean that it left her breathless. Now she saw that same kind of breathless response in Leslie: it was unexpected coming from this great lady of reason, order, and sensibility. "What about the night of the murder?" Robin asked, changing the subject.

"She was there all right. But no one can swear that she might not have left for awhile still, no one there is going to testify that she wasn't there. She might as well own the place; she's the one in charge. She licks no one's boots."

"But she could have left?"

"It's common for her to disappear for an hour or two in some private room. The way the place is arranged, it would be easy to create a perfect alibi and then slip out to do some murderous deed."

"Did anyone remember her being in a private room?"

"She's into a girl named Chris. Was with her that night. I managed to get Chris to tell me that she and Jane had quite a scene going, but is sounded like Chris was too far gone to testify to anything. I suppose you know what that means?"

"You mean she was likely bound and blindfolded and off in another world? Yeah, I understand that," Robin said. "So Jane doesn't really have an alibi at all. That makes it very interesting."

"But I don't think she killed Felicia," Leslie quickly added.

"Why? Because she had the capacity to care?" Robin asked.

"Because I couldn't imagine her doing it," Leslie said.

"Now you're sounding like me," Robin said. "My intuitive abilities must be rubbing off." She chuckled under her breath. "So tell me, how did you like surrendering your ass?" she asked, reminding Leslie that she hadn't forgotten her earlier announcement.

Leslie thought for a minute. "I was dumbfounded," Leslie admitted.

"And…"

"Puzzled. It was bizarre. But it wasn't all that different than slapping asses when I make love to someone. I even did that to you," she reminded Robin. "I guess because it was the club and there's all that SM ambiance," she said tongue in cheek, "it took on a darker flavor."

"Well, did you *like* it?" Robin asked, frustrated with her partner's vague replies.

"Yes!" Leslie said.

"Good." Robin backed off, a pleased smirk crossing her face. "I would never have believed it," she commented.

"Well don't get too excited; it's not like I'm going back tonight," Leslie added. "But…"

"You might do it again?" Robin suggested.

"Let's just say the possibility is much more likely than it was a few days ago. So what have you uncovered?" Leslie asked, ready to talk about something else.

"My friend Diane called to report on Martha and Zelda at State U. Martha got her graduate degree there in 1976, but as far as Diane could tell, Zelda was never there, at least under that name. Betsy was pretty clear that Martha wasn't telling the truth when she called them friends. I think there's a lot those two are hiding. Remy too."

"So we still have four suspects," Leslie stated.

"We do, and none of them with a reasonable alibi, including Jane, and any of them could have a reason to murder Felicia. Jane's could be a number of things, from money to sex. Remy might well have been jealous, and Martha and Zelda are both suspect because of their affection for Remy."

"So where do we go from here?" Leslie asked.

"Well, I've done some checking on Brightwood. There's a Brightwood Hospital, a private mental institution in New Hampshire that might just have some answers."

"One of our suspects was a resident, you think?"

"I think so," Robin said.

"Which one?" Leslie asked.

"I'm not sure, but the way Martha was almost afraid to let Remy talk…"

"Afraid she'd incriminate herself?"

"Or both of them. I think it's very possible that one of them could have some secret they wouldn't want anyone to know, especially when it concerns this case. How about a little side trip?" Robin suggested.

Several hours later Leslie and Robin were making their way north in Leslie's pickup, chattering back and forth about the case. Revelations about Leslie's experiences the night before went undiscussed, creating an ever-mounting tension between the two.

"Do you suppose there could be some conspiracy between the three ladies in question?" Robin asked.

"What makes you think that?" Leslie asked.

"I'm not sure, but if we believe it's not Betsy, and we know instinctively that it's not Jane, because she's too sweet to do it…," Leslie laughed at the remark, "then, it would have to be one of the other three, and for the life of me, I can't quite figure which one could do it. They all seem to be rather mild-mannered women. Hardly your killer type."

"Well, when you rule out the 'killer type' because she's got a soft side," Leslie said, referring to Jane, "maybe you can include the mild-mannered, because underneath there's a hidden darker side," Leslie suggested, her eyes glowing with a mock-horrified glimmer.

"I guess we'll have to see if we can get something really concrete on this trip. We could use something really solid, and soon," Robin said.

They drove along in silence for some time, with Robin turning in her seat after they were another fifty miles down the road. She put her hand on Leslie's thigh, enjoying the warmth of her partner's body. "You want to stop at a motel and take care of this 'stuff' going on between us?" Robin asked.

"What stuff?" Leslie asked.

"You can't feel the tension?" Robin asked.

"I got to you, didn't I?" Leslie said, feeling almost triumphant that she'd given her partner a taste of the same jarring discoveries she'd been treated with in the past. Robin's sordid sexual disclosures had left her with her mouth on the floor on more than one occasion.

"You've wanted me back on *your* terms," Robin suggested, "now you want me back on mine, perhaps? You're not too good at lying about these things. Your revelation this morning was a pretty blatant come on."

Leslie turned and smiled. "I know, and it was probably stupid, because I'm quite prepared to love you again, but I'm not prepared for the sex. Not yet anyway. I know that it sounds absurd, but this is all really strange to me, that I'd respond this way to SM, when I did a pretty good job of feeling rather bored about it while the two of us were together. I'm still not sure about you and me and how that would feel. Besides, I do have a relationship with Rosalie."

"Rosalie didn't seem to bother you last night," Robin pointed out.

"I know. But that was practically anonymous, and it was work. Rosalie wouldn't have any problem with that. Sleeping with my former lover and business partner—that's something different. I'm not sure Rosalie would be that open."

Robin snickered, listening to Leslie defend herself. "I think it's you that has a problem, just like always. Rosalie is a convenient excuse. You never thought the two of you would be together for long in the first place. You don't really love her—mutual respect maybe, but love? Come on Les." Robin turned back in her seat and stared out the window, watching as the sunny countryside rolled by, thinking for just an instant that it would be nice not to go back to this case at all, for all the weird things that it had seemed to spawn.

"I'd like not to make any mistakes with us," Leslie interjected after about ten minutes of silence.

Robin listened impatiently as Leslie went on about her fears, finally interrupting, "What does it matter if we do make a mistake? It's not going to change anything, is it? We've already kept the partnership together with one breakup." She shook her head angrily. "I don't know why I'm arguing with you. Listen to yourself! This doesn't sound like you at all."

They arrived at the mental hospital an hour later, after riding in a prickly silence the rest of the way.

Leslie flashed her identification to the woman at the front desk; and after sitting in the lobby to wait, they were finally ushered into a pleasant office with an expansive set of windows that overlooked an all-too-passive scene. Brightwood's grounds looked like a stereotypical movie-set version of psychiatric hospital serenity. A few people strolled the landscaped lawns, though at lunch hour most of the staff and patients were in the dining room.

"I'm Jessica Crandall," a stately woman said, rising to shake their hands. She was a gracious woman, dressed in a plain gray business suit, her hair tied back in a bun at the base of her neck. She did look austere, making the detectives immediately doubt her usefulness to their investigation.

"Robin Penny and Leslie Patrick. We're private investigators looking into the death of Felicia Roman. We have reason to believe that one of the suspects in this case was a former patient at Brightwood."

"It was my understanding from the papers that the murderer is in custody."

"It's our belief, Ms. Crandall, that the woman in custody may very well be innocent."

"I see. But then, how can I help you? Our records are confidential, so there would be very little I could tell you."

"Perhaps you could just look up these names and see if any of these woman have a connection with this hospital."

"And they are?"

"Martha Quigley, Remy Thurston-Moore, and Zelda Wing."

With a grim expression on her stern face, the administrator lowered her half glasses to the bottom of her nose, then turned to the keyboard where she typed into her computer. She watched the screen for a few moments, then turned back to the investigators with a shrewd look on her face, as if she were trying to determine exactly what to say to them.

"Remy Thurston-Moore was a patient here for two

years. I do remember her. She was discharged in stable mental health five years ago. Martha Quigley was an attendant here for nearly a year. I remember her too. She did her job well but had career plans outside the medical field."

"Were the two women here at the same time?" Robin asked.

"Yes they were. In fact, they left within days of each other, but that would appear to be coincidental since they were in different sections of the hospital. I doubt they had any contact, if that's what you're trying to establish."

"And Zelda Wing?"

"Our records show that she was also here as an aide, very short term."

"And that was during Remy's stay?" Robin asked.

The administrator turned back to the computer. "Yes. At the very beginning she did work on the ward where Remy was assigned. But she was there only about five months."

"At the same time Martha Quigley was here?"

"No, she left several months before Martha joined us."

"You can't give us anything else?"

"I'm afraid not. The courts might be able to open my files, but I'm rather a stickler for rules. If you had a warrant, then I might help you more. Now, if you'll excuse me, I have to meet someone in the dining room."

"I'll say she's a stickler for rules," Leslie said sarcastically, as the two detectives walked out of the building. "She certainly wouldn't want to be out on a limb to be useful in an investigation."

"But we did establish that Remy and Martha likely met here, not at school. It seems our dour shrinking violet Remy has a past that bears more looking into," Robin said. "And we seem to have the beginnings of Remy and Zelda's friendship, though I wonder what would bring them together so quickly in a place like this, especially with Remy in the violent ward?"

"I wish we had more," Leslie mused aloud.

They stood together in the parking lot for some minutes, Robin looking as if her brain were working overtime.

"Just give me a minute," Robin said. "I think I'll try a long shot." Leslie watched her partner quickly dump her jacket in the back of the truck, along with the red cap she was wearing. Robin hastily swished her blonde hair to reveal a woman in a white blouse and baggy navy pants that would hardly stand out in any crowd. She could even pass for someone who belonged on the hospital grounds, which was exactly what she intended. She left Leslie standing by the car and walked toward the footpath that traversed well-manicured lawns.

There had always been a little bit of an actress in Robin, and it was suddenly ready to appear again. Leslie watched her partner, admiring her style. For a moment, Robin appraised the landscape carefully, thoughtfully eyeing a number of patients and aides. Finally approaching an older female aide, Leslie saw her partner strike up a casual conversation. She knew right away that Robin had picked the woman for her easy, jovial personality: she looked every bit the gossipy kind of person who would spill everything she knew as long as someone paid attention to her stories.

"You hear about the murder down south?" Robin

asked the bubbly gray-haired woman, after the two had exchanged pleasantries. She watched the woman's eyes light up as she stopped to sit on a bench. The detective was pleased to see a twenty-five-year pin proudly displayed on the lapel of the woman's white uniform, along with a name tag reading Joan Barnes, LPN. Her big, thick glasses assured Robin that she wouldn't be able to recognize people by sight all that easily.

"I sure did, noticed the names right off. Doesn't surprise me in the slightest, that Martha Quigley. She was an interesting one from the beginning. Kind of odd, but pleasant enough. And she wasn't one of those girls that hardly lifts a finger around here. Kind of strange though, the way she got all attached to that girl, she was always doting over her like some mother hen. It was really funny if you ask me. What was that girl's name again? Funny name." The woman screwed up her face trying to think.

"You remember the girl, the patient?" Robin asked.

"Naw, she was in another ward. I guess she only knew Martha, because she put in some extra time, doing research of some sort with the violent ones."

"I'm surprised the two weren't suspects in the murder," Robin suggested.

"Isn't that amazing? Hard to picture that one being violent, even when she was here. Few times I saw her, I remember her being real sweet, kinda quiet though. But you know those quiet ones." She rolled her eyes. "You know, I thought about calling the police when I saw they arrested the lover of the murdered lady. You think they'd know about that girl—what was her name again?"

"Remy?" Robin asked, as if she were also in doubt.

"That's right. Kind of nice name, I think. I figure

Martha and Remy musta ended up lovers. I mean with the victim and that suspect being lovers. Stands to reason that they were all lesbians, living together."

"I guess so," Robin agreed.

"You know, when I read about the murder, it reminded me of this woman who was here a while back. Eve was her name. Oh, I'll never forget her. They put her in this place for murdering her lover. Just like this case, she tied up the poor girl, went really crazy and stabbed her. Now there's a real loony. Not a sane bone in her body, though you wouldn't know it to see her."

"What happened to her? She still here?"

"No," Joan Barnes said. "Dead. A couple of years ago she got out and really went plum crazy. Jumped out of a building, I think. You wonder sometimes what makes people do things."

"Did you see that other woman who lived with them at that big estate? She used to work here too," Robin continued baiting her subject.

"Oh, yes. Now I didn't see the picture in the paper, but if that was Zelda Wing, I'm hardly surprised. That woman was kind of funny, too." She leaned into Robin whispering. "You know, I think we all get a little funny in the head working here," she said with a smile. "Never heard from her after she left, and then she shows up at a murder."

"You kinda wonder," Robin said shaking her head. She would keep the woman talking as long as she could, but Joan Barnes seemed to be ready for something else, since she rose from her seat on the bench.

"Hope they got the right woman. Would be terrible wouldn't it, if it was Remy?"

Robin smiled as she joined Leslie at the car.

"So…" Leslie asked anxiously.

"Didn't get much, but I did find out that Remy was in the violent ward," Robin said with her eyes glimmering happily. "Martha apparently had a fixation with Remy right off, so this lady says."

"Why was Remy committed?" Leslie asked.

"She didn't say," Robin shrugged.

"And Zelda?"

"She remembers her, but not well. She remembers that she was strange, but then she thinks everyone's a little crazy around here," Robin said.

"She's probably right. So what's the next stunt you plan to pull?" Leslie asked, still a little in awe of her partner's fact-finding genius.

"I think we need to do some further checking on Remy. See what the DA's office has on her. We might just have our killer," Robin said.

The two climbed in the truck and headed back home.

When they were nearly back in town, and the quiet between the two of them became too much for Robin to bear. "When do you think you'll be ready for me again?" she asked. "Or are you saving your dominant/submissive tenancies for strangers?" The idea that Leslie would even consider the SM left her with an incredible longing. She almost wished Leslie had never gotten into this at all.

"Don't be difficult, Rob, I've got to get this clear in me first. Then we'll talk." Leslie drove up to the office, pulling the truck next to Robin's Suzuki.

Robin nodded. "Whatever you say, love. I'll just forget about it."

"So, I'll see you in the morning at the Hill?" Leslie asked. "A few cards to lay on the table?"

"Maybe, but I'm sure not about confrontations just yet. I want to get some more information on Remy, if the police have anything. And I want to check around the estate." Robin replied.

Leslie nodded, knowing that her partner had something churning through her head, but as usual she was keeping mum, probably because Robin wasn't even sure yet what she was looking for. Funny, Robin's dilemma about the case matched Leslie's own about sex. She guessed they both had some thinking to do.

Leslie drove off, leaving Robin wondering if she might visit Britta again. She hadn't had back-to-back sessions in some time, but she was feeling as raw as she had just after she'd learned of Felicia's death. She didn't know what she wanted from Leslie, but this impasse certainly wasn't it!

Leslie drove toward home realizing that she was so torn between conflicting desires, she had no idea what to do. A big part of her wanted to go back to Robin and find some way of making mad, passionate love to her, though strangely now, she would hardly know where to begin. To Leslie's amazement, she was nearly as motivated to go to Jane Hugh's cottage on the Hill and seek out the dom's advice. But that seemed pretty stupid. She couldn't imagine a dom giving advice. Jane would probably as likely beat her ass as talk to her. But then again, maybe that's what she wanted. As Leslie approached her apartment, however, she gazed up to see that the lights were on in both the living room and bedroom.

"My word, Rosalie's home," she thought, suddenly very relieved.

"Home early?" Leslie said coming in the door with a smile on her face.

"*Ah, mi señorita*," Rosalie said in her thick Spanish accent, "you look so flushed tonight."

"You been speaking Spanish all day?" Leslie asked, as her arms surrounded her lover. Rosalie was warm as always Leslie noted as her lover's hips moved against her for a luscious tango.

"*Sí*. With my old *amiga*," she said, smiling brightly.

The look in her eyes was definitely carnal.

"Had a good time?" Leslie asked.

Rosalie shook her head and pouted, "No sex: she was on the rag."

"That's better for me. I need you," Leslie said, drawing the warm body closer to her.

"Of course you do," Rosalie said.

"I always want you, but I need you now," Leslie clarified. "This case is just too strange. I'm getting a little spooked."

"The murder?" Rosalie asked.

"Yes, in fact, I spent last night in a lesbian S&M club," she explained.

"Oooo, the nasty stuff? You play too?"

"A little," Leslie admitted. "I was wearing my leather pants, and your vest and earrings."

"And you don't do that for me, you naughty bitch," Rosalie replied, half angrily. She shoved her lover away with a playful push.

"It would have been better if it had been you," Leslie tried to assure her, even if it wasn't true at all. She couldn't imagine anything more perfect than Leta's kind dominance. She was certain Rosalie would be a much different dom, if she would be dominant at all. And she couldn't even imagine her being submissive.

"You could spank my bottom," Leslie offered, thinking that, regardless, she wanted sex now.

"And you can spank mine," Rosalie retorted.

It was just a big tease, the two of them beginning to laugh as they traded slaps and raced each other to the bedroom. Leslie tumbled in first, ripping her clothes away. Rosalie dove for her puss, licking it from top to bottom.

"God that feels good, do it more, Rosie," Leslie cried.

Rosalie looked up, winking at her, then patted Leslie's pussy as if she were spanking it.

"Oooo, yes," Leslie said, jerking with the slaps that began to sting.

Rosalie inserted two fingers into Leslie's cunt and fucked her nastily, while Leslie grabbed her lover's hair and pressed her further into her wet cleft.

Rosalie bobbed up and down on the throbbing clit, though a second later, she backed off. "Not so fast. You're not gonna get off that easily you little slut!" she said. Rosalie then drove her fingers deeper yet, Leslie opening wide to accommodate them. "You take it all tonight," Rosalie said, removing her hand and pulling a bottle of clear grease and a smooth latex glove from the bedside table.

Leslie watched as Rosalie prepared her slim hand for the assault on her cunt. This was the one thing Rosalie did so well, one thing other lovers had problems forcing on her. A most submissive kind of sex, fist-fucking. She needed it tough, especially right now. Leslie felt herself juice at merely the suggestion, her cunt relaxing to open wide for Rosalie's entry.

Then her lover descended on her, with her Spanish eyes flashing gaily, her red lips lustily descending on Leslie's clitoris.

Three fingers in her pussy became four, became Rosalie's full hand pressing at the gate, seeking entry all the way inside. There was a burn, a pressing-pulling-reaching sensation, so hard to describe afterwards, but so glorious for the instant it happened. With Rosalie's fist at last inside, the two rocked about the bed, while Leslie moaned from the amazing feelings that split her in two. She loved being fucked this way, rutting like some wild animal.

"Oh, yes, Rosalie, yes!" Leslie screamed. She felt waves passing through her as her muscles pulsed and the orgasm washed over her. Rosalie licked every bit of the pussy juice splashing out over Leslie's clit, her tongue not ceasing until her lover was finished, her body limp.

Leslie's eyes opened to see a smile on Rosalie's face—worth the violation. It was the perfect reward for a savage moment of bliss, seeing her lover's lusty, bright lips beam at her.

"You kinky slut," was Rosalie's favorite compliment.

"No nastier than you," Leslie charged back. Rosalie withdrew her hand, leaving Leslie's cunt empty, noticeably empty. Too quick, it was always too quick, Leslie thought to herself.

"I could do the same for you," Leslie said, as she lay side by side with Rosalie, their breasts pressed together, their arms and legs intertwining as their tongues met.

"I should have done it in your ass, little naughty bitch that you are, going out and getting yourself screwed by some dyke in a nightclub. What did they do to you?" she asked.

"Leta spanked my bottom."

"And you like that don't you?" Rosalie asked.

"I'm not sure. Do you?" Leslie asked, giving Rosalie a whack on the rear.

"Only as long as you use your hand. I love hands. I love yours. I love being mauled." Her voice disappeared into soft cooing moans, traces of unintelligible Spanish words on her red lips. Leslie kissed them while her hand worked Rosalie's softly swaying cunt. She pinched her clitoris, rubbed her tender folds, and toyed gently with her opening. Leaning back, Rosalie let her coming sounds ripple joyously through the air, tiny spasms giving her away. She always came so softly, and Leslie always loved the moments after resting in the soft surrounding essence.

How many more times they'd be together like this, Leslie wasn't sure. In the past it had been Rosalie who played around, Leslie by choice remaining faithful to her sweet Spanish lover. It was just simpler and more convenient for Leslie to have one lover at a time, even though relationship commitment was not a concept that honestly applied to Rosalie.

Now thoughts of Robin and Jane held her fascination, so that she knew Rosalie wouldn't be around much longer. Rosalie sensed things; she'd be moving on by the end of fall, if not before, Leslie guessed—just because Rosalie wouldn't stay around to any bitter end. The flirtatious woman would find someone else to catch her interest, and then she'd be gone.

Leslie lay back, relaxing, letting her mind drift away, coming back to the reality of this murder investigation and its need for a solution.

CHAPTER EIGHT

"We're going to look through Felicia's room," Robin announced as she met Leslie on the steps of Roman Hill the next morning.

"Her room? What are your searching for? The police have probably taken everything of interest. They confiscated all the pictures of Felicia with Betsy and Martha."

"I know that, but Felicia used to hide stuff," Robin explained. "She had her little treasures planted all over the house. I'm counting on the possibility that the police missed a few things. Once they decided on Betsy, I don't think they did much searching after they had the evidence they wanted."

"What are you looking for?" Leslie asked.

"In general, anything. Specifically, more pictures. It struck me last night, all this photography. That wasn't something Felicia ever did with me. But she had a real obsessive side to her; once she started something like this hobby of hers, she became insistent on duplicating the same thing over and over. Like the way she used to tie a bow around my neck. It didn't matter what kind of sex she wanted, it was always the same, Felicia signaling her intentions. She'd take a slip of ribbon and tie it around my neck, then she'd flash her eyes at me and giggle in a very provocative way. Sometimes she'd wait for hours before she made the next move. She even performed her little gesture with people around. 'Our little secret,' she'd tell me."

"Did she ever not make a move?" Leslie asked. "I mean after she put the ribbon around your neck?"

"No, but it did make things awfully suspenseful."

From what Leslie knew of Felicia, she had to admire her sexual theatrics. No wonder she could string so many women along at once.

"So you think the pictures could be another fetish with her?"

"Yeah. It could also have been a spur of the moment thing, some wild idea because she had an expensive new camera and wanted to try it out."

"She did have quite an elaborate setup with the tripod and the delay timer and all that," Leslie added. "It would suggest that she really spent some time thinking about what she wanted to do with it."

"I'm thinking that going to the trouble to take these pictures of her with her lovers that there had to be more than just the ones with Betsy and Martha. The camera was at least five years old, and knowing Felicia, she had photographs of every one of her lovers during that time. One thing I know for certain—she'd never hide all her 'evidence' in one place. She was never that organized. She stashed things of all kinds everywhere. The police were probably lucky to find what pictures they did. And those were probably the most obvious."

There was no sign of life around the house as Leslie and Robin climbed the front stairs. The morning was brisk for the time of year. There seemed to be a clarity in the air, and a crystal clear quality to the sky so that even in this muted place of savage wildness, things stood out rather starkly. By afternoon, everything would muddy considerably.

"Wonder what will really happen to this place when this is all over?" Leslie said.

"After she's buried today, I guess they'll read the will—that should be interesting."

"You going to the funeral?" Leslie asked.

"My love, I wouldn't miss it," Robin said. According to Robin, funerals were the best source of clues possible. She prided herself on studying patterns of grief, since it was so often associated with their investigations.

After waiting for several minutes at the front door, Leslie turned the knob and called into the musty air, "Anybody here?" Hearing no response, she and Robin stepped inside the hallway. They shut the door, hearing a heavy click as it latched tight. The screen door banged outside a few seconds later. They were surprised that still, with all the annoying sounds, no one answered.

"Martha, Remy!" Leslie called. They finally heard a shuffle upstairs. Through the hallway they thought they saw Zelda slipping out the back, though at the same time their attention was drawn to Martha coming down the sweeping staircase.

"May I help you?" she said politely, though she didn't seem particularly happy to see the two detectives.

"We'd like to take a look at Felicia's bedroom," Robin said.

"Oh?"

"Betsy assured me that we could have free access to the room, since, of course, it was hers too."

"I doubt Betsy really has the authority to allow anything regarding this house, but go ahead if you want. I assume you'll stay clear of our room. We really have nothing to hide; and, since the police went through everything, including underwear drawers, before they finished their investigation, I can't imagine there's anything left to find."

"We won't be long," Robin said, ignoring Martha's editorial. The two detectives mounted the staircase and made their way down the massive hallway, entering the spacious apartment that had always been Felicia's bedroom—and that of whatever lover shared her bed.

Robin made a first perusal of the room, noting similarities and differences between its present state and when she used to share it with Felicia Roman.

Leslie watched her partner work; Robin had this theory about climbing inside a person's psyche and waltzing around in their point of view so she could figure out how they thought. Leslie had heard of people, psychologists in general, talk about doing this; but she'd never seen anyone but Robin do it with such startling and immediate results.

Robin gave the room a thorough scrutiny. There was a round turret that was set up like a sitting area with two chairs, a small footstool, and a table with an antique lamp. The bed was to the right against the wall, an enormous antiquated four-poster bed with a canopy and drapes that closed around it. Leslie had seen pictures of the bed with Felicia in it, but in person, it looked even more imposing. Now, stripped of all its sheets, the bed looked stark and wholly uninviting without the soft aura of pillows and comforters.

There was a dressing table and mirror on the far wall, and an enormous wardrobe to the left of the doorway. On the near wall were doors to closets and the bathroom. With the door standing open, Leslie and Robin could see inside the stark white-tiled room which had already been cleared out and cleaned.

The blonde detective moved around the room slowly, opening doors and drawers but not really looking beyond the surface of things. Occasionally she looked back at the turret sitting area as if there were something there that she was trying see, and yet hadn't been able to. She went about the whole room with this strange cursory inspection. Her mind was obviously churning madly. Leslie was certain that her partner would spin out of control if she didn't come to a verdict soon.

"Robin...?" Leslie said, wanting to hear her partner speak her mind.

"You know I can almost hear her laughing at me right now, as if we're little kids playing hide and seek, and she's giggling in some dark corner. I know there's something in this room that no one has seen. It's like she's toying with me. I've got goose bumps all over."

That was Robin's sure sign of cosmic truth about to descend.

"So, what's going on?" Leslie prompted her quietly, not wanting to disturb Robin's mood.

"It's so strange in here," Robin started. She was opening more of the infinite cubbyholes and hiding places scattered around the room. "I guess I'm time warping, remembering this room. It hasn't changed very much since I was here. Funny, don't you think, that there's really nothing that personal around here, certainly nothing of Betsy's? And all these things, these pictures and figurines around here, they're all the same as they used to be. Isn't that kind of strange? I wonder, in all her jumbled disordered life, if this room wasn't the one place that was stable for her. Perhaps this house was her anchor, what kept her from really getting out of control. I was thinking about what Jane said, that she couldn't give this up. I can't imagine Felicia ever living anywhere but here; she was a very provincial woman." Leslie could have commented, but she didn't want to break Robin's train of thought.

"She liked it here; she used to like to sit in the window...." Robin's voice drifted off as she moved toward the turret, her eyes on the footstool. She had found something. Suddenly grabbed the small piece of furniture and pried the top of the cushioned seat off the four-legged base. It came loose with little effort, spilling a white, dog-eared envelope onto the floor.

"I knew it!" she exclaimed, throwing the stool aside.

Picking up the envelope, she sat down in a chair and began to open the packet. Leslie sat across from her, anxiously watching Robin's hands pull out the contents.

"Your source at Sapphos was right. Look," Robin said. She handed Leslie the photographs after she looked at each one. They were pictures of Felicia tied to her bed, not unlike the pictures of her at her death. The delayed action of the camera had caught Jane Hugh in the act of whipping Felicia's rear end. In other pictures Jane was shoving a dildo into the woman's ass, while still another showed Felicia at Jane's feet, her head pressed to the carpet with a riding crop at her back. Red marks showed that this was no passive staged pose: Jane was in the process of punishing her. It was remarkable the expression on Felicia's face: a little anguish, a little pain and fear, and a degree of contentment that was appalling. Frozen in the white frame of the photographs, Felicia looked as if she could walk right out of the picture as big as life. So very different from the violent peace of her death, though that death seemed all the more fitting after seeing these photos.

"How did you know these would be here?" Leslie asked.

"I'm not sure exactly, except that I flashed on this picture of Felicia sitting by these windows—she loved this view of the grounds. She'd meditate here for hours sometimes: I often wondered what she was cooking up in that creative little brain of hers. I remember walking in on her one day; her hand was at her cunt playing. I watched, just stood stock-still and watched her masturbate. She knew I was there, but she kept going, not for an instant missing a stroke. It was really lovely...Felicia there in her paisley print dress, the skirt pulled up, her naked cunt, all pink and wet, responding to her thoughts and playing hands."

"Perhaps she was looking at pictures then?" Leslie asked.

"No, I don't think so. There weren't any that I remember, but I can imagine her sitting here in recent weeks, looking through these photographs, getting recharged by the scenes she played out. I was wondering, where would she hide them? Some place close seemed like an obvious choice."

"Well, you got results," Leslie said happily.

"Did you notice the ropes this time?" Robin returned to a picture of Felicia tied to the bed.

Leslie studied the color pictures for a few moments. The ropes were tied the way they were tied in the photographs of her dead body. "Exactly the same knots the murderer used," Leslie said. "More reason to implicate Jane."

"Looks that way, doesn't it?" Robin answered.

"Time to talk to her?" Leslie suggested.

"It's getting very close," Robin replied.

CHAPTER NINE

Zelda walked along the garden path, making her way toward Jane Hugh's cottage. She was purposeful in her intentions, knowing exactly what she wanted after having been at Roman Hill for the last dozen days. She hoped that she would have made as distinct an impression on Jane as Jane had made on her. Not seeing the dom anywhere around, Zelda knocked on the cottage door. She knocked again when no one answered.

"You looking for me?"

Zelda turned to see the object of her search standing behind her some five feet, looking lusciously handsome as usual. "In fact I was," Zelda replied, flashing the woman a charming smile.

"And why's that?" Jane asked directly. She was wearing a pair of jeans, her cowboy boots, and a plain black shirt. There were small silver hoops in her ears, one with a dangling cross. Otherwise she was as plainly dressed as usual. Her close-cropped hair had its usual spiked look on top.

"I thought, perhaps," Zelda hedged as she batted her eyes at Jane, "maybe we could spend some time together."

"What in heaven's name for?" Jane asked.

"I think we have some common fetishes," Zelda said.

"You want me to make you submit? That would be the only thing we have in common."

"I think we could have some fun."

"I don't do just anyone," Jane said. "I have to have some motivation. Your little games with Martha were hardly inspiring."

"That's what I mean. Martha is rather uninspiring. And she's kinda pent up about Felicia's death. I thought perhaps we could enjoy ourselves a little." She batted her eyes again, which Jane thought was rather silly.

"I'm going to the funeral," the dom informed her. "I really don't have time."

"I'm going too, but maybe after?" Zelda suggested. "It would release a lot of tension."

"I see your point. But why would I want you?"

"You don't know how inventive I can be, how much I like to be whipped and played with and pinched," Zelda said.

Jane passed her on the walkway and opened the cottage door.

"You can suck my cunt, bitch, and bring me off. Then I'll do what I can do for you later," Jane said.

Zelda smiled happily. Walking through the cottage door, she was about to close it.

"No, leave it open. Anyone here can see what you're like."

"Oooo, my, you are devilish," Zelda whispered.

"I'm more than that; get on the floor, slut."

Zelda instantly dropped to her knees and crawled to Jane, whose pants were already open, her wet pussy waiting to be served.

"You fuck this up, bitch, you'll get nothing," Jane charged. Taking a handful of Zelda's hair in her hand, she pulled the woman's head to her cunt.

Zelda squealed with delight and planted her mouth on Jane's puss. Jane hadn't liked the woman from the moment she'd first met her, but she was the kind of lesbian the dom liked to be nasty with. That weasely affectation in her voice, those rolling eyes, and suggestive body language were all so repulsive to her that she would love to slap the woman's face, and keep her on her knees, making her crawl for weeks and eat off the floor before she'd give her one ounce, one iota of consideration. She'd wipe that flippant grin off Zelda's face.

The woman did have a way with her tongue, obviously well practiced. She knew how to flick Jane's clitoris as if she'd been doing it for years. And then fingering her around her sensitive hole, she quickly had Jane on her way to an orgasm. Zelda was right about one thing, Jane thought—the tension reliever would be welcome after all the rigmarole they'd been through in the last few days. She wasn't particularly looking forward to Felicia's funeral.

Zelda continued her play with equal enthusiasm, beginning to end, her submissive inclinations obvious, as was her ability as a cuntsucker.

"Keep it up, bitch," Jane said.

Maybe she wouldn't be so bad to top. Jane didn't really think she'd be up for the club that night, unless she raged through the place and kicked ass with all her favorites. They'd probably be waiting for her, in fact, but then again, maybe she'd surprise them all, including herself, and stay home, dispensing a week's worth of whippings on this voluptuously contemptible creature.

The more the woman sucked her, the hotter Jane got; the dom pulled at her hair with such abandon that Zelda should have squealed in protest, though she remained attentive to her task.

"Goddamn fuuuucccck!" Jane blurted out, her only exclamation of pleasure as she rocked against Zelda's perky face with a whorish glee, spewing cum on the woman's soft pink cheeks.

Jane shoved her away roughly, and Zelda sat back meekly on her haunches with cum still on her face.

"Have I pleased you, sir?" Zelda asked.

"No," Jane answered. "You talk too much, slut. But you come to me tonight at eight and I'll teach you a few lessons in manners. And don't bother wearing any clothes. I'd burn them in the fireplace if you did."

"Yes, sir," Zelda replied, pleased.

"Did you get me right? You show up at my door naked."

"Yes, sir," Zelda shivered.

"We'll confront her after the funeral," Robin suggested, as she sat back in Felicia's chair looking out on Felicia's world, the pictures still in her hands. The eroticism of the photos turned them both on.

"You think she's guilty?" Leslie asked.

"Frankly, no, but we wouldn't be doing a very good job for Betsy if we ignore the fact that Jane didn't offer any information on her relationship with Felicia, and that she lied to us about her SM and Roman Hill. That's not even considering the ropes, which she seems to think aren't important."

"Well, the woman seems to be good at explaining: let her explain all of this," Leslie suggested. She stared down at one picture of Jane, a particularly intimate pose between dominant and submissive with Jane's expression grim and caring all at the same time. It was the one expression that sent Leslie's sexual desire flying every time she'd seen it. "Does Jane turn you on at all?" Leslie asked, looking at her partner very carefully.

"Does she you?" Robin returned the question immediately.

Leslie stared at the picture again. "My honest answer? Yes," Leslie reported.

"That's a switch," Robin replied, thinking of the many years of Leslie's denials. Never would a butch leatherdyke catch her attention, let alone engender her lust. "All that leather is much too much," she'd say.

"How about answering *my* question," Leslie said, jerking her partner from her thoughts.

Robin looked up at her. "Does *Sir Jane* turn me on?" Robin repeated. "I imagine she could top me in a second, and I'd do everything that woman said. I don't know what it is about her, but she's got some kind of genius about her sexuality."

"I didn't think you went for her type any more than I do."

"Everyone's different, Les, and she certainly is. If

you can change your ideas about what turns you on, don't you suppose I can too? Jane Hugh's about the most exciting dominant I've ever been around. But frankly, I'm not sure why."

The funeral was an exquisite piece of theatre, planned by Betsy though she wasn't in attendance. Felicia's death managed to attract a number of community celebrities, a few writers of some prominence, and a wide range of personalities that made her finale with the world an interesting, though uneventful parting. The service was simple, elegant and understated, especially given the overstated way in which Felicia lived her life.

"She looked rather like herself, don't you think?" Robin said, as she and Leslie walked away from the chapel. "I'm amazed what a mortician can do with a dead body. He certainly didn't take away any of her haughtiness; it was all there as plain as day."

"But not her mirth," Leslie suggested. "I think that's what I remember about her the few times I ran into her."

"Her haughtiness was more genuine," Robin said.

"I don't agree, but then I didn't know her the way you did. So what great revelations did you get from the last hour?" Leslie asked.

"None," Robin replied. "Our little women, Jane included, were on their best behavior, don't you think?"

"Perfect. If Jane had all this affection for Felicia, she didn't show much."

"Maybe just showing up was important for her. If she had the nasty kind of relationship with Felicia that everyone thought, she wouldn't be here at all," Robin reasoned. "If Felicia was a particularly special submissive in her host of submissives, then showing up at the funeral was a sign of respect that Jane wouldn't give to just anyone."

"Maybe she was really gloating because she murdered her. She is the suspect with the most motive, opportunity, and circumstantial evidence in her favor, outside of Betsy of course."

"Too bad Betsy couldn't make it."

"Yeah, she cried her eyes out with John yesterday, he told me," Leslie said. "She may have been on her way out Felicia's door, but I don't think she wanted anything to end like this."

The two detectives watched the crowd at the chapel leave for the cemetery. Martha, Remy, and Zelda left together in Martha's car. And Jane roared away in her old beat-up coupe.

"Looks like we won't be talking to Jane until later," Robin said. "Maybe we can find her at the Hill tonight?"

"I'll meet you there," Leslie said.

The two left in separate cars.

CHAPTER TEN

Zelda could not believe what luck she'd had to attract Jane's attention for the night. This was one woman she'd lusted after since her arrival, though she was also one woman she assumed would be off limits to her. The thought of being Jane Hugh's slave for the night had her mind reeling at the deliciously dark possibilities.

Such a nasty touch Jane had, making her strip before she even knocked at the door, Zelda thought, as she made her way into the garden in the dusky evening light. Taking off her dress, a little slip of a thing with nothing underneath, she stuffed it behind a bush to find later when her session was over. It was not completely dark, a fact that made Zelda's nakedness all the more wicked to her. Stepping into the path, she hustled quickly to Jane's cottage and knocked on the door. Gazing around, Zelda looked for someone who might see her, not sure whether she wanted a voyeur or hoped she'd remain undiscovered. It could be a messy situation being found out like this.

Not surprisingly, Jane made her wait for several interminable minutes before she finally opened the door.

"On the floor, bitch," Jane ordered immediately, and as Zelda had done with other lovers at other times, she instantly heeded this new dom's command.

Jane clamped a collar on Zelda's neck and led the willing submissive to an empty space. Jane's cottage was one large but functional room, complete with living room, a bedroom area, and a kitchen with a small dinette in a bay window that looked out on the wooded grounds of the estate. In addition to the usual furniture, it was also furnished with rings embedded into the brick walls, a pulley hidden cleverly in the ceiling, and a couple of odd-looking benches that were designed for specific purposes. All these things were throwbacks to the years before when Felicia had used the cottage for her secretive S&M games. Left in the cottage when Jane moved in, the new tenant appropriated them for her own use.

Opening a cabinet on the wall, Jane revealed the implements of her craft—whips, chains, leather, and ropes in an abundance of sizes and arrangements that would please any dominant. There were ball gags, collars, clothespins, and, for this occasion, a long, thin riding crop which she withdrew from the cabinet.

Zelda could see the three-inch tasseled end of the crop, which now dangled by the side of her face. Jane ran it along the surface of the submissive's skin, against her shoulders and back, and then even across her brow and lips. It was as tender as any lover, though she knew it would bite like fire.

"Well, my little bitch, you suck pussy well."

"Thank you, sir," Zelda instantly replied.

"I'm not about to spend my time with you unless I know you're worth it. But the way you move, I imagine that you're an experienced little slut, aren't you? Know just what to call me."

"Yes, sir," Zelda replied. This was going as she hoped it would.

"I wonder why you bother coming here, throwing your brash little bitch body at me, when you know I don't like you," Jane mused aloud.

Zelda didn't reply.

"You going to answer, or shall I send you away now?" Jane prodded the kneeling woman with the crop, though she still hadn't administered one blow.

"I've seen you at Sapphos, I want what you can give me, and I'll do anything to have you," Zelda answered.

"Anything?" Jane took notice of the sweeping declaration. "I don't think there's anyone that could take anything I'm inclined to give them."

"Please, Sir Jane," Zelda looked up, beseeching her cold mistress.

"You could slave for me for a year, and you wouldn't please me," Jane retorted, as she walked away then looked back to appraise the bent-over woman. Zelda's head was nearly touching the floor, and her ass was waving in the air so that, looking at her from behind, Jane could view both the naked pussy and anus exposed for her. "I don't like women who throw themselves at me. Is this display suppose to turn me on?" Jane asked. She didn't wait for a reply this time. "Come here," she ordered.

Zelda crawled to Jane's feet, making an even greater effort to bow before the dom with just the right attitude of surrender.

"You want your ass punished, don't you?" Jane said. She ran the crop over the exposed rear, for an instant pressing the tasseled end of the thing against Zelda's anus.

"Ouch!" Zelda said without thinking.

"Women like you make me want to puke," Jane said. "All dolled up like whores, as if that's what's going to get me excited."

It was a waiting game for Zelda, a little tenuous to start, not knowing how Jane would respond to her.

Jane reached down and ran her fingers along the woman's pink-white flanks. For all her revolting mannerisms, Zelda had the most satiny skin. Jane could imagine it marked with red lines made by a biting cane. She smacked the fleshy thigh with her hand, then sat back in a chair and watched the red imprint appear like magic on the white. Reaching down again, she fondled Zelda's rear cleft: there was enough juice at her cunt to lubricate her asshole. She pressed her index finger at the anus, and it slipped inside. Jane fucked the woman with her finger, listening to Zelda's lusty moans.

"Like this, don't you?" she charged.

"Yes, sir," Zelda answered promptly.

Two fingers slipped inside easily. This was a well-worked hole. It must have been violated many times. If Zelda were to remain compliant, Jane could find herself liking the bitch. Of course there were a few habits that needed changing, but she needn't worry. That would be easily accomplished. A gag would shut her up if she whined too much, and a few chains in the right places would remind her of her place. Perhaps she could have the woman work at the club, where this great ability of hers would stand out.

Outside the cottage, the dusky shadows had given way to darkness. Lights gleamed brightly through the windows, and on approaching the place from the garden, Leslie and Robin could easily see inside.

"My god, she has Zelda in there!" Leslie exclaimed.

"Shush," Robin said.

The two approached quietly, the intent of their meeting suddenly altered, a conversation with Jane highly unlikely at the moment.

"Not much reverence for the dead," Leslie said.

"Don't say that. People mourn in different ways, and we're not sure Jane is mourning at all." Robin thought of her own night following the revelation of Felicia's death. Might be good for both women, though she wasn't sure if Zelda even knew Felicia enough to grieve her passing.

"I suppose we'd better find another time," Leslie suggested.

"Don't you want to watch?" Robin said.

Leslie could tell by the tone of voice that her partner was aroused, the darker husky timbre familiar to her. She had to admit that she was aroused too.

"You had no trouble watching the other night at Sapphos, calling it part of the investigation. Besides, you'll never now what you can learn."

"About the case or sexually?" Leslie whispered.

"Either," Robin whispered back, giving Leslie the raised-eyebrow look.

The two remained in the shadows. With the window open, they could hear as well as see what was going on inside the cottage.

"Over the bench," Jane ordered, prodding Zelda in the ribs with her crop. She flicked the woman's thighs with sharp, biting snaps. Zelda responded, her body jerking though her arousal was apparent; the erotic movement of her limbs was mesmerizing. Once on hands and knees on top the two foot wide bench, she waved her bottom lewdly as if to taunt an uncaring Jane. The dom was as likely to walk away and smoke a cigarette as pay any attention to the her; but for reasons she would hardly admit to herself, Jane was intrigued with this bottom. Even more annoying than the intrigue, Jane was turned on.

Using the crop on Zelda's ass again, this time Jane ripped off a half-dozen cuts that made the woman yowl in pain. The red stripes that followed were easily visible to the two detectives on the outside.

"Damn that hurts," Robin whispered, as if she had taken Zelda's place on the bench.

Leslie felt it, wincing herself, not because she'd ever known that much sexual pain, but simply because it looked so painful.

Jane pressed her hand into Zelda's ass again, inserting three fingers and fucking her deeply.

"Put your head on the bench," she ordered, as she reached to the woman's head and pushed her down roughly, leaving Zelda's ass even more vulnerable to attack.

How convenient that Zelda's ass faced the windows, Robin thought. She wondered if the two realized that they were being watched so closely, every move scrutinized for clues to a murder and to fuel the detectives' own erotic pleasure. If Zelda and Jane did realize that their sex was a show, would they care, or simply find it a part of the scene to be as enjoyed as much as the act itself?

As far as Leslie could see, Sir Jane was no different with Zelda than she was at the club. She wore her dominance well; not the kind of woman to waver or for a second consider turning the tables.

Jane greased her hand with a slick, clear fluid and began to probe Zelda's rear deeper still. There didn't seem to be any way she could thrust her whole fist inside Zelda's ass, but she was not beyond trying. It would be a good time for a smaller woman to assist her, since she wanted to see the little bitch driven to the edge by an offending fist stretching her to her limit, and then just beyond.

Zelda groaned even as she winced. Used to violation of this sort, she was willing to take it all, if it was possible, even if it ripped her apart. Jane worked her hard for several minutes, then abruptly pulled out. Taking a strap from the wall, she beat Zelda's ass until it was a savage red. Zelda's screams were useless, as this an easy pain to give and to take. After one ruthless journey, Jane began another, until the white alabaster was scorched with raw welts that would take days to heal.

"Turn over, bitch," Jane ordered.

This was not to Zelda's liking, though she was obliged to obey. Moving awkwardly, she complied. Lying on her back against the hard bench, she felt her ripped backside sting with pain, a constant sensation of discomfort to tease her mercilessly. Jane fastened

Zelda's arms overhead so her full breasts were stretched tightly. Still, they lay against her chest, her nipples erect, her flesh jiggling with each move. The dom spread her submissive's legs apart and tied each ankle to a leg of the bench, fixed efficiently with ropes.

"See the knots," Robin whispered from her view outside the window. "What did I tell you about clues," she chided her partner.

"She does them so easily," Leslie remarked.

"Of course she does, she's done them a thousand times, if she's done them once."

Jane left the woman's side and strolled to the back of the cottage, disappearing for while into the bathroom.

"Sir Jane," Zelda called out after some moments alone. She squirmed uncomfortably in her bonds. "Jane, please don't leave me here." Zelda called out, louder this time.

Jane returned seconds later, quickly clamping the woman's nipples with raw-edged pincers.

"I'm going to gag you," Jane said almost kindly.

"I have to pee," Zelda replied.

"That's okay, I'm almost finished with you. You pee on my floor and you'll lick up every drop," she warned. A ball gag in her hand, she fixed it Zelda's mouth with a rubber strap that fit securely around the woman's head.

Picking up the riding crop once more, Jane rapped at Zelda's cunt, an event the other woman did not enjoy. But her hips bucked wildly, and her cunt reached ever higher to greet the small leather end as it stung her tender lips and inner thighs. She heaved at last, a strange muffled cry muted by the gag, but a cry of pleasure nonetheless.

Whatever look appeared in Zelda's eyes invited more, which Jane gave her. Ruthless cuts were leveled at her inner thighs. In the middle of the punishment, Jane picked up the chain that was attached to the nipple clamps. She pulled it tightly so that Zelda's breasts were stretched taut. Jane beat the stretched-out breasts with the end of the instrument: the pain had to be excruciating. But even though the submissive screamed behind the gag, her whole body seemed to be asking for still more.

Jane paused for an instant and stared at the woman, and then dropped both the chain and the riding crop.

She walked away.

Leslie wondered where the more vibrant woman at the club had gone. No tenderness, no obvious self-satisfaction, this must have been a different kind of rush for Sir Jane, if there had been a rush at all.

At the kitchen counter, Jane poured herself a shot of bourbon and downed it in one gulp, then returned to her well-bound submissive. Zelda's cunt still looked raw, as she stared in vacant anxiousness at the woman above her.

"Had enough?" Jane asked.

Zelda shook her head no, much to Leslie and Robin's surprise.

"Well I have," Jane answered. She leaned down and loosened the bonds, letting the woman's ankles and wrists free. She let Zelda remove the gag herself. The redhead sat up and looked at Jane with an expression as deliberately seductive as her earlier one. She acted as if the scene that had just played out had never happened, as if she could start all over again from the beginning. As raw as her body was, Zelda wanted more.

"We should cut out of here," Leslie suggested. Robin nodded and the two quickly walked to a safer place, though their gazes were still fixed on the women inside the cottage. The exchange they saw between the two women was cryptic. An almost pleading Zelda looked up at Sir Jane, imploring her...another demand perhaps, another order, another whipping?

Jane shook her head. She listened to the pleas the woman gave back and just shook her head again.

"This is really strange, don't you think?" Leslie murmured.

"Yeah, it is," Robin answered. Something about this scene was not quite what Jane thought it should be, though Robin wasn't certain what it was that bothered the dom so much.

Moments later, Robin and Leslie watched as a naked Zelda ran from the cottage. She dashed toward the garden, finding a dress under a shrub, and then, without bothering to put it on, she made her way briskly toward the house, her white, raw body disappearing out of sight, her red curly locks bouncing, just as her red-marked breasts bounced in the night air.

"So, do we confront Jane now?" Leslie asked.

"I think I want to wait until tomorrow," Robin answered. She was still troubled by the finale of this scene, as troubled as Jane appeared to be.

Leslie nodded her agreement, sensing Robin's uneasy mood.

CHAPTER ELEVEN

After a night of letting scenes and pictures of SM dominate her dreams, Leslie rose from bed feeling as if she'd lived in real life all the nightmares that she had dreamed of. She was glad that Rosalie was off on business again; she'd rather not bring her into the confusing picture of murder suspects and clues and crazy sex practices.

Going to the bathroom, Leslie splashed some water on her face, then went to her closet to find something to wear. With her jeans, she decided to wear a sweater that dipped low in front, revealing the tops of her jiggling breasts when she walked. For reasons she wasn't ready to admit, she was dressing to tease Robin, or maybe even Jane, she wasn't sure which, though she was sure her motives were shameless. By choosing a sweater she hardly ever wore, she hoped that either or both would notice.

It seemed to Leslie that this case was going nowhere, loose ends everywhere, suspects only more probable all the time, with Remy institutionalized for some as yet undisclosed violent encounter, and Jane looking like a sitting duck with photographs of sexual scenes between her and Felicia that seemed to duplicate the murder scene. Not to mention what role the overprotective Martha and the curious Zelda might have had in this drama.

And of course there was the sexuality surrounding the murder, something that was becoming more intriguing all the time—a fact Leslie wasn't sure how to handle. Watching Zelda and Jane was even more enticing than her voyeuring at the club. It wasn't Zelda she was so much interested in as Jane's style, the way she moved, the expression on her face, and the sternness in her voice. Jane's personality had gotten inside Leslie, strangely working on her the way that new lovers always did. She hoped this wouldn't skew her viewpoint of Jane as a murder suspect. It could be a dangerous mistake.

To make things even more confusing, the way she and Robin had left each other the night before had made *their* relationship as much a mystery to her as the case itself.

When the phone jangled it took her four rings to get it as she stumbled over the bathroom rug.

"Hello," she answered breathlessly.

"What's going on?" Robin asked.

"Ah, it's you," Leslie said, recognizing her partner.

"I got a call from Hannah in police records. She did

a little more checking on Remy for me. I wanted to see if she could find some police report to confirm the violence that put her in Brightwood."

"And?"

"Remy was arrested for slashing her lover with a knife, caught her in the thigh and abdomen."

"Whoa. Was the other woman tied up?" Leslie asked.

"No."

"Did the victim die?"

"No. She was slashed a little but survived. Apparently Remy went nuts, inexplicably, all of a sudden. Then, at the last minute, she panicked, and thankfully couldn't go through with the murder. Remy was sent away for psychiatric evaluation and never made it back to court after the initial proceedings. She was committed to Brightwood and stayed there for two years."

"Was there any indication as to why she wanted to murder her lover?" Leslie asked.

"She was losing her to another woman," Robin said.

"How interesting. You know, Rob," Leslie said, hearing the story, "I think it's time we confronted the ladies on the Hill a little more directly."

"Remy and Jane both," Robin agreed.

"And no Martha this time," Leslie added.

"I'll pick you up at one," Robin said.

When Robin and Leslie arrived at Roman Hill that afternoon, they were in luck, finding Remy outside in the big garden by the roses, with a pair of trimmers in her hand. Thinking of Robin's report on the slashing, Leslie shivered seeing the sharp shears.

"I thought a few flowers in the house might brighten things. I don't know how we're going to get over the gloom there," Remy said, trying to put on a pleasant face.

"Do you have a minute for some questions?" Robin asked, speaking to her kindly.

"Sure," Remy answered. Her eyes twinkled softly. It was hard to believe that this woman had a history of crazy behavior. Remy appeared to be a shy woman, peaceful, but shy; and her quiet didn't seem to be at all a disguise for a violent, troubled soul. Hopefully, she had been cured in her two-year stay at Brightwood.

"We understand that this murder has really shaken you," Robin said.

"Wouldn't it upset anyone?" Remy said, her expression suddenly quite sad.

"I'm sure, but perhaps this reminds you of your past?" Leslie continued probing gently.

"My past?" The woman looked instantly distraught.

"Let's not beat around the bush. Perhaps you could tell us about your stay at Brightwood Hospital?" Leslie asked.

Remy's eyes changed immediately upon hearing the name. She lowered her head as if she were going to cry. "Please, please, I don't really want to think about this, it does remind me so much of that time.... The people around me were dying left and right. My mother, my brother. My father was terrible. My sanity got away from me. Sometimes I still struggle with it, but I didn't kill Felicia, I couldn't." She was instantly anxious, looking as if she had been accused. "I could never do anything like that, tie her up, never." Remy paused, looking guilty just talking about it.

"We know Martha had played some S&M games with Felicia. Were you jealous of that?"

"Oh, no, not really. Martha is wonderful to me," Remy's eyes brightened. "She's taken care of me since Brightwood. I don't know how I could have done things without her, have my job and everything. I've gotten much stronger because of her."

"But weren't you jealous of her attention to Felicia?"

"I can't do those things, and she enjoys it," Remy explained.

"Doesn't that cause problems in your relationship?"

"No, no it doesn't," Remy said, trying to answer with a firm denial.

"You knew Zelda from Brightwood too," Robin moved on.

"Yes. That was a long time ago."

"But you must have stayed in contact with the woman for her to come here several years later?"

"She was very sweet to me at the hospital, the first friendly face I remember. Just that face, those lovely eyes—she does have lovely eyes, don't you think?"

"Yes, she does," Robin agreed. She was afraid of flustering the woman more. No wonder Martha didn't want her talking. "So you must have written regularly?"

"Well, not really until recently. But I was very excited when she wrote. Then she called. She is one of the best friends that I've ever had. She and Martha both, of course."

"Were you two ever lovers, you and Zelda?"

"Oh, no! I was a patient, she was an aide. You didn't do those sorts of things with the staff."

"But your relationship with Martha?"

Remy smiled, confused, the expression on her face becoming more perplexed each moment. "But Martha's different..." Her soft eyes drifted away.

"How is she different?"

"She loved me; she's given up so much, and I'm so grateful." There was a singsong sadness in her voice, and she looked as if she were going to float away. The woman, with her instability clearly showing, didn't seem capable of continuing the conversation.

Martha looked out of the window at the three women in the garden.

"Damn! Those detectives."

Zelda sidled up to her, putting her arms around her.

"You're scared of what she'll say?"

"Damn right I am. Remy's still not right. Those women will twist her words, assume all the wrong things from her confusion."

"But you don't believe she killed Felicia," Zelda said. "I wouldn't worry, she'll only tie her tongue in knots the way she usually does. What on earth would she say?"

"She didn't kill her," Martha insisted.

"Of course she didn't," Zelda assured her, though there was a hesitancy in her voice. "I still think it was Betsy, unless it was Jane. But I wouldn't worry about Remy. She's more savvy than you give her credit for. I think you're too concerned about her." Zelda rubbed at Martha's breasts, feeling for the nipples that grew instantly hard to the touch. "Since we have a few minutes alone right now, why don't we have some fun?" She rubbed her body seductively against Martha's.

"I don't know. I'm not up to spanking you, Zelda. I need to lie back and relax. The tension of this is sometimes more than I can handle. Keeping Remy together—it's so hard."

"I know, but you do it very well. Remy's so lucky to

have you. You were really all she wrote about," Zelda said, as she planted soft kisses on Martha's neck. "But now that she's so occupied, you can take some time for yourself. Maybe turn the tables?" she suggested.

"You do that? I mean, you'd be the aggressor?"

"Sometimes, with the right person. I've never been one for hard and fast rules."

Right now Zelda's warm body felt good to Martha. She had little trouble with the idea of lying back and being taken by another woman. It could be just what she needed.

"You just relax and let me take you someplace special," the warm-bodied woman purred in her ear. Zelda's hands were inside Martha's blouse, pulling at both her nipples. She stretched them long and slow until they hurt. But the ensuing pain was delicious. Martha had only had such attention on rare occasions. Once she remembered Felicia gave her this kind of exquisite little torture, but just once. Felicia was only occasionally dominant with her—she often wondered why, when Felicia herself was known to be dominant. "You like this?" Zelda asked.

"Oh, yes, keep going," she said, falling back against the woman. One of Zelda's hands dropped down to Martha's crotch and began to fondle her there. Then her hand moved to the waistband of her pants and pushed its way down inside.

"My, how wet you are!" Zelda said. "Pent up again, are we? You shouldn't wait so long to take care of these things, but don't worry, I'll just have to take care of what you need." Her voice was so soft and commanding. Everything Martha needed. "First thing, you need to relax," Zelda continued whispering in her ear, as Martha moved against the cushion of her body.

"Oh, yes," Martha moaned. The lusty redhead had played an unexpectedly needed role in the last few days, giving her what she was unable to find elsewhere, and what Remy would never bless her with. Martha started to turn around and face her.

"No, no, stay right where you are," Zelda said, continuing to whisper in her ear. "You let me be in control this time. Just you relax and get into it." She moved with Martha to the nearby sofa, laying the woman down on the thick, comforting cushion. She tugged at Martha's blouse, pulling it up to find the woman's sumptuous breasts. "Just keep your hands over your head," Zelda said, smiling, "and let me do all the work." Martha gazed up into Zelda's eyes, letting the feel of the woman's hands on her flesh warm and arouse her.

"This is so lovely," Martha moaned.

"Of course," Zelda said, with a voice that faded away as her red curls descended to Martha's chest, her lips kissing her a dozen times. Her teeth captured a nipple and held it tightly, while she looked up at Martha's rapturous face. Martha saw the smile behind the teeth, the dark, delicious smile that made her new lover look so wonderfully wicked.

"Martha?"

She heard her name called from outside the room and jumped. Zelda's teeth dropped the nipple, letting the breast fall back against her chest. "Oh, my god!" Martha bolted from the sofa and pulled down her blouse.

Zelda stood up at the same time and was almost laughing. "My, aren't you nervous. The door's closed, silly."

"I know, but we should be more careful with this.

Damn! I bet it's those two detectives." She quickly glanced out of the window to see Remy still working on the roses. The woman was by herself.

The two detectives stood in the hallway, waiting for Leslie's call to be acknowledged.

"Remy was very odd, wasn't she?" Robin whispered.

"Still a little wacko, I'd guess."

"Definitely," Robin agreed. "I kept thinking as she was praising Martha that Remy really is a very unhappy woman. I think her doting lover's wandering has bothered her much more than she admits."

"I agree with you there. I wonder if she wasn't under the same kind of stress seven years ago when she tried to kill her previous lover. Perhaps she snapped again."

"Killing Felicia would make a lot of sense for her—get rid of the competition."

"Anybody here?" Leslie called again, as they waited in the foyer for Martha or Zelda to appear.

The door to the study suddenly opened, and a disheveled Martha stood there with a pleasant expression plastered on her face, a hand running through her messed-up hair. "May I help you?" she asked. Zelda stood behind her with a broad grin on her face.

"I'm sorry if we've interrupted something," Leslie said, thinking that they had just walked in on some erotic interlude.

"No, no, not at all," Martha answered politely. "I see you were talking with Remy in the garden."

"Yes," Leslie said. "She was very helpful."

"Oh? And how's that?"

"She confirmed some information we have about

her past, and yours, and yours too, Zelda," Robin said, nodding to the other woman.

"About her past?"

"Yes. Things you've been hiding from us and the police."

"I don't know what you could mean," Martha replied defensively.

The two detectives made their way beyond Martha and into the study. Zelda had taken a seat by the window and was looking out to the garden. Martha backed off, intimidated by Leslie's remarks.

"We know that Remy was hospitalized at Brightwood Psychiatric Hospital for a violent incident with a former lover. Her condition was described as extremely confused and volatile."

"Are you suggesting that Remy killed Felicia?"

"We're suggesting that, with a violent history the possibility is not unlikely."

"Remy's problems were years ago," Martha reminded them. "And except for the use of the knife, I don't really see how the two crimes compare."

"Regardless, I think the police will be interested in this information."

"I think you're just complicating something that's already been resolved," Martha charged, regaining some of her composure and her protective attitude.

"That's possible, but you've been less than candid with us. Perhaps you can explain that."

"Well, doesn't it stand to reason?" Zelda suddenly interjected. "Remy would obviously be a suspect if the police knew about her history. Why would we want to offer that information?"

"So the two of you have been making up stories to keep Remy from suspicion?"

"That's about what it adds up to," Zelda replied flatly.

Martha looked at the redhead, annoyed by the way she was talking. "I think it's more a situation of not placing undue stress on Remy. She is still a delicate woman. I know that she didn't murder Felicia, so why put her through hell? She's had enough in her life."

"Do you really know she didn't commit the murder?" Leslie asked. "Or are you just hoping that she didn't?"

"I beg your pardon, but Remy did not kill Felicia!" Martha snapped.

"Because you know who did?" Robin asked, with a soft but very incisive voice.

"I think that Betsy is the murderer. I've thought so from the beginning. The only possible other suspect would be Jane."

"I've thought about that," Robin said kindly. "But I'm not so certain anymore."

"You can't go telling the police your half-cocked story. I mean, look at the murder scene—so precise, so perfectly executed. Do you think for minute that Remy would have been that careful with the details? You're right that she's not a completely well woman, but she doesn't have the temperament for the crime."

"You speak very passionately for her innocence," Leslie said. "I admire your loyalty to her, but your story doesn't completely add up."

"What do you mean?" Martha said suspiciously.

"Remy is a chemist, is that not so?"

"Yes."

"There are not too many fields that require more precision than chemistry. I'd say that our innocent, shy, confused woman has a side to her personality that is very sharp and meticulous. The precision of the bondage and the wound does not necessarily rule out your lover."

"But *I* can rule out my lover. She was in bed with me," Martha said, practically shouting.

Zelda moved off the sofa and put her arm around the woman. "I think we've all been stretched to the limit, ladies. Any further conversation about this is not going to get us anywhere. Do what you have to do with your information, but please leave us alone. We've said all we're going to say." She stared at the two detectives with very intent eyes. As far as she was concerned, the conversation was over.

"We're sorry to have bothered you," Robin said, as she followed Leslie, who was already out the door.

"They were quite a pair," Leslie said, as Robin joined her on the front porch and they briskly walked back toward the garden on their way to Jane's cottage.

"One protecting the other, protecting another, I agree," Robin said.

"A little strange, don't you think, those two together? It looked pretty sexual to me when Martha opened the door."

"I wonder what that means?" Robin pondered.

"Perhaps Martha misses the sex with Felicia. Looks like Zelda might be up to the same antics. There sure is a lot of bed hopping in this little S&M community," Leslie said.

"Is that some sort of judgment?" Robin asked.

"No, no, not at all; just an observation," she replied with a sigh. "They were right about one thing," she went on. "The police will chew up Remy in seconds, if they start to interrogate her."

"I think it's time we had a talk with our detective friend downtown," Robin said.

"Perhaps he won't think it's such an open and shut case anymore," Leslie replied.

"Isn't it strange," Robin commented. "Two such very different women being the two likeliest suspects?"

As the two retraced their steps to the garden, they spotted Remy some distance away, moving around to the back of the house with a bouquet of flowers in her hand. "Maybe Remy and Jane aren't so very different; they're both duplicitous women. They're just duplicitous in different ways," Leslie suggested, as they watched Remy slip out of sight on her way to the garden shed at the back corner of the property.

Reaching the cottage, Leslie rapped loudly on the door. "Jane?" she called, hoping to find the woman at home. "Doesn't look as if she's here," Leslie said. She put her hand to the knob and turned it easily. "Maybe not."

When the door swung open the two women looked inside.

"Jane?" Robin called this time. She stepped inside. "C'mon," she said, looking back to her partner.

Inside the cottage they had a different view of Jane's life than the one they had witnessed in high relief, when they watched Jane and Zelda engaged in their sexual interlude. The place was much prettier than they expected. Of course it was without the fussy flowers that were splashed throughout the big house, but Jane's taste in interior decoration included a dozen well-tended houseplants, and soft, sumptuous leather that was a cozy accompaniment to her earthy style. Two large abstract oil paintings hung on the one wall, companion pieces: they depicted nude women in states of bondage, though so uniquely rendered you had to look at them closely to see what the wild shapes represented.

"Tasteful, don't you think?" Robin said.

"Yeah," Leslie replied, feeling a cold shiver race down her back. "I think we should go."

"Why, what's the problem?" Robin asked.

Leslie looked at an empty place on the wall where there were rings embedded in the brick, remnants of the cottage's former use. She spied the cabinet where the crop Jane had used on Zelda came from. The bench that Zelda had mounted sat innocently in front of Jane's leather chair.

"You want to submit to her here?" Robin asked, wishing she could really press Leslie on her newfound desires.

"Maybe, but I'm feeling very uncomfortable being here."

"Since when has snooping around bothered you?" Robin queried.

"What's there to look for?"

Robin didn't reply but continued a typical "Robin" perusal of the place, as if the walls were telling her their secrets. "The more I'm in her environment, the less likely I think it is that she murdered Felicia," Robin finally said.

"I agree, but our strongest evidence still implicates her," Leslie reminded her.

"Then perhaps we should go to the police now," Robin suggested, turning around to face her partner.

"I still want to talk to her one more time," Leslie said. "I just want to see the look on her face."

"You're sounding like me," Robin said with a laugh in her voice.

"I guess I am," Leslie concurred. "Is that bad?"

CHAPTER TWELVE

"I don't think we're going to find her tonight," Robin said, as she looked at the outside facade of Sapphos.

"Yeah, it's been two hours and there's obviously not much going on around here." The two detectives sat in Robin's Suzuki waiting for Jane to show. After a quick dinner, they'd checked inside the club and were told she was expected, but their waiting outside proved fruitless

"We could check back at the estate," Robin suggested.

"Or we could give up for the night and look for her in the morning."

"I'd rather see if we can find her tonight," Robin said. "We need to get this resolved quickly, get to the police, see if they'll look at the evidence a little differently now. Maybe we can get Betsy released."

Leslie nodded her agreement.

"But say," Robin went on, "I want to change clothes. I'm getting cold. Let's stop by my apartment for a few minutes, and then we'll drive to the estate."

Robin drove to the old brownstone neighborhood where her apartment was located, finding a parking place just in front.

Leslie gazed up at the quaint building, remembering when Robin had moved out of their shared apartment and into this place. How she'd cried. Now the warm yellow lights that glowed in several windows gave the place a welcoming appearance.

"I'll wait for you here," Leslie suggested.

"Hey, I'm going to be a few minutes—how about a cup of coffee?" Robin countered. "If we're going to be on this all night, we don't have to hurry."

Leslie agreed.

Robin served her partner a steamy cup of espresso and went into her bedroom to change. She returned with a heavy sweater replacing the thin blouse and grabbed a coat from the closet, tossing it over the back of a chair. Then, sitting down opposite Leslie, she took a sip of her coffee.

"You were kind of spooked at Jane's cottage," Robin said.

"Can't hide much from you, can I?" Leslie shrugged, looking rather sheepish for the normally self-assured detective.

"No, you never could. Thinking about Jane and her sex games perhaps? About being in Zelda's place at Jane's feet the other night?"

Leslie chuckled. "I can't get away from it," she

said. She didn't want to look directly at Robin. Anytime in the last few days they got to the subject of sex, the most awkward moments followed. This time she felt a strange prickly heat between her legs. It shouldn't feel so strange, for it was a feeling that had been present a half-dozen times since the case began; at the club, when she looked at the murder photographs, the photos in Felicia's room, the sex in Jane's cottage, and then this morning when they obviously interrupted Martha and Zelda in the middle of something sexual.

"Why are you avoiding this?" Robin asked.

"It looks fascinating and provocative, but I can't believe I'd crawl on the floor for any woman or want to make another women crawl at my feet. Somehow all that posturing—I think I'd loose my sexual excitement," Leslie replied.

"Funny, Les, you played around at the club and had no problem," Robin reminded her. She had a way of making Leslie look into her eyes, into the vast depths of that haunting blue.

"Yes, but the atmosphere in that place—how could I not? And Leta was hardly your typical dom. She certainly wasn't Jane. It was just one of those things that happens, like suddenly finding yourself in bed with people you never expected to be attracted to. A little drink and you'll do most anything."

"But you weren't drinking that night," Robin said, knowing Leslie would never drink on the job.

"Of course I wasn't. It was the place; just being there is like being drunk, soaking up the vibes. It was an experience, not a life pattern."

Robin flashed her a haughty grin. "You're making excuses," she said. She rose from her seat and went to the couch where Leslie sat: she knelt on the floor to one side of her partner, leaving her espresso cup on the coffee table. Her gentle hand stroked Leslie's thigh. "I think we need to take care of this now. I can't wait any longer, and you're being silly for being so cautious."

There was too much longing for Leslie to protest, too much pent up desire burning between her legs and in her cunt. The thought of making love to Robin again, any way she wanted it—Leslie didn't care—was too much to reject. "So who's going to be in charge?"

"It doesn't matter," Robin said, leaning forward. She touched Leslie's lips with hers, letting her former lover explore the soft inside flesh of her mouth.

Leslie's initial reaction was to dive right into Robin's body for a quick fuck, but she didn't. Subdued, Leslie lay back passively on the couch, letting Robin make love to her. Such a submissive position to take, one she'd rarely assumed with Robin in the past, yet it seemed to be what they both needed at the moment.

Robin took Leslie's half finished cup of espresso from her and put it on the table. Then, taking Leslie's hands in hers, she pinned them over the other woman's head, moving aggressively to her lover's lips, kissing them, her tongue forcing its way into Leslie's mouth.

Robin backed away ever so slightly, then bit the brunette's lip with her teeth.

"Ouch!"

"Leave your arms there," Robin ordered, as Leslie was about to revolt. Leslie put them back above her head, too mesmerized by Robin's surprisingly dominant attitude to do anything else. "You've wanted to have me again for a long time, so tonight you will."

"But this way?" Leslie said shaking her head. "I didn't imagine it like this."

"Too bad," Robin retorted. "I promise you one thing though—you will enjoy it." It was as much a command as it was an assurance.

"I always thought it would be the other way around," Leslie whispered, dazed by the bold advance.

"It will be, just not tonight," Robin replied. Leslie had the feeling that any protest would be countered. Robin was pulling Leslie's sweater over her head so that her naked tits fell lazily against her chest. "It's been so long," she murmured softly, as her head descended to Leslie's perfectly round breasts. She squeezed them together and licked them both, her mouth moving from one to the other as she bit both of them with soft nibbles. She sucked so there were little red marks left behind. Each nipple became hard when she blew her warm breath on it. She pinched each one hard with her fingers. "You've never been tied up, have you?" Robin asked.

"No."

"I want to tie you so you can't move, so you're mine to do with as I please. I want you to lie back and let me have you."

"And you promise it won't hurt?" Leslie asked.

"No. I won't promise anything, but I will start very gently."

Robin rose, darting away to a closet in the kitchen, then returning with several lengths of soft nylon rope. "Come with me," she said, taking Leslie by the hand and leading her into the bedroom.

"My lord, you have a new bed," Leslie said, seeing the mahogany four-poster in Robin's room. "This looks like a regular pagan den." She looked around, seeing the dark papered walls, all burgundy red, forest green, and gold: a thick, dark paisley comforter covered the bed. The blinds were closed, and a single bedside lamp gave the room a mellow light. Black lace diaphanous curtains circled the bed, so it looked like some harlot's lair. Leslie shivered at the way it made her feel like some raunchy whore.

"I treated myself last winter. Do you like it?" Robin said, with her eyes flickering on dim. Something in her was going darker with each moment.

"But you're not going to tie me to that," Leslie said, a little appalled. "It's a little too reminiscent for comfort." She was thinking of Felicia's pose at the time of her death.

"Oh, stop it," Robin said, reading her mind. She pushed Leslie toward the bed. "Take off your jeans."

Leslie stared at her. Such a strange way to begin sex, yet her cunt was throbbing. She removed the jeans and panties without thinking. She stared at Robin, who returned her look with the most wicked gleam in her eye and the most decadent smirk on her lips.

"Lay down and spread your legs," Robin said, as she looked at Leslie's brunette snatch which was already beginning to glisten with juices, fragrant, pungent, and sticky. How many times she had buried her face there?

"You're really going to do this?" Leslie whispered.

"I'm going to be gentle, very gentle, and you'll love every minute of the feeling. You need this, Leslie, and so do I."

Leslie wasn't sure, but seeing Robin strip down to nothing before her eyes, she wasn't going to miss an opportunity to be close to her again. Leslie was hot between her legs, her body obviously more enthusiastic than her mind. Perhaps her mind would just have to catch up or fly off somewhere else for a while.

Leslie crawled up on the bed, Robin taking her by surprise before she could turn over, catching her with a hand.

"Stop right there," Robin said.

"I thought you wanted me spread-eagle?"

"Later," she replied.

"What are you going to do?" Leslie asked, as she remained stock-still on her hands and knees, her ass end waving in the breeze in front of Robin's appreciative eyes.

"Shush!" Robin ordered. She accompanied the sound with a smack of her hand on Leslie's ass. She continued her slapping, each one more intense, more biting, more filled with enthusiastic passion. "You're getting very red," the blonde detective announced. "How does it feel?" She kept slapping Leslie's bouncing skin while the brunette moaned without protesting.

"Ahhh, please Robin, it stings," she groaned at last.

"So much the better. You can stand a little pain, just know there's lots of delicious sensation coming after." She slapped Leslie even harder, a vibrant warmth rising on Leslie's rear to match the vibrant red hue.

"You're very wet down here," Robin said, fingering the brunette's cuntlips. She pulled the labia while at the same time pinching them hard. "You like this too, don't you?"

Leslie didn't answer. It was not a sensation she would call pleasant.

"You like this, don't you?" Robin repeated, insisting on a response. She continued pulling at Leslie's labia while she slapped her bottom hard again.

Yes," Leslie replied loudly.

"Don't ignore my questions," Robin said, in a voice as nasty as Leslie had ever heard from her.

"You're very good at this," Leslie murmured, realizing that her once very submissive lover was doing a more than adequate job of making her submit.

"That's not for you to comment on. Of course I'm good. But I'm going to have to use something else on your ass. This is getting to hard on my hand."

"Robin, no, I can't take any more."

Robin backed away and stared at the splash of color on Leslie's bottom. "That's really too bad," she said, "because it really looks beautiful. But I can stop now, since what I really want is your cunt." She moved in and played with the juicy place, pushing her hand against the opening door. "You still take fists?" Robin asked.

"Yes," Leslie answered, as she felt her cunt being violated by Robin's hand, knowing it was exactly what she wanted right now. Robin had made her open herself this way: she'd been the first woman to fist-fuck her. Now, she rocked against the loving hand that pressed into her. "Please, yes," she purred, as she waited for the entry. She pushed her cunt back on fingers that, one after another, slipped inside. When the whole hand crossed the door, Robin fucked her, moving herself in and out of the warm, tight place.

Full.

Consumed.

An extraordinary peace pervaded Leslie in every little place.

"My God, keep going, yes." Leslie was coming, her bottom pulsing as the fist inside her continued to prod her deeply. She shivered everywhere, then collapsed to the bed as Robin's hand slipped out.

Leslie felt as if she'd passed out. There was nothing in her mind for such a long time, even though she was aware of her body and the soft pulsing that continued through her. After effects, ripples, little pains, twinges in her empty cunt. She hadn't had enough. This just pricked the boundaries of her need. She wanted to be filled again.

Leslie wasn't sure where Robin was, but she felt her near. Something slipped around her ankles, then around her wrists.

"What are you doing?" she managed to whisper.

"Tying you up," Robin replied in a whisper.

"But I just came."

"And that's just the start; you'll come again," Robin assured her. "Turn over."

"You're really doing this?"

"Of course—it's what you want. I just got carried away taking you so fast to start. It's been so long since I've had the pleasure of my hand in your cunt. Now move over."

Leslie smiled as she followed Robin's orders. Scooting over, she had to avoid the ends of the ropes now attached to her.

"You may want to keep denying it, but I've seen the way you've stared at the pictures."

"Oh, please, let me forget them?" Leslie groaned, thinking that the case was the last thing she wanted to think about right now.

"Don't worry, you'll forget: just give me your wrist."

Robin fixed it to the bedpost with a quick, simple knot. She moved to the end of the bed and fixed Leslie's ankle. "I'm glad your knots are sloppy," Leslie said, thinking of the pictures again.

"Oh, you want me to make them like Jane's?" Robin asked with a devious smirk on her face.

"How do I know you're not the murderer, going back to all your old lovers and knocking them off?"

"Great idea," Robin said. "You really ought to have thought of that before, don't you think?" Only one free hand remained. When that was tied, too, Robin's naked body immediately descended on her. "Relax, darling Leslie, the only crimes I want to commit are outrageous acts of hedonistic lesbian lust." Her lips came down and pressed themselves on Leslie's. "Close your eyes."

"Is that when you strike?"

"Sure," Robin said. "I'm not going to blindfold you, just close your eyes and feel."

Leslie obeyed, even though she was inclined to peek. She wasn't used to being this out of control. But all that her lover had in mind for her was in the snap of a little whip that Robin held in her hand. It came down on Leslie's thighs and she jerked. Then on her breasts, and she jerked more.

Robin waited each time to watch the little red marks rise on Leslie's white skin. She wanted to leave a little bit of herself on these tits especially. She planned to lay on six sharp cuts.

"Yeeeeawww," Leslie cried when Robin had laid on the first two. She opened her eyes to see a wilting smile on Robin's lips.

"I've always wanted to mark a woman's breasts," she said.

"You're leaving marks?" Leslie asked.

"Beautiful ones," Robin told her.

She snapped the whip again, twice. Two lines both women could distinctly see rose on the surface of Leslie's flesh just above the nipples, right next to the first two. Then with quick snaps of her wrist, Robin followed with two sharp raps right on Leslie's nipples.

"God, stop!" the bound woman shouted. Her nipples stung with a vicious, sweet pain that made them burn.

"Got your attention," Robin mocked her.

"My god, what do you want from me?" Leslie cried, the tears in her eyes genuine, just as was the little hint of fear.

"Are you turned on?" Robin asked.

"Yes!" Leslie answered. "Are you going to toy with me forever?" Her hips bucked as if to prove the arousal mounting steadily in her loins.

"Maybe," Robin purred, "but first you're going to suck my cunt." She climbed up on Leslie, facing the submissive's cunt, pressing her own into the brunette's mouth. Leslie's tongue was instantly doing its job, finding places she should easily remember for the many, many times they'd made this journey before.

"Oooo, yes," Robin cried softly. She ground her hips against the busy face. "Use your tongue, bitch," she insisted, as if Leslie's tongue wasn't already working fast and furious to bring Robin to a climax. The blonde bucked again and again against Leslie's face, the wet spilling out covering the submissive mouth. Robin moaned softly as she finished, just small, simple sounds that Leslie remembered for the way they made her feel, knowing that her lover was being satisfied.

Pulling away from her, Robin began to finger the bound woman one more time, knowing that Leslie wasn't far from another orgasm. It didn't take her whole fist this time—Robin didn't have the energy for it, though she had plenty of energy to see it through until Leslie's body went limp, happily limp.

"You going to keep me tied this way forever?" Leslie

finally said, feeling Robin's nakedness snuggle against her own.

"You want me to take pictures?" Robin asked lightly, looking into Leslie's face and gazing at her outstretched limbs. "I kind of like you this way."

"Really?" Leslie replied. "But I can't touch you this way."

"That's true," Robin agreed. She slowly pulled herself from Leslie's side and began to undo the four haphazard knots. "You liked it, didn't you? Admit it."

"I liked being with you again."

"No, you liked this, the bondage. Admit it." Robin insisted.

"Yes, I liked the bondage, but I might have liked it even more if I'd been doing it to you."

"We'll get to that eventually," Robin told her.

"I bet sooner than you think, if I know you," Leslie countered.

Robin gave her a vicious grin as the last knot came loose. She collapsed against Leslie's familiar body and stroked it as if it had been days, not years, since they'd been in bed together. "So I guess unwritten rules are broken now," Robin said.

"About you and me together again?" Leslie said.

"What do you think I mean?" Robin said, slapping the other woman's thigh.

"There are just a few matters to be resolved before we start things again," Leslie reminded her.

"Like what?"

"Like Rosalie," Leslie said.

"She's easy; send her packing."

Leslie looked just a bit startled by Robin's seeming coldness.

"And the case," Leslie said.

"You mean Jane?" Robin said.

"I mean this case. I'm not going to get involved with you until we solve this thing."

"What in heaven's name does that have to do with anything? You're already involved with me."

"I just want to put some space between the case and my sex life. I don't want to be doing this just because I got a little horny while I was working," Leslie said.

"That's the stupidest thing I've ever heard," Robin said.

"It probably is, but it's what I want. I like things settled, you should know that."

She did. Robin remembered other times when Leslie had had a problem responding sexually while they were in the midst of a sticky case—though there had never been quite a case like this one, with all of its very sexual aspects.

"Okay, I can live with that," Robin replied. "We'll hold off until things are settled. By the feel of it, that might be tomorrow."

"Just one more thing," Leslie added.

Robin didn't say anything. With her head resting on Leslie's soft chest, she could feel her lover's breath and hear her beating heart. There was a steadiness about Leslie she loved, but she knew that steady person had her limits, and this case had taken her partner right to the edge.

"It's Jane, isn't it?" Robin said.

"Yeah, kind of. I don't know what it is about that woman, but as long as she's not the killer—and you never know, she just might be—I've got to find out what it is I want from her."

"I think it's pretty obvious. I know what *I* want from her," Robin said.

"We'll see. I've told you before, women like that don't really excite me."

"Except that one," Robin suggested.

"Except that one," Leslie agreed, instantly seeing the woman's mannish face appear in her mind, as if Jane had taken up residence and was watching her now.

After an hour, in the twilight that faded to darkness, Leslie jiggled Robin's sleeping body. It was the first time in a week, since the case began, that Leslie had felt this peaceful. She knew it was the sex and Robin that made her feel this way, but she also knew that the feeling would be short lived, and this brief respite would only add to the confusing mix inside her.

"Don't you suppose we should go find Jane now?" Leslie said.

"Why?" Robin asked opening one eye.

"I thought you were the one that wanted to take our findings to the police right away."

"Oh, it can wait," Robin said, stretching lazily against Leslie's warm body.

"It's only..." Leslie reached for the clock by the side of the bed "...eight o'clock. We still have time to check on her."

"My, how time flies," Robin said, stroking Leslie's thigh. "You did pretty well for your first time in bondage."

"Maybe it wasn't the first—how do you know?" Leslie joked.

"I'd know. I'd see it in your eyes."

"Yeah, you probably would," Leslie agreed. "So do we go stake out the mansion and wait for Jane to come home, or do we lie here in bed all night together?" Leslie asked.

"I'm opting for the latter. I guess I'm a slut at heart: if you hadn't taken off your clothes for me, I'd say we ought to go back to work, but since you're naked and I am too, and we can do anything our hearts desire all night long, I think we should just stay."

"Well, I don't know about anything our hearts desire," Leslie countered, "but I do like the prospect of spending the whole night in this bed. I've slept in a four-poster before, and this is downright…" she searched for a word "…bohemian." She stared up to the dark canopy, a deep black hole that seemed to be dropping down to surround them both.

"I'm glad you like it. I thought you might," Robin said, almost as if she'd planned this place especially for Leslie. "We'll see what other possibilities evolve. How about a little break—some decaffeinated cappuccino?"

CHAPTER THIRTEEN

Leslie opened her eyes in unfamiliar surroundings. There were four posts around her that for an instant made her think she was in the midst of a bad dream, in the middle of Felicia's last nightmare. Feeling another body beside her, she looked over to see Robin's back. The soft, lovely lines, so memorable, made her smile seeing them in their sweet repose once again. She would have reached out and stroked her, but thinking this was likely a one-shot moment, she didn't want to spoil the picture too soon. She was content just to stare at Robin's back, the lovely curve at her waist, the undulating mounds of her asscheeks and their pink cleft, and, at her head, the way her hair was in the most beautiful disarray.

She wished they didn't have the awkward moments together that always came with beginning anew, but there were things they couldn't avoid. She hoped that Rosalie hadn't come home the night before. Her Spanish lover wouldn't worry about her being gone, but it would make Leslie feel guilty if she knew Rosalie was wondering where she was. And here she was whooping it up with another lover.

The truth was, Robin was a better lover than Rosalie, not that Rosalie wasn't wonderful in her own endearing way. But Robin was always the best: she always had been and likely always would be. That was probably because, even with all their conflicts, Leslie still loved her.

The night before, after sex and drinking their decaffeinated cappuccino in the nude, and showering and giggling like school girls about some really stupid old horror movie on TV, they'd tumbled in the bed. This time, Leslie tied Robin's hands above *her* head. She'd slapped the blonde's breasts until they were red all over. Robin kept encouraging her to go on. "Don't stop, don't stop, don't stop," she'd cried again and again. The sensation that rose in Leslie was remarkable. The woman was at her mercy, unable to move from her place. The feeling of power that raced through her was as good an aphrodisiac as any sex act she'd ever experienced. It was sexual, but it was also power.

Was this what Jane felt when she grabbed at chains suspended from nipples or raised a whip against immobile, submissive flesh? Did Jane come just from the sensations of power that being dominant created? Leslie didn't orgasm in the midst of abusing Robin's tits, but she might have. She stopped short of it, needing to take baby steps into this crude world. At least for now.

They went on long into the night, long after the clock across the street struck midnight. Sometime in the morning's wee hours they collapsed into a heap, exhausted, and fell asleep.

Even when they were living together, they hadn't had sex like that, that long or that wild, Leslie mused. Maybe Robin was right, maybe she needed this too.

Now she wanted to know everything about Robin's SM scene. What her doms were like, and who'd put the marks on her breasts, those marks that were now just faint lines. How had Robin felt when the blows were delivered, and how long ago had it been? By the looks of them, it couldn't have been too long ago. It gave Leslie an excited rush to think that in just the last few days her partner had submitted to another woman. Who was she? Leslie looked at her own breasts, still able to distinguish four of the six cuts Robin had laid on them the night before. They gave her the most incredible feeling, a very submissive feeling. She wondered if she would feel the same way when Jane marked her breasts with a crop.

Leslie pulled herself from the bed; she didn't want to but she had to pee. Returning to the room, to Robin's peacefully sleeping body, Leslie stared at her lover's gentle face before she reached down to pick up the alarm clock that had fallen to the floor sometime in the midst of their wild battles the night before.

"Damn," Leslie said aloud, seeing that it was nearly nine o'clock. It had been weeks since she'd slept in that late.

The phone rang and she answered it, even as she watched Robin open her eyes and stare up at her.

"Leslie?" the woman's voice asked.

Damn, it was Rosalie.

"Yeah babe, we got exhausted casing out a suspect and just crashed here. I'm sorry I didn't leave a message. I didn't think you'd be home." Leslie was sure that Rosalie didn't believe her story.

"Yeah, that's why I was calling," Rosalie said. "I was worried when you didn't come home."

"I thought you were gone for another week."

"Things pooped out, but hey, I thought maybe I'd take off for Sonora. See my brother."

"Really?" Leslie answered cautiously. Rosalie didn't go to see her brother unless something was bothering her. "Anything wrong?"

"No. Just not seen him in awhile. I miss Mexico. You want to go?" she asked as an afterthought.

"God, Rosa, wouldn't I love it, but we're still working on this case. It's a real nasty one, but I think we'll have all the answers we're going to get in about two days. Then it's do or die."

Leslie looked down to see Robin with eyes open looking up at her in the middle of her lies.

"I'll be about a week. You take care, pretty buns," Rosalie said. "I love you."

"I love you too," Leslie answered. She heard the phone click, and she hung up. "How did I do?" Leslie asked the watching woman on the bed.

"I would never have bought your story. I suppose it depends on how much she wanted to believe you."

"I don't think she did. She's going to see her brother."

"So?"

"She's ready to split, I can tell. Last night was just the icing on the cake. I feel it in her voice."

"Just your intuition?" Robin asked.

"Maybe you're rubbing off on me, but Rosalie is *not* hard to figure out. But hey, we don't have much time, it's already nine. Jane's probably left, and we'll be on a wild goose chase all day finding her."

Martha was finishing the breakfast dishes in the kitchen when Zelda came up from behind her and grabbed her ass playfully. "You going to the library this morning?" she asked her.

"No. At one," Martha replied. "Though I must admit, it will feel good to get back to work."

"Remy leaving soon?"

"She's due at her lab at ten I think," Martha answered.

"Ah, then we have time together alone," Zelda said. "Do what we couldn't do yesterday." Her face flashed with a bright smile.

Martha turned around and gazed into the redhead's eyes. They looked green today, but they often changed color. Maybe it was the bright green shirt she was wearing. They were thinking the same thing, about what they missed the day before. Their sexual attempt had been ill timed: they should have guessed that Leslie and Robin would be nosing around their lives again. By the time detectives Patrick and Penny were done, they'd upset everyone so much that getting back to sex was impossible.

Martha still wanted some time with Zelda, still wanted to lie back in that female tenderness. That kind of sexual release was something she longed for which didn't happen often in her life. She was the kind that gave and gave and gave, taking little for herself. Felicia would talk about giving her what she wanted, but other than that wild woman demanding that Martha abuse her, and having the satisfaction that came with that, Martha usually brought herself off. Felicia was always too strung out to even tongue her pussy at the finish. Did all submissives act like dominants right in the middle of a submissive scene?

One thing for sure, Zelda wasn't demanding the way Felicia was. Whether she took a dominant or submissive role, Zelda would give to her without asking everything in return. She'd seen the woman nurture Remy, how lavish she was in her sensuousness. Martha couldn't wait for that for herself.

"You really think we'll finally have the privacy?" Martha asked, leaning in to kiss Zelda's very soft lips.

"Oh, I think so. We'll go upstairs, take the phone off the hook, not answer the doorbell, and even Jane won't be around to ruin things," Zelda suggested.

They played with breasts, caressing each other through their clothes, their lips meeting tenderly time after time. "Remy won't be gone for a few minutes yet," Martha said, pulling away reluctantly. Her thighs were trembling, her heart pounding with need: she wanted Zelda now.

"Well then we'll wait. It won't be long," Zelda returned, giving her a delicious grin, her eyes glimmering and thoughts of sex motivating her to blow a meaningful kiss in Martha's direction as she left the room.

Robin and Leslie drove to the Hill after they'd quickly showered and dressed. They didn't talk about sex, the night before, or being tied to the bed. By mutual agreement, it would be awhile before they'd share a bed together again. That fact made their morning another bittersweet moment, halting and uneasy.

At the base of the hill, they spotted the little red compact car that Remy drove turning right onto the street and moving away from them, in the direction of the lab at the university.

"Must be going back to work," Robin said.

"She looked a little flustered," Leslie said. "Didn't even see us."

"Just as well, our business is not with her. If she'd seen us now, she'd probably have an accident. I'm surprised that Martha doesn't drive her."

"Perhaps she's not as confused as she sounds. It wouldn't surprise me if she has spells of very clear thinking."

"You think she's guilty, don't you?" Leslie asked.

"I think we'll know more after we've finished with Jane," Robin assured her.

They drove up the long driveway to the top of the hill. Roman Hill stood like a monolith. Its purpose didn't seem as clear to Robin as it once had been. She was thinking of it as a relic that would best be bulldozed away once the murder was solved. A bed and breakfast? She wasn't sure it would fly, unless someone wanted to give ghost tours or mystery nights or something like that.

They parked close to the garden, just a short walk to Jane's cottage, both detectives hoping that Jane Hugh was still at home. There was no excuse for not having been there bright and early, except for the simple lust which had overcome them both.

"I wonder if Martha is back to work, too," Leslie considered aloud. She stared up at the at the dark windows that looked out onto the garden, thinking of Martha's disgruntled face staring down at them the day before. Perhaps the woman didn't realize that

Leslie had seen her scowling at them from her perch. Later, when they seemed to interrupt her and Zelda, the same scowl was thinly disguised.

Reaching the cottage, they could see a light still on. A knock on the door and Jane answered moments later.

"My, to what do I owe this return visit?" she said. Her eyes were without a hint of malice, her tone not in the least accusatory, just curious.

"We've made some discoveries that we'd like to talk to you about," Leslie said. "May we come in?"

"By all means," Jane said. Holding the door wide, she let them pass first.

There always was an air of authority about her that suggested she would be in control of any situation. Robin wondered if she would still be in control if the police arrested her.

"I'm surprised you two can confront me at all," Jane said, with a pleased smirk. "You look as if you're creaming in your pants."

Leslie was taken aback, not realizing that she was so obvious with her lust. The truth was, she *was* "creaming" in her pants. Just seeing the woman, it was difficult not to think of being dominated by her.

"Is that suppose to disarm us?" Robin readily replied to the sarcastic remark.

"Just stating what I see. It doesn't bother me," Jane said. "If I was prone to be flattered, I suppose I would be now."

"You're assuming a lot," Leslie said, trying to regain some of her typically aggressive attitude.

"Am I?" Jane's eyes flashed.

"There are some things we have to ask you, Jane," Robin said, changing the subject. "Some very curious holes in your story, lies in fact. We'd like some explanations."

"Why don't you just take this to the police?" Jane asked.

"Because, frankly, we don't think you murdered Felicia," Leslie jumped in.

"But you have to ask? So ask."

Jane moved to her leather chair and sat down. Robin and Leslie sat down on the couch opposite her.

"We found pictures of you and Felicia in her room. You had her bound just like she was when she died. The very same knots that her murderer used."

"That is curious, isn't it?" Jane said, though she was not at all perturbed by the information.

"You were having sex with Felicia here at Roman Hill, what appears to be many times, and you brought her to the club. I would guess your relationship with her was more than just a sour business partnership." Leslie was on the offensive.

Jane stared at them, her forceful eyes hard to look into. The sensuality of her masculine allure and the way she seemed to remain in command made Leslie shiver and Robin flinch. For Leslie it was the beginnings of sexual awakening and arousal, and for Robin—well, she knew what Jane could do; she'd seen this kind of commanding dom many times before.

"Yes, we did have quite a relationship. We'd had one for several years. I would often dominate her, pretty much anywhere I wanted—here, the club, other clubs, in public. She loved semipublic venues to proclaim herself. Nothing made her hornier than showing off in front of people, baring her tits, flaunting her ass. She was shameless," Jane said, sighing wistfully.

"If she was reputed to be dominant, why do you suppose she wanted to be submissive?" Leslie asked.

Jane eyed the detective and chuckled at herself, obviously holding back some personal remark. "Beats me why she switched the way she did. She saw me at a club somewhere and came to me wanting to be taken and abused. I did it. Gladly. She told me I was her balance, I kept her from going crazy. I gave her limits. It's not an easy relationship to describe. But then, you had to know the woman to understand her."

"I understood her very well," Robin said. "I lived with her here for two years."

Jane was surprised and impressed. "Then this case has personal implications for you," she said.

"Some, though it was quite a while ago. I do want to find her killer."

Jane nodded. "Well then you would understand what she needed in me," Jane said.

"I think so," Robin agreed. "And did she pay you for dominating her?"

"No. I gave it willingly. I didn't want her money. In fact, I don't take money for sexual favors. I play my games because it pleases me, nothing else."

"Why did Felicia owe you so much money?" Leslie asked.

"Bad investments," Jane said.

"Bad investments?" Robin repeated.

"I'm a stockbroker when I'm not doing other things. I've dabbled very successfully for years. Felicia kept coming to me with really boondoggle ideas, and I'd make some investments for her, and she kept losing. She ran up a tab for awhile. I advised her. She didn't listen. I finally quit making the investments for her. But by that time she had to sign over half the house to me. The rest she tried to pay back a little at a time out of her trust. That's dwindled down pretty low. I'll get back what she owed me, but I don't need it. I'd rather have her alive."

She was very believable: if she was lying, she was very good at it, Robin thought.

"Did you business dealings start before or after the sex began?" Leslie asked.

"It was pretty much simultaneous. We had great sex: I've never known a better submissive. It wasn't that she submitted all that well—in fact she struggled like hell—but she liked the confrontation, and I liked the way she'd go really deep into everything. I love women that act like hellions."

"Were you in love with her?" Robin asked.

Jane gave her a curious look.

"Someone at Sapphos suggested you were," Leslie explained.

Jane looked genuinely surprised, as if it weren't a proper question to ask a dominant. "Yes I was," she finally admitted. The silence that followed was awkward until Jane lit a cigarette. "I mourn in my own way," she continued. "And I suppose I loved her in my own way. I've never really been as taken by any submissive as I was by her."

"But being dominant, you can do scenes even when you're in mourning?" Leslie said with a sarcastic ring.

"It's a release," Jane said.

"Pretty damned good release with Zelda the other night," Leslie said.

Jane looked at Leslie curiously.

"We were on our way to talk with you and saw your lights. It wasn't hard to see your scene. We thought since you were leaving the lights on and the drapes open that you didn't care who saw. I would assume you would welcome an audience."

"I suppose that was part of the point," Jane agreed, "though up on this hill there aren't many who would have the opportunity to watch." Jane's eyes glimmered. "I hope you enjoyed yourselves." She looked directly at Leslie, stared right at her chest and then moved her glance to the other woman's crotch. "You two ever get it on?" she asked.

"We're asking the questions," Robin said.

Jane shrugged. "Then be my guest, but remember, next time I'll be doing the talking," Jane said. She said that, knowing that there would be a next time, speaking as if there were a relationship developing between the three of them that only she was yet privy to. At the moment, however, she only had eyes for Leslie. As she talked, her gaze did not waver from the brunette detective—from her breasts, her crotch, and her sumptuous lips.

"Are you and Zelda having a regular relationship now? Is that why she's still staying here?" Robin asked.

"I had her the other night, but never again. Never. If she's involved with anyone it's Martha."

"Martha?" Robin asked. She recalled the interruption the day before.

"I saw them together a couple of days ago. They'd had quite a session on the back porch. A little tame for me, but they were obviously into it."

"Why would you never have Zelda again?" Leslie asked.

"She didn't have any limits. I don't like that."

"Was that any different than Felicia?" Robin asked.

"Much. I always knew how far to go with her; she

never gave me any doubt. She may not have seemed like the kind of woman you could trust, but she had her sexual boundaries. I could trust her. There's a safety for me in that, you know. I'm not out to harm anyone. Most of it's psychological. The physical can be rather mild and a scene still very provocative if the mental aspects are properly seen to."

"And Zelda isn't aware of her limits?" Robin suggested.

"No, not physically. She didn't want me to stop. That woman will keep going on until, someday, someone's going to kill her."

"You don't mean that?" Leslie said.

"I do. And it's not going to be me."

"Why on earth do you think that?"

"I can't really tell you, it's just a feeling that I have. A real spooky, eerie feeling. I didn't like the vibes I was getting. The scene was alright—of course you know that, don't you," she said with a sly grin, though she returned quickly to a serious expression. "She went really crazy because I wanted to stop. I wouldn't take her as far as she wanted to go. And then she kept pleading with me, 'Do it for Eve, please, do it for Eve.' She was nuts. I asked her who the hell Eve was, and she gave me this really stupid look, like she was crazy, crazier than Felicia ever was. I had to back off. I couldn't get into some scene that I didn't understand. She was really weird." Jane looked as troubled as the two were ever likely to see the woman.

"You say she wanted you to call her Eve?" Robin asked, her eyes widening.

"Yeah, Eve."

"What else did she say about that?" Robin asked.

"She rambled on about maybe we should trade

places, that I should let Eve tie me up, that Eve would give me a really good time."

"Did she tell you who Eve was?"

"I guess it's her. Maybe she's a split personality."

"My god, maybe she's Eve. Maybe she's our killer," Robin said, her heart beginning to thump excitedly.

"Who the hell is Eve?" Leslie asked.

"An aide at the hospital, the woman I talked to on the grounds," Robin explained, "told me about a woman, Eve Delisle. She'd been a patient at Brightwood who'd killed her lovers, tied them up and stabbed them. She escaped. According to the woman she died, but I'm beginning to wonder...."

"You're not kidding about this, are you?" Leslie said.

"No, I'm not."

Robin was on her feet. "And we know that Zelda and Martha are having sex. We saw them yesterday in a compromising state of disarray. C'mon Leslie," Robin said anxiously, "we need to go to the big house. I don't want to wait."

Martha and Zelda raced upstairs after Remy left and went immediately to Zelda's room.

"We could do it in Felicia's room. I've really wanted to try that great big bed of hers," Zelda said.

"No, for heaven's sakes no," Martha flinched at the thought. "She died there; it really should be burned, the whole room dismantled. This will do just fine," she remarked, looking at the lovely brass bed in Zelda's room. "I've always loved this room. It's so bright, kind of like you," she told Zelda.

She looked at the woman's eyes, seeing how dark they had become. The light in them wasn't the pretty green she'd seen downstairs in the kitchen earlier that morning.

"Well, my dear Martha, you just lie back on my brass bed and rest yourself. You're in for one terrific treat." Zelda went to a closet and brought out some rope.

"You're going to tie me up too?" Martha asked. She was trembling inside, thinking that she'd never been submissive this way. She'd dreamt about it many times, even suggested it to Remy once, thinking that the two should really broaden their sexual horizons. But Remy shirked away so badly at the idea that Martha knew never to bring up the subject again. There had never been anyone else to try these things with. Maybe if Felicia had remained alive there would have been the opportunity for Martha to be submissive. Felicia certainly had her dominant reputation, but she only seemed to want Martha's control, nothing more.

"I'm going to love you like you've never been loved," Zelda assured her. Laying the ropes down, she climbed on the bed with Martha and caressed the woman's body carefully. The two embroiled in a sensuous moment that could have easily brought them both to a climax.

"Oh, we're not going to go too fast today. Let's see how we can stretch this out," Zelda said. She picked up one rope and took Martha's right wrist, tying it ever so carefully with a neatly tied knot.

"You've done this before?" Martha suggested.

"A few times. I know you have to tie the knots right, or your wrists will have marks after, and I wouldn't want that." Taking Martha's right ankle, she repeated the process, first binding it with the length of rope and then securing it to the brass footboard. She repeated the process until all four limbs were securely fastened.

"Feel them—are they too tight?"

"No, they're perfect," Martha said, moving against the binding ropes. Her body was trembling with anticipation. The wait was as delicious as the act itself. Seeing Zelda's vibrant eyes glimmering so beautifully with all that dark, purposeful light in them, she was transported into a world she'd always longed for.

"You like being helpless, don't you?" Zelda purred.

"Oh, it's wonderful," Martha replied, as she sank into the feeling of being out of control. How long had it been since she'd been treated to this kind of selflessness? Her body was clamoring for more.

"Just close your eyes and relax," Zelda purred. "You're totally in my power; just let go and let me have you." Zelda had picked up a soft deerskin whip. She stroked Martha's aroused body with the instrument, gliding the soft talons over the woman's tender skin. Martha twitched excitedly, a smile breaking out on her face. She opened her eyes to see Zelda grinning at her with a nasty stare. "Just keep your eyes closed and let me caress you," she purred at the submitting woman.

Martha closed her eyes again, feeling as if she might float away. "Whip me more," she groaned. "All over, please." The whip continued its journey over Martha's breasts, down her belly which moved erotically to each stroke, and then across her thighs and between her legs where her pink cunt lay exposed.

The groans from the surrendering woman were beautiful music to Zelda's ears. She listened for the mounting arousal, then whipped her hard, the talons cutting ever so wickedly in some soft places. Martha's groans became more vibrant. But the submissive woman didn't say stop. She didn't protest. She was loving it and wanting more, exactly what Zelda wanted too.

Zelda knew when to end it. There seemed to be that happy oneness between the two, as Martha drifted away, lost in the sensations, and Zelda's eyes darkened to a hard edge, a necessarily determined edge taking control. She'd know when to end it, and she knew Martha would take much more before that moment came. And when the time did come, she'd give her that last exquisite finale, that final moment of passionate release.

"You really think we have to rush so fast?" Leslie said, as she struggled to keep up with Robin who was quickly making her way to the house.

Jane had stood at the cottage door with an uncharacteristically confused look on her face, then decided to follow the two detectives. She was used to gauging female emotions, and she could see that Robin was terrified. From what she knew of the detective, Robin had strong gut instincts.

"I thought you said this Eve was dead?" Leslie asked.

"How do we know that for sure?" Robin said. "Remy's gone. We interrupted Zelda and Martha yesterday...if we're going to find out if Zelda is Eve, it'll be now. We could be stopping a murder!"

A horrid shiver raced down Leslie's back as Robin ran into the house, while she followed close behind.

"Upstairs," Robin said, leading the way. How she knew where to go Leslie wasn't sure, but she would follow. God, she hoped that this was a silly goose chase.

They turned at the top of the stairs, moving away from the front of the house, away from Felicia's room to the rooms at the back. They passed Martha and Remy's room, the door standing open. It was empty. The door the end of the hall was closed.

Robin stopped to listen.

"I hear her voice," the detective said, pressing her ear against the door. "Zelda's."

"They could be in the middle of an innocent scene," Leslie said.

"Or Zelda could be killing her," Robin said. She was certain of herself. The knob turned and the door opened easily. The two detectives stood at the doorway, looking in on Martha and Zelda. Yes, they were in the middle of sex, a scene, S&M in bold relief; but not the S&M of games of fun and playtime and erotic adventure. This was something more.

Martha was tied to the bed, eyes closed, writhing in lewd abandon, her body glistening, hot with sweat and sexual fever. She moaned lustily and loud. Robin gazed at the bondage, seeing the knots tied to the bed's brass footboard. Yes, as she expected, they were the exact same kind of knots that had bound Felicia when she was murdered. But, though Robin noticed the knots immediately, it was not the knots that concerned her.

Zelda stood at the far side of the bed, her eyes glazed over, her attention unwavering, not even the sounds of the door opening shaking her spellbound stare from Martha's undulating form. The smirk on her face was otherworldly.

Something was very wrong, Robin was sure, and then she saw it. The glint of a knife, a long, slim knife, grasped in the redhead's chubby hand, poised and ready to strike the unsuspecting woman on the bed. "Zelda, no!" Robin shouted. She leaped inside the room, racing for Zelda's outstretched, knife-wielding hand. As she reached the side of the bed, Zelda's eyes suddenly turned, fixed intently on her. With her free hand raised, Zelda delivered one powerful punch that landed across Robin's face, throwing the detective off balance and knocking her against the far wall. Robin was in the corner on the wings of strength she never imagined possible from the diminutive woman. Falling hard against the wall, she banged her head and slumped to the floor, momentarily too dazed to get up. All she could think was, how can I get up, I've got to get up, but her body wouldn't move.

Focused on just one thing at a time, Zelda's concentration immediately returned to Martha. The bound woman, who had been moaning so lustily, waiting for another blow of the lovely whip, waiting to go deeper still into her erotic ecstasy, momentarily opened her eyes, sensing something wasn't right. She looked up at Zelda, her gaze abruptly frozen, fixed in horror on the glint of the knife poised high above her body.

Leslie, having followed Robin to the far side of the room, grabbed for Zelda's arm and turned the woman around on a dime. Zelda yelled something unintelligible, interrupted in her task, and the knife dropped from her hand, clattering against the floor. She lunged for the weapon, landing hard against the wooden floor.

"No you don't!" Leslie screamed, and she covered Zelda's falling body with her own.

Zelda's outstretched hand reached for the knife. Finding it, she held the handle in her fist, clutching it with every bit of strength she had. With Leslie's body weight on her, she could hardly breathe, her gasps for air becoming desperate as Leslie struggled to keep her down and take the knife from her at the same time.

Zelda was mad, insanely mad, the knife flailing about her. She had to find the target, she had to find the flesh, she had to find that soft, tender, giving flesh in which to sink the blade. Such a pretty polished blade, so bright and glaring, harsh, very harsh. If only she could complete her task, take the woman away with her. Her mind was sinking, going somewhere far, far away. It was difficult to breath, every breath heavier still, heavier still. She could hardly breathe at all, but she couldn't stop. No, never, she couldn't stop until it was finished. She had to finish her task, she had to take the woman away with her.... Yes, take the woman away with her. This would be the last time, the very last time....

Leslie almost had the knife in her hand. She reached, but she couldn't grasp it. The angle was all wrong: she struggled to get closer, but she couldn't allow Zelda to escape. She held down one flailing arm, but not the one she wanted. She had to reach farther, just an inch farther.

At that moment Jane was in the room, at Leslie's side. She dove for Zelda's flailing wrist, clutching it so the pinned woman couldn't move it or the knife. "Drop it, Zelda," she said quietly. The flailing crazy woman wouldn't let go. She hadn't even heard the quiet command. Then, all of sudden, the knife was gone, wrenched abruptly by Jane's sure fingers.

The redhead went limp under the weight of Leslie's body. The knife was gone, it must have hit home, it must have found flesh, it must be over, Zelda thought...it must be over now, no more sense in breathing anymore.

For a moment the scene froze—Zelda fainted on the floor with Leslie, numb, on top of her, Jane standing over them, Robin still recouping in the corner, and Martha seeing little but the flash of polished metal in Jane's large hand. For a moment the action stopped cold, frozen in time, as it would always remain frozen in the five minds of the five women, each with different vantage points, each with different angles of perception, each with different versions of the truth.

CHAPTER FOURTEEN

Robin climbed from her car and looked at the familiar setting of Roman Hill Estate. It was getting all too familiar, though this should be the last time she had to make this trek, at least for awhile; that is, if all the loose ends had been wrapped up as neatly as they looked. Staring up at Felicia's turret bedroom once more, she flashed on the first time a week ago that she and Leslie had arrived to investigate the murder. It made even more sense to her now that Felicia had died in such a enigmatic way, with a host of odd women surrounding her, interplaying with her very complicated life. She like complicated things, and so it was when she died.

"Feeling better this morning?" Leslie asked as she joined Robin, the two walking toward the house.

"I'm okay, a little headache, but it was mostly gone this morning. I still can't get over that I didn't get that knife from Zelda...Eve...whoever she was," Robin said.

"Oh, that doesn't really surprise me," Leslie replied. "You're out of shape, need to brush up on some basic karate: you're getting too lazy. A little too much laziness could kill you."

"Well, you didn't get it away from her either," Robin reminded her partner.

"We can thank Jane," Leslie said.

"Want to thank her personally?" Robin asked in jest.

"Maybe, just maybe," Leslie replied.

"Is she going to be here this morning?" Robin asked.

"I called to tell her we we'd be here. She was rather noncommittal," Leslie replied. "But at least it's over. Betsy should be here any minute."

"Over, that's right it's over," Robin said.

"What's the matter? I'd think you'd be happy."

"I should be, shouldn't I?"

"But you're not," Leslie queried.

"No, I just have this weird feeling that it's not over yet."

"Weird feeling about what?" Leslie asked.

"I'm not sure yet," Robin answered.

"Something we've overlooked?"

"I don't know. I think we'll just see how things are when we confront them all. I have a feeling we still don't have the whole story."

As they talked, a car pulled up the long driveway, and John Longcore and his sister Betsy got out.

"Just who I wanted to see," John said, giving first

Leslie and then Robin a big hug. "Thank you for saving my sister."

"It's always easier to save the innocent," Leslie told him with a smile. She gave Betsy a warm kiss on the cheek.

John reached into his pocket and pulled out a check that he handed to Leslie.

"Very nice, thank you," Leslie said, looking at it, then handing it to her partner.

Robin pocketed it without seeing the amount.

"Listen, Betz, I've got to go," John said, turning to his sister. "We'll have dinner tonight, okay?"

"Sure."

"You going to be all right?"

"I think so," she replied, looking up at the old house. "I have my things to pack, then I'll take a taxi to the cemetery and give Felicia my last kiss." There was a sad look on her face.

Robin looked at the small woman, trying to imagine her with Felicia. For all the sexual partners that Felicia had, Betsy seemed the oddest. She wasn't the kind of woman that Felicia was usually attracted to. Not that there was any particular type: Felicia's tastes were obviously broad and wide. But Betsy seemed too conventional for Felicia's kind of lifestyle. Maybe there was a siren under all that quiet and composure. She had a lusty reputation, but even so, Betsy seemed too sensible to be attached to anything as bizarre as Felicia Roman. Where would she go now? That was a mystery as interesting as the case.

"Don't worry, Sis, we'll find a place for you. I think there's an apartment near mine that's available. I'll do some calling this afternoon," John assured her.

"Thanks," Betsy said with a tentative smile. John

gave his sister a hug and then climbed into the car and drove away.

"Good morning, ladies," Leslie said, entering Felicia Roman's study to see Martha, Remy, and Jane sitting in an awkward, though relieved silence.

Robin and Betsy followed Leslie into the room.

"Oh, Betsy," Remy raced toward the pale but smiling woman. The two hugged warmly at Remy's insistence, though for Betsy the display was obviously forced.

"This has been all my fault," Remy began. "I've been over and over it in my mind. I should have known, please can you forgive me?" She was in tears again, just as she'd been for nearly the entire twenty-four hours since Zelda's unveiling.

Betsy stroked the distraught woman's mop of hair because she really had no other choice, even though the gesture seemed fake.

"Remy, leave Betsy alone for awhile, she needs a little space," Martha reminded her lover.

"Oops, I'm sorry," Remy said pulling away. The woman fidgeted nervously with the cotton handkerchief in her hand, wringing it, pulling it through her fist.

"Eve was a cunning impostor, and it was a confused time for you back then, Remy. How would you have known?" Leslie said, as the whole room watched the anxious Remy return to her place beside Martha on the sofa.

Betsy sat down in the high-backed chair that had always been Felicia's. She didn't look like the grand dame; she wasn't even trying to. It was simply pleasant to sink herself into something familiar. She smiled at the others, feeling as if she would prefer being there alone, not with five women eyeing her.

"We've checked things at Brightwood," Leslie said, jumping into the uncomfortable silence. "Eve Delisle escaped from Brightwood just at the time that Zelda Wing left her employment there. Apparently she stalked Zelda, killed her, maimed the body beyond recognition, dumped it, and then assumed Zelda's identity, which she's maintained now for at least four years. Before Brightwood she killed two lovers, just as she killed Felicia and was attempting to kill Martha. Unfortunately we don't know what set her off this time. One thing for certain—she's smart, clever, and extraordinarily ruthless. She had an uncanny way of covering her tracks for a woman so mentally disturbed. Of course it helped that she bore a strong resemblance to the real Zelda."

"Where is she now?" Martha asked.

"There will likely not be a trial, but that will take months to decide. She'll probably be locked up in a hospital for the criminally insane. When she was taken into custody yesterday, she'd regained some of her composure, but her mind was all over the place. Her gross failure with the murder didn't sit well with her psyche."

"Oh, my, I should have known," Remy said, with tears still falling from her eyes. Though she sat next to Martha, she seemed to cringe when her lover surrounded her with a comforting arm. She shook the woman off. "It was strange how she wrote to me out of the blue, a year ago. I thought it was a good idea for me, reacquainting myself with someone from Brightwood—that it might help me understand the past, help me heal even more." She looked up at Leslie and

Robin with an imploring look. "She was so gentle and reassuring, reminding me of private things we shared during that time. I wonder how Eve knew."

"The police found Zelda's diaries in her room. They were rather detailed regarding every aspect of the woman's life. She really hit on a gold mine, choosing to take the woman's identity. It was all spelled out in clear terms. All she needed was a little hair dye and the right haircut," Leslie said.

"Maybe you can tell us—what might have brought her to Roman Hill in the first place?" Robin asked the shivering woman on the couch.

Remy looked up at Robin nervously. "I really don't know," she replied. Her eyes refused to focus on anyone.

"Zelda—Eve, I mean," Martha began, "told me that you wrote her about strange things happening here. What did you tell her, dear?" Martha asked.

Remy's chin trembled. "Oh, I'm sure it was too much. I must have told her that you and Felicia were, you know…playing your games." Remy's voice turned cold, as if her entire body had suddenly been hit with a blast of snow. She shook, her arms drawn in close to her sides.

"Remy, hon, perhaps you need to lie down," Martha suggested, trying to comfort her again.

"No, I don't need to lie down," she said, wiggling away from the woman's grasp. Her eyes stared blankly ahead, then looked up as she realized that everyone was staring at her.

"You told her about the S&M?" Leslie asked.

Remy's eyes darted about the faces of the women looking at her. "Yes," she answered, "I told her that my lover was into S&M games with another woman, that I couldn't do those things, and I was very concerned about my relationship with Martha."

"But Remy, I thought we'd talked about this?" Martha said.

"How did she respond?" Robin asked.

"She wrote back not to worry, that there was nothing wrong with variety in sexual expression, that perhaps I should talk to Martha about my feelings."

"Quite a sane thing to advise you about," Leslie said.

"I can't believe how devious she was," Martha said, shaking her head. "I still can't believe that you three rescued me from this. I would have died." The look of shock on Martha's face was as real as the one she'd had the day before, when she was finally aware of exactly what had happened in the middle of her scene.

"It's going to take some time to get over, I'm sure," Robin said kindly.

"But Remy," Martha said, "you mean to tell me that you didn't have any doubt about Eve when she came here? I mean, did she really look that much like the real Zelda?"

Remy shook. "I told you," she said icily, "the woman looked like the Zelda I knew. But you know as well as anyone that I was not well when I knew her. Please, Martha, stop browbeating me!"

"Remy, please," Martha said, trying to calm the woman down, but it was obvious that Remy didn't want Martha's affection.

"Perhaps we could all use something to drink. I'll see if I can find something." Martha's discomfort was showing, and she rose from the sofa, patting Remy's hand softly. "I'll be right back. A little iced tea?" she said, addressing the whole room. There were enough nods to send Martha on an expedition to the kitchen. Remy quickly jumped up and followed her lover.

"Maybe she needs my help," she said nervously.

"You think that woman is going round the bend?" Jane asked as the two women disappeared into the back of the house.

"She doesn't look very sane," Robin agreed. "This has obviously shaken her badly."

"I'd put her back in the mental institution and let her calm down," Jane suggested. "But then, who am I to say anything."

"Did Zelda kill anyone else between her stay at Brightwood and Felicia?" Betsy chimed in. "I mean, is she some kind of serial killer?"

"That's not clear; the police will be looking into it as they check their unsolved murders," Leslie said. For an instant she caught Jane's attentive eye and stared at the dom. Jane's legs were crossed in a masculine way, her cowboy boots still caked with mud on the heels. She squashed a cigarette in the ashtray beside her, her husky finger pressing the butt into the glass while Leslie stared at her. The detective felt her body jump, as it had on so many recent occasions. Her mind fast forwarded to their private talk, the one they would need to have when this was all over. It made her nervous, even as the possibilities excited her.

"So what's your explanation about the those tricky little rope knots you two were so worried about?" Jane asked. She was smirking, almost anticipating the answer.

"Eve had seen the pictures," Leslie explained. "In one moment of lucidity, she spilled the beans to the police, started talking, told them all kinds of things. She thought she was quite clever pinning this on you,

Jane. Of course, when Betsy was arrested, she had no problem supporting that theory too. It seems that Eve had a penchant for being submissive to an extreme, then turning the tables, trying to top her dominants, even if it was just once. She did that with Felicia, and unfortunately it worked exactly as she planned."

"She tried doing that with me," Jane said. "I laughed in her face. She wasn't clever enough to know that was something I never do. In fact, using a little psychology of my own, I think she wanted a way out with me. She wanted me to take her hard, wanted the punishment to hurt her, really hurt her. It's too bad Felicia was so naive."

"Yes it is," Betsy said. There was a sadness in her eyes, a loneliness that seemed to bring the room down to her level of gloom. A respectful quiet followed…

…until the scream.

A bloodcurdling cry pierced the quiet calm in the study.

The four women jerked. Then Robin and Leslie immediately bolted to the back of the house, to the kitchen.

Remy had a kitchen knife in her hand, as if trying to reenact the failed moment in the upstairs bedroom the day before. For the second time in two days Martha found herself about to be the victim in a murder, the glazed-over eyes of a crazy woman staring into hers.

Strange the strength of madwomen with knives, Robin thought as she struggled to pull Remy away from Martha. Remy's strength was suddenly far beyond what anyone would have thought. She had her lover pinned to a kitchen counter, her smaller form leaning against the heavier Martha with a zealot's madness propelling her.

"You're suppose to be dead! Dead, do you hear!" she screamed at her frightened lover. "You run off screwing around with that bitch! You loved her didn't you? You said you loved me! But you lied, you lied to me, you bitch!" Remy tried to bury the knife in Martha's chest as Martha struggled for her life, barely able hold off the slowly sinking weapon.

Robin pulled at Remy's back, expecting Leslie behind her to have the knife in hand.

"You bitch, you lying bitch!" Remy screamed. She lunged again.

She was sobbing, her words garbled by her rage. Yet her strength was finally vanishing as her body collapsed back against Robin. The detective gave her one sharp determined tug, and the knife dropped to the kitchen counter, without having to be pried from her hand. And Leslie instantly retrieved it, taking it as far from Remy as she could.

"I brought her here," the woman sobbed. "I knew who she was from the moment she arrived." Regaining a degree of clarity, she looked up at Martha one last time, for one last verbal knife to throw at the object of her passion. "I knew she was Eve. I knew she hadn't died. I suspected it all along when I got the letters. I may have been insane then, but there were things about Eve you could never forget, even if you only met her once." Remy's eyes were still filled with hate. "It was Eve all right, and she was going to kill you, just the way she did Felicia, and I was happy about it. I wanted her to."

Martha hid her head, not wanting to look at Remy's twisted face. Robin pulled Remy away from the kitchen. More babbling, hurtful denunciations would be pointless. She led the dazed woman into the hallway, to the foyer, where she and Leslie would keep her calm. Jane had 911 on the phone, and Betsy comforted the shocked Martha. For the second time in two days, Martha been rescued, and a house full of women was left stunned. Hopefully this was the end at last, but an eerie silence followed, no one ready to let down their guard.

An hour later Leslie and Robin watched the red lights of the ambulance disappear down the driveway of Roman Hill.

"So this was your gnawing intuition," Leslie remarked.

"She was sadly unstable. I feel very sorry for her," Robin said, shaking her head. "Amazing, bringing a madwoman into this house to match her own madness."

"She'll go back to Brightwood, or wherever she belongs—certainly not among the sane," Leslie speculated.

"I feel sorry for Martha—did you see her in there? She looked horrible."

"She'll survive; she's the kind that does," Leslie said. "If Jane's smart she'll put Martha in charge of the renovations on the estate and have a top-notch showplace by the time it's done."

"I'm still not sure about the bed-and-breakfast idea," Robin said.

"I think you're right, but knowing Jane, maybe she'll open a new club. It would be perfect for that, don't you think?" Leslie said.

"Sure, and you'll be her first slave?" Robin said.

Leslie was startled by the suggestion. "I think you're jumping to conclusions," she answered. "I hardly know the woman."

"Really?" Robin replied, a devilish smirk on her normally soft face.

Leslie didn't answer. She took a deep breath instead and gave her partner a pat on the arm. "At least this time you did a better job, a lot more efficient subduing Remy," Leslie complimented her.

"Thanks, I'm glad I redeemed myself."

Leslie and Robin stared around the grounds of Roman Hill. The quiet that had been here so many times was pervading the place again. The house still threatened to fall into the earth, and the gardens were as wild as ever. It was a place they would never forget. They watched as Betsy climbed into a taxi that had just arrived. She waved to them but was too distraught to do more. They'd see her soon, but right now she wanted to be as far away from the place as possible. They didn't blame her.

"You know, I feel sometimes like I fly in an out of peoples' lives at crucial moments like these, and then they're left to pick up all the messy pieces, and I don't have to be accountable for it," Leslie said.

"I've never heard you talk that way," Robin said, looking at her partner with a degree of concern. "You okay?"

"Yeah, I'll be fine. I just need to shake the effects of these two days off my feet, if you know what I mean," Leslie said.

"I know exactly what you mean," Robin said. She was thinking that a visit to Britta that night would be a perfect remedy to the gnawing agitation that she was feeling. "So are you going to the office?" Robin asked her partner.

"No, not yet. In fact, if you don't mind, I need to take the afternoon off. I have something I need to do."

The SM Murder | 209

Robin nodded, knowing what her partner meant. "Watch yourself," she warned. "I want something left for me."

Leslie smiled and watched her partner climb into the Suzuki and drive off.

CHAPTER FIFTEEN

Leslie knocked on the door of the cottage.

Jane answered. "You didn't waste much time," she said, looking at Leslie standing before her.

"I need to talk to you." Leslie said.

"Of course," the woman replied, as if it were self-evident. "Why don't you come in." She opened the door wide and turned around, letting Leslie follow her inside, the two sitting down exactly where they'd sat the day before, Jane in her leather chair, Leslie on the couch. "So are the surprises over?" Jane asked.

"I should hope so. Remy didn't exactly come out of the blue. We suspected her of something, but she certainly did surprise us with her sudden move. Let's hope there aren't anymore unexpected knife-wielding conspirators. I'm not sure Robin or I could take another scene. You're likely not to be there to rescue us for the next one," Leslie conceded, with a grateful smile.

"Robin did well today," Jane reminded her. "Pretty sassy for a submissive I'd say."

"You like her?" Leslie asked, noting the lusty look on Jane's face.

"Why not?" Jane shrugged.

Leslie was feeling slightly embarrassed, not knowing why she'd suddenly turned the conversation to her partner. She looked nervously around the cottage, which at the moment was beset with a dull gray light to match a sky now shrouded by looming storm clouds. How apropos, Leslie thought to herself.

"So you need to talk?" Jane said, as she waited patiently for the conversation to resume.

"Yes, I do," Leslie replied. She liked looking at Jane, wished she could simply stare at her in silence, drinking in her powerful essence. She was the kind of woman Leslie had taken pains to avoid in her lesbian life. Jane stood for things she was unsure about, stood for sex that even in Leslie's unconventional lifestyle seemed strange to her, stood for a feminine model so "out there" it scared her, maybe because there was a little butch in her. Leslie liked a certain form in her life, and Jane's very presence seemed to do everything it could to shatter her well-defined ideas of how she wanted to live. Now, suddenly, she wanted to be near the woman, just to get used to the feelings that had been running rampant through her like some savage beast.

"I wonder if it's talk that you need or something else?" Jane pondered out loud.

"I don't know," Leslie replied. The pauses in their conversation spoke volumes. Jane knew more about Leslie's motives than she wanted any stranger to.

"This case has opened my eyes to lots of things," Leslie started, not having the faintest idea what she would say next. For a woman not unaccustomed to being in dangerous, threatening, and bizarre situations, this moment was one of the most intimidating she'd ever experienced.

"Our lifestyle on this hill a little odd for your tastes?" Jane asked. She was being totally noncommittal which made things that much more difficult.

"Seeing you at the club... I've thought about that, and..." She couldn't say what she was really thinking.

"You want sex with me?" Jane asked.

Leslie waited to reply. It was a daring thing to say, almost like she'd be committing herself if she let the words pass from her lips. "I think so," Leslie admitted at last.

"No," Jane countered immediately. "You either do or you don't. Guesses and thinking about it don't cut it with me."

"The truth is, I've had to put some things on hold till the case was resolved. That came first."

"I can see that. I suppose you needed to solve the crime before you engaged my services. Didn't feel comfortable cavorting with a murderer?"

"We never believed you did it," Leslie reminded her.

"That's what you said. But you still had to wonder. You had all your incriminating evidence; even I would have suspected me. I was surprised every morning to be sleeping in my own bed, not in some jail cell." Jane smirked.

"I never had any doubt about you," Leslie told her.

"Really?" the dom replied. She rose from her chair. "Sit tight a minute while I get us a beer."

"Not for me, please. I don't drink in the morning," Leslie called to her.

"Oh, but you will today," Jane assured her, calling out from the kitchen. Leslie heard the refrigerator open and close.

Maybe the beer would do her some good. She needed to relax. She'd relaxed with Robin two days before, but not since. The case had been an all-consuming drain on her, the nasty twists and turns taking even experienced veterans off guard by the very nature of the wild emotions behind them.

In many ways this case had been no different than others she and Robin had solved. They'd created their own clues and stumbled on pieces of information only because they put themselves in the right place at the right time. Solving a case was often a string of well-timed accidents, created, noticed, filed away and later brought together for the conclusion. This one had been no different. And the surprises? Leslie had grown to expect such minor flukes and miracles. Anyway, she knew that things would wrap the way they did, and sometimes, as in this case, with sudden lightning speed. Yet this case, with its overt sexual aspects, required a different finale. To put it to rest required more than just filing it away in a drawer with all the others. It required a visit with this woman and letting go desires that the detective been holding back from the start.

Leslie looked up at Jane as she returned with the two beers in her hand.

"Drink," Jane ordered gently, as she popped the lid

of the can and handed it to Leslie. "So, you didn't answer my question. Why were you so convinced I didn't murder Felicia when all the evidence pointed otherwise?"

"It was mostly Robin who it figured that way. She's more experienced in your S&M lore."

"Tell me what *you* figured," Jane said.

Looking at her sent new chills through Leslie's excited body. Jane had an intensity in her gaze that was uncanny, as if she had already read the next line of the script, knew exactly where it was going and was just toying with Leslie to make her say things that were so difficult to put into words. Leslie gulped her beer. "When I saw you at Sapphos, you were much different than I expected."

"Oh?" Jane said.

"You're not as tough as you think you are," Leslie suggested.

"I'm every bit as tough as I appear," Jane countered, as her eyes flashed.

"It was more than that. It was the affection, the tenderness, not the pain you gave Dagne, that impressed me."

"I give my submissives what they need, that's all," Jane retorted, as if her gift were nothing at all special.

"I can see that. But it was that other side, that softer side that I found so very appealing."

"Don't kid yourself, Leslie. For every ounce of tenderness, there's a pound of pain—real hard, biting, nasty pain. I'm not a gentle woman."

"Oh, but I know you are. That's why I know you didn't kill Felicia. You couldn't love her, even the way I saw you love Dagne that night, and then turn around and stab her. Besides, the crime was committed by someone who had unexpressed desires to be fulfilled, not by someone who regularly got what they wanted sexually."

"I commend your insight," Jane replied. "And so you come to me for what? Tenderness, love, pain?"

"All, I suppose. But understanding, mostly." The woman in the leather chair eyed her so carefully it was hard not to feel exposed, as if she were already naked before her.

"Understanding I can give you. But you want much more than that. You can have understanding from Robin or dozens of other women. But you came to me." Jane transmitted her quiet lust in a way that seemed to roar through Leslie's mind and body. "You're very transparent, Leslie Patrick. What's even better, you've given me lots of time to consider what I'd do with you, waiting as long as you have. Sometimes I have to make these spur of the moment decisions. But you've given me the opportunity to consider how I'll have you, what kind of torture I'll put you through. It's been a rather amusing week watching you."

"When did you know I'd be coming to you?" Leslie asked curiously.

"The first time I met you."

"The first?"

"It shouldn't be so odd. You've been climbing the walls of your psyche with curiosity about your Robin's desires for a long time. It's been years, hasn't it? I hit you in the face with it. Felicia, Betsy, Martha, this whole damned case hit you square between the eyes. You're ripe. You need me so you can have Robin again. You couldn't figure out how to have her on your her terms, and you want me to teach you, which is something that I can do very well. I'm an excellent teacher.

"But, there's only one way to get what you want, and you know what that is. You learn by being. You submit to me, there are no shortcuts in the game. It's got to be carefully learned. You have the desire now, but that's all. You have to learn to be cold and calculating, to mix your passion for dominance with the innate kindness in your heart and the love you have for Robin. She'll be licking your feet and loving it."

Leslie didn't disagree with anything the dom said. She knew Jane was right. "We've already played around together," Leslie offered. "We had sex together two days ago."

"Dabbling or real stuff?"

Leslie considered the question thoughtfully. "Dabbling, I guess."

Leslie felt hot all around her, like it was August, or better yet July in the desert, and a hot, white heat surrounded her, making her upper lip sweat and her palms wet and her legs burn right where she sat. She felt as if a heat lamp or the sun was shining on her back, the intensity was so strong. She knew it was just the fear creeping around her, but she wasn't sure what to do with the feeling. She wanted to pee. The beer seemed to go through her the instant she swallowed it, but she was afraid to ask permission to find the bathroom.

Jane was moving on her, blanketing her with words, each designed to draw her in closer to the dom's habitat where her rules were law, and she ordered things. Leslie had seen it at the club and with Zelda. In fact, in any situation it seemed that Jane was seducing the women around her with thoughts of their own need to submit to her. Something was happening to Leslie on a very primal level.

"What did you do to her?" Jane queried.

"She tied me to her bed," Leslie answered.

"She tied you?" Jane shot back.

"Yes."

"Why was that?"

"I wanted her."

"That's pretty shameless. You let a submissive tie you up?" Jane admonished her as if she were a naughty child. "What did she do to you?"

"She used a whip on me, on my thighs and my breasts."

"Did she leave marks?"

"Yes."

"Let me see them."

Leslie shuddered, thinking at first there was no way she'd bare her marked breasts for Jane's eyes. It was all happening much too fast. As much as she knew she had to face this woman's remarkable hold over her, she hadn't expected it quite so suddenly.

"Open your blouse, bitch," the dom told her, raising her voice to a slightly more intense timbre. As if Jane could read Leslie's unspoken protests in the hesitant expression on her face, she was quick to explode any hesitation. She expected unquestioning compliance. Her eyes demanded it. She didn't need to say more.

Leslie began slowly, her fingers finding the top button of her blouse difficult to undo. Jane stared at her impassively, just waiting. The second button was easier, and then the third. Leslie pulled the two sides of her pale blue blouse apart and revealed her white breasts, marked with fading red stripes.

Jane nodded, not saying a word, as Leslie started to close the blouse.

"Leave your blouse open. I want to see you," Jane countered her move. Leslie laid her hands nervously in her lap, not knowing what to do with them. "I'll make the cuts more distinct," Jane told her. "Then you'll show them off to my friends."

Leslie thought of the club. "Are we going to Sapphos?" she asked.

"Eventually, maybe," Jane said. She finished her beer and set the can on the table next to her. "Did you switch?" Jane asked.

"Switch?"

"Did you dominant Robin?"

"Some."

"But you were nervous. Didn't know what to do."

"Yes."

"How did it make you feel?"

"Slapping her tits?" Leslie said, as she thought of that moment. "It turned me on."

"A lot?" Jane asked.

"Yes, a lot," Leslie admitted.

"You understand, slut, this will take more than a day—you understand that? I can't make you who you are in one session. So you'll have to be patient. Let the feelings develop in you, create your own style of dominance. You'll do that by becoming my slave. It may seem like a contradiction, but it will work."

Leslie understood perfectly well. She was already feeling Jane inside he. She'd been there for some time, since Leslie first saw her working over Dagne that night at Sapphos. When Jane spotted her in the doorway with Leta, her hot-fired eyes reached right down and drew out her desire.

"It's all in the little things, the attitude," Jane continued. "Not how hard I'll beat your ass, how much pain I'll cause stretching your asshole, how far you bend to kiss my boots, or how many clothespins I can rip from your aching sides. It's the little things. The way you'll look at me, wait for me, defer to me; the way you'll want me to speak to you, instruct you."

Leslie looked at the woman, mesmerized by the way she talked and the way her body sat in the chair and the way her legs were crossed. She was already in a position to do everything the woman said. Jane seduced her with every move of her body, not like she'd ever been seduced before. Even though Leslie could never imagine being seduced by a man, it was Jane's masculinity that excited her most, that mysterious unknown quality she expressed so well in everything she did.

"I'm beginning to understand how I can submit to you, but I still don't understand how I'll ever do this with Robin. I never could before. We're partners in a very equal sense. Friends. We've known each other for so long, how can I make her submit?"

"You're in love with her?" Jane asked.

Leslie hadn't thought about love much, not recently and not concerning Robin. "Yes," she replied truthfully. "I've never stopped being in love with her."

"Does she love you?"

"Yes," Leslie replied, certain she was right.

"Then you'll work it out, trust me. It's just sex. Sex takes you places with people you'd never think of going in your regular life. You'll adopt your games when the time's right. Other times you won't even think of it. I've done this for years with women you'd be shocked to know how they'd crawled at my feet. I can walk into a room with them now and we're easy friends, and in some cases sure enemies, but we're equals. We've never been anything but, we just express ourselves differently. Right now, you need to forget about those things, Leslie: they're not important."

"No?" Leslie replied meekly.

"No," Jane said, gently shaking her head. "Right now you're going to follow my instructions to a T. You're going to do everything I say without question, and you're going to love it. You understand that?"

"Yes," Leslie nodded.

"You're not going to balk because I'll be even harder on you. I don't care how much you like or don't like pain. I'll give you what you need, you understand that?"

Leslie was quivering, biting her lip like a little child.

"You may have seen me be affectionate with Dagne, but be assured she deserved it because she had taken a lot of pain. She was a good girl, just like you'll be. You only get my loving care when you do what you're told. You understand that?"

"Yes."

"You're my submissive, and you belong to no one else unless I give you away. Your body is mine now. I don't care how much you want to fuck your little bitch-whore Robin: you don't give her anything unless I tell you to."

"Yes, sir," Leslie responded, the formal masculine form jumping out of her mouth unexpectedly, though it seemed as natural as if she'd used it with Jane from the beginning.

"I'm going to make it very easy on you; you won't have to ask any more questions, you won't have to stew in your head for days. I'm taking all those questions away. All you need to do is everything I say."

"Yes, sir," Leslie replied, hypnotized by the sexual sensations that Jane created in her just with the tone of her voice.

"Now, I want you to sit at the edge of the couch," Jane said.

Leslie complied, moving to the edge. She couldn't help but sit straight, straight as an arrow straight.

"Cup your breasts," Jane said.

Leslie responded, taking a pink-marked breast in each hand and pushing it up, presenting it to the scrutinizing woman before her. Jane rose from her chair and opened the cabinet with the whips. She drew from it a thin, canelike instrument, something Leslie had never seen before, though she could easily guess its intended use.

Arriving at her side, Jane looked down at her calmly. Drawing the instrument back, she brought the cane down on Leslie's left breast with a quick cut. An immediate second cut followed.

Leslie gasped. The cuts stung. Looking down she saw that they left their marks too, ones she suspected were much more precise and distinct than the ones Robin had left before. Jane was quick to follow with a twin pair of cuts, the same startling effect quickly apparent. Another two and there were six neat lines on her cupped breasts, three on each one, supplanting the cuts that Robin had willfully administered two days before.

The pain was excruciating, fiercer than the pain at Robin's hands; but in reply she only winced, squelching the desire to cry out.

Jane backed away and replaced the cane in the cabinet while Leslie still held her red-marked breasts, feeling the sharp pain shoot fire through her whole body.

"I want you to meet me at The Arrowhead tonight," Jane said. "You know where that is?"

"Yes."

"Let's say seven."

Leslie nodded.

"You hot?" Jane asked her.

"Very," Leslie answered.

"Good, but don't let that pussy of yours insist on coming. I'll tell you when you can come, you understand?"

"Yes," Leslie replied. She sat waiting for a few seconds as she watched Jane return to her chair.

"Get me another beer, will you?" she said sitting down.

Leslie scurried to the kitchen and found Jane's stash of beer. She thought of getting one for herself, but she had the feeling that Jane would have told her to, if that's what the dom had wanted. Was being submissive always this hard? Knowing when to make decisions and when not to? Jane had said she'd take away all those decisions, but it seemed to Leslie that she had even more to think about now. She didn't want to do this wrong. In the last ten minutes she'd suddenly discovered that pleasing Jane was the most important thing in her life.

On the way back, Leslie popped the lid on the can then handed it to the dom. She stood for some time, silently waiting for further instructions.

"You can go now," Jane said at last.

"Go?" Leslie questioned. She didn't want to leave. Leaving meant waiting, and she couldn't wait any more.

"It's what I said, isn't it?" Jane answered sarcastically. "Get some rest. You'll be up most of the night."

"Yes, sir," Leslie replied. It was over as simply as that, Leslie scurrying outside and closing the door, not knowing what else to do. She had until seven o'clock before she'd be with Jane again. She was halfway to her car before she realized that she had forgotten to button her blouse.

Spending the day obsessing on the possibilities of servitude to Jane, Leslie was in her car driving to The Arrowhead at 6:30. The club was a lesbian meeting place with no specific agenda other than providing its clientele with a private place to meet other lesbian woman. There were no SM overtones. In fact the club seemed rather bright and cheery in tone compared to Jane's somber purposes. Leslie wondered if Jane chose it for that reason. But an afternoon's worth of second guessing, trying to figure Jane's motives, had only left her more anxious, second guessing her own reasons for submitting to this woman.

What it finally came down to was that Leslie wanted Jane. Desire, lust, longing, that strange concoction of arousal that had accompanied her since she first met the woman, couldn't be denied. It didn't even matter about Robin anymore. Oh, yes, Jane was right, Leslie wanted the dom to teach her how to love Robin more; but at the bottom of it all was Leslie's own desire to be used by this remarkable master. She wanted to be taken, abused. and then deeply loved.

Leslie had never felt about anyone the way she felt about Jane. Maybe this would be a long term relationship, maybe not; it didn't matter. All she cared about was now, and how the fervent butch woman would subdue her. She wanted to crawl at her feet, be at her mercy, and experience her tender care once the blows had driven her over the edge.

Arriving at The Arrowhead at the stroke of seven o'clock she walked in the door, not immediately seeing the object of her search. Trying to decide how to proceed, she heard her name called.

"You're Leslie?" a quiet voice asked.

Leslie turned to a woman just behind her.

"Yes."

"Jane's expecting you."

She led Leslie into the club which, for seven o'clock, was still not too dark, though it was already filled with cigarette smoke. The music playing in the background was erotic.

Jane was at a table with another woman who looked a good deal like her. Not in appearance, but in attitude. They were obviously both doms, masculine, but with the same possibility for softness inherent in their expressions.

"This is Leslie," she introduced her to the woman, though she didn't introduce Leslie in return. "Sit down," she ordered. Jane pulled out a chair next to her which Leslie immediately took. The two women talked for sometime, ignoring Leslie who listened attentively to their conversation. They were talking about people Leslie didn't know.

"I think she's going to bring her tonight," the other woman said.

"I doubt it. She'd never come with her," Jane replied. "The little one is hardly submissive."

"Maybe this time Sybil doesn't have a choice," the woman said.

"She never should have in the first place," Jane responded, taking a long drink from the glass in front of her. She turned to Leslie. "Open your blouse." Jane sat back in her chair and stared at Leslie with a stony cold expression. Not a hint of affection: the discipline had commenced.

The club was open, the lights still bright enough to see clearly, and she was being asked to expose herself in a public place, something she had never done before. She shivered nervously, wanting to hesitate, but it was time to comply. Looking at Jane's expression she saw that there was no room to waver; and the excitement racing through her seemed to rid of her of all trepidation. The submission was the most important thing to her now.

Leslie began unbuttoning her blouse. Jane's intent gaze did not waver from her for a second, as if it were there to give her courage, or an ample threat to ensure her obedience. With three buttons loosened, Leslie's blouse was wide open. The marks of the crop were still there, as both women knew they would be. The red lines on each breast stood out for Jane's friend to see.

"Impressive," the other dom said, admiring them. "Put some on her ass too, why don't you?"

"In good time, when she earns it," Jane said. She reached out and grabbed one of Leslie's breasts in her hand and squeezed the sore flesh. Watching Leslie's expression closely, she waited for the tiny wince of pain. It took some seconds before Leslie responded, the submissive wanting to prove herself brave enough to take what her dominant required.

"Close your blouse," Jane finally said, satisfied with her. "Now go to the bathroom and wait for me in the far stall."

"Yes, sir," Leslie replied.

"And take off your pants," Jane added.

Leslie nodded.

She waited at least twenty minutes until Jane joined her in the far stall of the rest room, an extra-large one, no doubt picked to accommodate their activity, but still cold, as cold as the tiny square tiles on the floor were stark and cold. Leslie waited, sitting with her naked ass on the toilet seat.

When Jane finally came crashing through the door, she jerked Leslie up by the arm, the stall door banging, though remaining open.

With Jane's foot on the toilet, Leslie was flung over her dom's hard leather-clad thigh, so that the submissive's ass was well exposed. "Her cunt's yours," Jane told the woman who'd followed her in. A hand quickly reached in and felt for the wet hole between Leslie's thighs. Her labia were pulled hard, her clitoris pinched, and her pussy violated by fingers with rings that scratched her. She hesitated to protest, though the intrusion was difficult to bear in silence.

"You need grease?" Jane asked the other woman.

"No, this one's flooding." The hand penetrated deeper, pushing its way inside, all the way in; after three fingers there were four, then the whole hand pushed its way past the small opening. Not the biggest fist to screw her, but the meanest the way it demanded quick entrance.

"Been fist-fucked before?" Jane asked. She had her hand at Leslie's neck, massaging her ever so gently as the rude hand behind her probed her insides.

"Yes," Leslie managed to gasp.

Taken by the anonymous fist, her body heat rose to a point where she thought she would pass out; but something cold abruptly hit her anus, and more fingers—Jane's or the woman's other hand, Leslie couldn't be sure—breached her rear.

"She'll take a lot," the other woman said.

The rape was ruthless, without any compassion except what tenderness Jane delivered with her warm fingers at the base of Leslie's neck and the back of her head. It was hard to believe she could orgasm this way, but a surge of energy shot through her lightning fast. She bucked noticeably as she withstood the fierce pain, feeling a pleasant surge carry her away.

"Such a slut you are, Leslie," Jane said. "Now lick her fingers dry."

Still bent over Jane's leg, still gazing at the toilet below, anonymous fingers clamped her mouth, and she tasted her own juices on the latex-covered hand. Latex and female come were an odd combination.

"You got your work cut out for you," the woman said, sarcastically. Leslie felt the woman draw away from her, and she listened for her to exit the rest room.

Leslie didn't move because Jane didn't move. Jane's one hand rested on her neck, the other on her bottom. Such a gentle touch. She now realized it had been Jane's fingers in her ass, for they were still working there.

"You mind well for a novice," Jane said. "I'm glad I don't have to beat you for disappointing me. We'll see how wide open you can be tonight, see how much your body can manage at once. I'll see what you can take, and then I'll push you harder." It was a threat. "You have a nice ass, and now it's my ass. I'll do anything I want to with it." She continued with her fingers pressing into Leslie's anus deeper still. "I love brutalizing bottoms the best of all, I think: they can take so much punishment."

The sound of women coming and going, peeing, flushing toilets, running water in regular intervals, made Leslie wonder how many had spotted her there in the open toilet stall with Sir Jane's hand at her ass. How many women had seen the other dom take her with the fist? Such a fine thing, oblivion; being able to think of nothing but sex and body heat. A crude place for love, but she felt it nonetheless.

"Stay as you are," Sir Jane ordered. Her fingers vacated Leslie's bottomhole, and she wiped them on toilet paper. Something cold, smelling of leather, stiff to her senses, circled her neck. She was collared. Jane's leg suddenly dropped from the toilet seat to the floor, and she pushed Leslie to the cold tile with a firm hand.

The collar jerked. She was on a leash being led like a dog through the rest room, to the carpeted hallway, to a stairway leading up, to a room where she was shown to a corner.

"Keep your head on the carpet," Sir Jane ordered.

So poised, Leslie's naked, greased rear remained higher than her head, signifying its importance. Jane walked away, and Leslie peered out of the corner of her eye to the center of the dimly lit room where a submissive was bound to upright wooden beams. The woman was stretched out, with ankles fixed at the base and arms fastened overhead.

The bound woman faced Leslie. Her broad breasts had been marked, as had her entire body. The red marks appearing on her white flesh reminded Leslie of Dagne and Zelda and the others she'd seen punished this way. The woman's breasts reminded her of her own. The submissive woman had been gagged, blinded by a mask, her head now flung back as she was deeply engrossed in her scene. She bucked against a whip that was thrust into her cunt by a dom with a nasty scowl.

Leslie heard a climax in the bottom's muffled voice and saw a surge of pleasure move through her imprisoned form. The woman shivered and collapsed against her bonds. Her dom withdrew the whip, flailing the spent body front to back until the submissive woman was at the desired state of surrender. Then she was freed, falling to the floor. When prodded with the whip, she quickly moved away from the apparatus.

Leslie studied the empty rack, assuming she was next, though it was a long time before Sir Jane tugged at the leash again. In the interim, Jane adjusted things until they were the way she wanted them.

Returning to Leslie's side, she pulled up on the leash again, leading her submissive to a stool between the wooden beams.

"Sit," Leslie was ordered.

Jane knelt on one knee in front of her, putting clamps on Leslie's nipples. She screwed them down till Leslie winced. Jane stared at her with eyes fixed, as if she were reading Leslie's thoughts of fear and lust.

Kindness surrounded her, and a surprising respect seemed to come from Jane to Leslie, though it was all unspoken.

Yes, little things. It was the little things, grabbing her in the middle of her cunt, making her want what she'd never wanted before. She was surprised how much she throbbed between her legs. Jane's hand parted her thighs carefully. Leslie hadn't realized how tightly they'd been pressed together. Opening them, she relaxed.

There was no one else in the room. Just her and Sir Jane. It felt so damned intimate. Without the electricity of Sapphos or the comfort of Jane's cottage, in just the barren emptiness of the room, she and Jane alone,

Leslie felt closer to this woman than any soul on earth.

Jane's fingers pushed inside her again, her cunt this time. Leslie scooted on the stool to accommodate her more easily. Withdrawing her fingers, Jane pressed her nails into Leslie's fat labia till the submissive jolted, and a funny-sounding cry came from her lips. Jane reached out and stroked Leslie's neck and ran her fingers through the woman's hair, even as she pinched her very hard down below.

Leslie was having it both ways. At once tender and punishing, the message so distinctly clear. She remembered how much she wanted this. It wasn't disappointing.

"Come to my lips and lick them," Jane said, drawing Leslie's head to hers.

She had fine breath, no bitter cigarette flavor, just a simple, natural aroma and womanly soft lips that belied her masculinity. Leslie liked the curious opposites of this woman's body.

"Get on your knees and suck my breasts," Jane ordered.

The fingers at her cunt remained, and the tender hand at her neck still cupped her gently there. As Leslie slid off the stool, dropping to her knees, she eyed Sir Jane's simple vest: it would be easy to undo, and she couldn't wait to bare her lover's breasts. Such a lovely form, Leslie thought as she exposed the round, white tits, the pert nipples already scrunched into tight buds. Leslie lowered her mouth to Jane's waiting breasts, her meandering tongue and her lust guiding her. She moved her mouth lower still, down Jane's belly to the top of her leather pants. Down lower still, Jane's hand pushing her all the way to a cunt that was still covered with leather.

Leslie fumbled with brass buttons that started at Jane's waist and proceeded down to her crotch, ones that continued between her legs, and up the back side. With deft fingers, Leslie opened each one until the two sides of the pants began to pull away from each other and a naked cunt peeked out. A slit with soft brown, silky, damp, musty hair came into view.

Leslie's tongue slipped between the thin labia to taste Jane's surprisingly sweet juice as her hands finished the little buttons. The pants slipped free and Sir Jane's entire cleft was exposed. She slid onto her back with her face at Jane's cunt, then watched as her dom lowered herself to be serviced.

The territory familiar.

The feelings new.

Leslie lapped eagerly, giving the woman that now owned her all the satisfaction she demanded. Jane's climax was as silent as her nature; but as Leslie's fingers slipped in and out of her dom's cunt, she could sense the satisfaction rise and fall from deep within. Leslie felt the hard body tense, and a remarkably quiet, strong come roar through her master.

The dom moved off of Leslie's mouth without giving herself time to rest. Standing, she pulled on the collar, bringing her submissive to her knees again.

Lengths of soft, thick rope went around Leslie's waist and through her cunt, pushed up tightly on either side of her clitoris, almost cutting where it's most tender. Leslie's arms were fastened above her, widespread. Her knees spread, she was divided, stretched and secured, immobile.

Jane stood over Leslie's bound body with her cunt exposed wide to be serviced again. She rocked against Leslie's face, washing her submissive in warm, sticky juice, making it even wetter as the dom took her pleasure. She took a long time this second time, savoring the way her little bitch could suck and suck well. At least this was not something she had to be trained to do. Leslie knew how to please a throbbing clit.

"Don't go anywhere," Jane said when she was finished and rebuttoning her pants. The tongue in cheek remark was almost laughable, but Leslie didn't think Jane was laughing.

The lights were dimmed lower still, and Sir Jane left the room. The darkness seemed to eat away the empty spaces around Leslie, leaving her bound body as the center of a tiny universe. She remained alone, and lonely.

Leslie preferred her eyes closed, preferred to feel the bonds and the pressure they applied in the complete darkness. She struggled for awhile to feel how tightly she'd been secured. Very tight. A good feeling, not being able to move. She couldn't think, being suspended like this. Thinking seemed insipid, except the one thought of when Jane would return—it was the only thing in her mind.

The collar jerked.

"Keep your eyes closed," the voice said.

Leslie came to realize that her body was being prodded at her cunt and ass with a double dildo. A blindfold slipped over her eyes, doing what she'd already been doing with her eyelids. Arms untied and stretched forward, her chest was thrust over something cold and hard.

The sting of a whip made her cry. A dozen sharp stings at once penetrated the peace with a roaring pain. One throbbing rush proceeded after the pain, then warmth, just warmth flooded everywhere, around her, in her body, and, for all she knew, emanated everywhere in the atoms that made up that plain dark room.

The cold prick in her ass popped free, pulled out by someone's hand, then was replaced by something smooth, heavily greased, and pressed to the hilt inside her ass. The dildo moving in and out of her, she was fucked, as someone else's arms held her steady over the hard, round thing supporting her.

Leslie screamed, or so she thought. Yes, it was more than one woman: one with the prick and one holding her hands. Her face burned, her ass burned—a whip still cut her with one cut after another. She must be raw. She burst inside, climaxed and wiggled lovingly against the thing that abused her.

Her ass friend slipped away with her prick, and there was just the woman holding hands with her. Her silent lover caressed her sweating palms as Leslie poured her tears of joy, tears of pain, and tears of relief into the fabric of the blindfold that covered her eyes.

"You sleep on the pad," she was told. She recognized the voice, thinking what heavenly thoughts Jane's husky voice inspired in her.

How quickly she'd become devoted! She wanted to be held by her, caressed by her, loved by her yet more deeply, but it was too soon. She had more to prove, and she would prove it.

Some bonds would remain all night—those around her waist and through her cunt. Jane fixed her wrists together, and she left the room, her submissive slave sleeping peacefully on a cool, hard mat.

Several days later Leslie rapped on the door of the cottage.

"Betsy Longcore asked me to give you the keys and this note," Leslie explained when Jane answered. She dropped the items into Jane's palm, the woman's well-remembered fingers closing around the hard metal keys and the envelope, the paper crunching in her grasp.

"She should have stayed," Jane said.

"It's too lonely, she told me," Leslie replied.

Jane nodded. "You want a beer?"

"No. I'm meeting Robin—a new case downtown; some messy divorce which I'll hate."

"Why bother?" Jane asked.

"Sometimes I have to eat real food," Leslie answered.

Jane smirked at her joke.

"I am feeling raw tonight," Leslie continued. "Rosalie left with her Spanish tongue wagging. She thinks I'm stupid. She was going to leave in a month anyway, but I hate when it's messy." Leslie was hoping for an invitation. She missed Sir Jane's touch, both cruel and tender. The stripes on her flesh had almost faded away altogether and she wanted more.

Jane looked into Leslie's longing eyes. "Be at Sapphos by ten tonight," she said.

Leslie smiled, trying not to look too eager. "I'll be there as soon as I'm finished work," Leslie replied.

"You'll be there by ten," Jane repeated. "No excuses."

"Oh, and I have date with Robin Saturday night. Totally platonic of course—unless you want me to take her?" Leslie asked hopefully.

Jane looked pleased. "Beat her ass for me."

"Maybe I should give her to you first," Leslie said, knowing that what was hers would be Sir Jane's too.

"I'd like that, and so would Robin," Jane said. "But you make her sweat first. Get her ready for me."

Leslie nodded, happy that Sir Jane approved of her plans, happy that she didn't have to keep her night with Robin platonic.

"Ten tonight," Jane reminded her. "You won't want to be late, even if you have a good reason."

Jane's cold threat sent a welcoming chill through her devoted slave. Leslie had been wanting a session at Sapphos, sort of as an initiation. Nothing made her happier than the thought of getting over Rosalie under Jane's whip, under Jane's watchful and stern command, under Jane's boots. Sleeping tonight with Jane's large hands stroking her neck and hair would be the perfect balm to soothe her.

The Masquerade Erotic Newsletter

◆◆◆◆◆◆◆◆◆◆◆◆◆◆◆◆◆◆◆◆

FICTION, ESSAYS, REVIEWS, PHOTOGRAPHY, INTERVIEWS, EXPOSÉS, AND MUCH MORE!

"One of my favorite sex zines featuring some of the best articles on erotica, fetishes, sex clubs and the politics of porn." —*Factsheet Five*

"I recommend a subscription to *The Masquerade Erotic Newsletter*.... They feature short articles on "the scene"...an occasional fiction piece, and reviews of other erotic literature. Recent issues have featured intelligent prose by the likes of Trish Thomas, David Aaron Clark, Pat Califia, Laura Antoniou, Lily Burana, John Preston, and others.... it's good stuff." —*Black Sheets*

"A classy, bi-monthly magazine..." —*Betty Paginated*

"It's always a treat to see a copy of *The Masquerade Erotic Newsletter*, for it brings a sophisticated and unexpected point of view to bear on the world of erotica, and does this with intelligence, tolerance, and compassion." —Martin Shepard, co-publisher, The Permanent Press

"Publishes great articles, interviews and pix which in many cases are truly erotic and which deal non-judgementally with the full array of human sexuality, a far cry from much of the material which passes itself off under that title.... *Masquerade Erotic Newsletter* is fucking great." —*Eddie, the Magazine*

"We always enjoy receiving your *Masquerade Newsletter* and seeing the variety of subjects covered...." —*body art*

"*Masquerade Erotic Newsletter* is probably the best newsletter I have ever seen." —*Secret International*

"The latest issue is absolutely lovely. Marvelous images...." —*The Boudoir Noir*

"I must say that the *Newsletter* is fabulous...." —Tuppy Owens, Publisher, Author, Sex Therapist

"Fascinating articles on all aspects of sex..." —*Desire*

◆◆◆◆◆◆◆◆◆◆◆◆◆◆◆◆◆◆◆◆

The Masquerade Erotic Newsletter

"Here's a very provocative, very professional [newsletter]...made up of intelligent erotic writing... Stimulating, yet not sleazy photos add to the picture and also help make this zine a high quality publication." —Gray Areas

From **Masquerade Books**, the World's Leading Publisher of Erotica, comes *The Masquerade Erotic Newsletter*—the best source for provocative, cutting-edge fiction, sizzling pictorials, scintillating and illuminating exposes of the sex industry, and probing reviews of the latest books and videos.

Featured writers and articles have included:

Lars Eighner • *Why I Write Gay Erotica*
Pat Califia • *Among Us, Against Us*
Felice Picano • *An Interview with Samuel R. Delany*
Samuel R. Delany • *The Mad Man* (excerpt)
Maxim Jakubowski • *Essex House: The Rise and Fall of Speculative Erotica*
Red Jordan Arobateau • *Reflections of a Lesbian Trick*
Aaron Travis • *Lust*
Nancy Ava Miller, M. Ed. • *Beyond Personal*
Tuppy Owens • *Female Erotica in Great Britain*
Trish Thomas • *From Dyke to Dude*
Barbara Nitke • *Resurrection*
and many more....

The newsletter has also featured stunning photo essays by such masters of fetish photography as **Robert Chouraqui**, **Eric Kroll**, **Richard Kern**, and **Trevor Watson**.

A one-year subscription (6 issues) to the *Newsletter* costs $30.00. Use the accompanying coupon to subscribe now—for an uninterrupted string of the most provocative of pleasures (as well as a special gift, offered to subscribers only!).

Free GIFT

WHEN YOU SUBSCRIBE TO:
The Masquerade Erotic Newsletter

Receive two **MASQUERADE** books of your choice.

Please send me Two MASQUERADE Books Free!

1. _____

2. _____

☐ I've enclosed my payment of $30.00 for a one-year subscription (six issues) to: *THE MASQUERADE EROTIC NEWSLETTER.*

Name _____

Address _____

_____

City _____ State _____ Zip _____

Tel. (____) _____

Payment ☐ Check ☐ Money Order ☐ Visa ☐ MC

Card No. _____

Exp. Date _____

Please allow 4–6 weeks delivery. No C.O.D. orders. Please make all checks payable to Masquerade Books, 801 Second Avenue, N.Y., N.Y., 10017. Payable in U.S. currency only. Order by phone: 1-800-375-2356 or fax, 212 986-7355

W74L

ROSEBUD BOOKS

THE ROSEBUD READER
Rosebud Books—the hottest-selling line of lesbian erotica available—here collects the very best of the best. Rosebud has contributed greatly to the burgeoning genre of lesbian erotica—to the point that authors like Lindsay Welsh, Aarona Griffin and Valentina Cilescu are among the hottest and most closely watched names in lesbian and gay publishing. Here are the finest moments from Rosebud's contemporary classics. $5.95/319-8

LOVECHILD
GAG
From New York's thriving poetry scene comes this explosive volume of work from one of the bravest, most cutting young writers you'll ever encounter. The poems in *Gag* take on American hypocrisy with uncommon energy, and announce Lovechild as a writer of unique and unforgettable rage. $5.95/369-4

ALISON TYLER
THE BLUE ROSE
The tale of a modern sorority—fashioned after a Victorian girls' school. Ignited to the heights of passion by erotic tales of the Victorian age, a group of lusty young women are encouraged to act out their forbidden fantasies—all under the tutelage of Mistresses Emily and Justine, two avid practitioners of hard-core discipline! $5.95/335-X

ELIZABETH OLIVER
THE SM MURDER: Murder at Roman Hill
Intrepid lesbian P.I.s Leslie Patrick and Robin Penny take on a really hot case: the murder of the notorious Felicia Roman. The circumstances of the crime lead the pair on an excursion through the leatherdyke underground, where motives—and desires—run deep. But as Leslie and Robin soon find, every woman harbors her own closely guarded secret.... $5.95/353-8

PAGAN DREAMS
Cassidy and Samantha plan a vacation at a secluded bed-and-breakfast, hoping for a little personal time alone. Their hostess, however, has different plans. The lovers are plunged into a world of dungeons and pagan rites, as the merciless Anastasia steals Samantha for her own. B&B—B&D-style! $5.95/295-7

SUSAN ANDERS
CITY OF WOMEN
A collection of stories dedicated to women and the passions that draw them together. Designed strictly for the sensual pleasure of women, Anders' tales are set to ignite flames of passion from coast to coast. The residents of *City of Women* hold the key to even the most forbidden fantasies. $5.95/375-9

PINK CHAMPAGNE
Tasty, torrid tales of butch/femme couplings—from a writer more than capable of describing the special fire ignited when opposites collide. Tough as nails or soft as silk, these women seek out their antitheses, intent on working out the details of their own personal theory of difference. $5.95/282-5

LAVENDER ROSE
Anonymous
A classic collection of lesbian literature: From the writings of Sappho, Queen of the island Lesbos, to the turn-of-the-century *Black Book of Lesbianism*; from *Tips to Maidens* to *Crimson Hairs*, a recent lesbian saga—here are the great but little-known lesbian writings and revelations. $4.95/208-6

ROSEBUD BOOKS

EDITED BY LAURA ANTONIOU

LEATHERWOMEN II
A follow-up volume to the popular and controversial *Leatherwomen*. Laura Antoniou turns an editor's discerning eye to the writing of women on the edge—resulting in a collection sure to ignite libidinal flames. Leave taboos behind—because these Leatherwomen know no limits.... $4.95/229-9

LEATHERWOMEN
These fantasies, from the pens of new or emerging authors, break every rule imposed on women's fantasies. The hottest stories from some of today's newest and most outrageous writers make this an unforgettable exploration of the female libido. $4.95/3095-4

LESLIE CAMERON

THE WHISPER OF FANS
"Just looking into her eyes, she felt that she knew a lot about this woman. She could see strength, boldness, a fresh sense of aliveness that rocked her to the core. In turn she felt open, revealed under the woman's gaze—all her secrets already told. No need of shame or artifice...." $5.95/259-0

AARONA GRIFFIN

PASSAGE AND OTHER STORIES
An S/M romance. Lovely Nina is frightened by her lesbian passions until she finds herself infatuated with a woman she spots at a local café. One night Nina follows her and finds herself enmeshed in an endless maze leading to a world where women test the edges of sexuality and power. $4.95/3057-1

VALENTINA CILESCU

THE ROSEBUD SUTRA
"Women are hardly ever known in their true light, though they may love others, or become indifferent towards them, may give them delight, or abandon them, or may extract from them all the wealth that they possess." So says The Rosebud Sutra—a volume promising women's inner secrets. One woman learns to use these secrets in a quest for pleasure with a succession of lady loves.... $4.95/242-6

THE HAVEN
J craves domination, and her perverse appetites lead her to the Haven: the isolated sanctuary Ros and Annie call home. Soon J forces her way into the couple's world, bringing unspeakable lust and cruelty into their lives. The Dominatrix Who Came to Dinner! $4.95/165-9

MISTRESS MINE
Sophia Cranleigh sits in prison, accused of authoring the "obscene" *Mistress Mine*. For Sophia has led no ordinary life, but has slaved and suffered—deliciously—under the hand of the notorious Mistress Malin. How long had she languished under the dominance of this incredible beauty? $4.95/109-8

LINDSAY WELSH

ROMANTIC ENCOUNTERS
Beautiful Julie, the most powerful editor of romance novels in the industry, spends her days igniting women's passions through books—and her nights fulfilling those needs with a variety of lovers. Julie's two worlds come together with the type of bodice-ripping Harlequin could never imagine! $5.95/359-7

THE BEST OF LINDSAY WELSH
A collection of this popular writer's best work. This author was one of Rosebud's early bestsellers, and remains highly popular. A sampler set to introduce some of the hottest lesbian erotica to a wider audience. $5.95/368-6

ROSEBUD BOOKS

PROVINCETOWN SUMMER
This completely original collection is devoted exclusively to white-hot desire between women. From the casual encounters of women on the prowl to the enduring erotic bonds between old lovers, the women of *Provincetown Summer* will set your senses on fire! A national best-seller. $5.95/362-7

NECESSARY EVIL
What's a girl to do? When her Mistress proves too systematic, too by-the-book, one lovely submissive takes the ultimate chance—choosing and creating a Mistress who'll fulfill her heart's desire. Little did she know how difficult it would be—and, in the end, rewarding.... $5.95/277-9

A VICTORIAN ROMANCE
Lust-letters from the road. A young Englishwoman realizes her dream—a trip abroad under the guidance of her eccentric maiden aunt. Soon the young but blossoming Elaine comes to discover her own sexual talents, as a hot-blooded Parisian named Madelaine takes her Sapphic education in hand. Another Welsh winner! $5.95/365-1

A CIRCLE OF FRIENDS
The author of the nationally best-selling *Provincetown Summer* returns with the story of a remarkable group of women. Slowly, the women pair off to explore all the possibilities of lesbian passion, until finally it seems that there is nothing—and no one—they have not dabbled in. A stunning tribute to truly special relationships. $4.95/250-7

PRIVATE LESSONS
A high voltage tale of life at The Whitfield Academy for Young Women—where cruel headmistress Devon Whitfield presides over the in-depth education of only the most talented and delicious of maidens. Elizabeth Dunn arrives at the Academy, where it becomes clear that she has much to learn—to the delight of Devon Whitfield and her randy staff of Mistresses! Another contemporary classic from Lindsay Welsh. $4.95/116-0

BAD HABITS
What does one do with a poorly trained slave? Break her of her bad habits, of course! The story of the ultimate finishing school, *Bad Habits* was an immediate favorite with women nationwide. "Talk about passing the wet test!... If you like hot, lesbian erotica, run—don't walk...and pick up a copy of *Bad Habits*."—*Lambda Book Report* $4.95/3068-7

ANNABELLE BARKER

MOROCCO
A luscious young woman stands to inherit a fortune—if she can only withstand the ministrations of her cruel guardian until her twentieth birthday. With two months left, Lila makes a bold bid for freedom, only to find that liberty has its own excruciating and delicious price.... $4.95/148-9

A.L. REINE

DISTANT LOVE & OTHER STORIES
A book of seductive tales. In the title story, Leah Michaels and her lover Ranelle have had four years of blissful, smoldering passion together. One night, when Ranelle is out of town, Leah records an audio "Valentine," a cassette filled with erotic reminiscences.... $4.95/3056-3

RHINOCEROS BOOKS

DAVID MELTZER

UNDER
The author of **The Agency Trilogy** and **Orf** returns with another glimpse of Things to Come. *Under* concerns a sex professional, whose life at the bottom of the social heap is, nevertheless, filled with incident. Other than numerous surgeries designed to increase his physical allure, he is faced with an establishment intent on using any body for unimaginable genetic experiments. The extremes of his world force this cyber-gigolo underground—where even more bizarre cultures await.... $6.95/290-6

ORF
He is the ultimate musician-hero—the idol of thousands, the fevered dream of many more. And like many musicians before him, he is misunderstood, misused—and totally out of control. Every last drop of feeling is squeezed from a modern-day troubadour and his lady love. $6.95/110-1

EDITED BY AMARANTHA KNIGHT

FLESH FANTASTIC
Humans have long toyed with the idea of "playing God": creating life from nothingness, bringing Life to the inanimate. Now Amarantha Knight, author of the "Darker Passions" series of erotic horror novels, collects stories exploring not only the allure of Creation, but the lust that follows.... One of our most shocking and sexy anthologies. $6.95/352-X

GARY BOWEN

DIARY OF A VAMPIRE
"Gifted with a darkly sensual vision and a fresh voice, [Bowen] is a writer to watch out for." —Cecilia Tan
The chilling, arousing, and ultimately moving memoirs of an undead—but all too human—soul. Bowen's Rafael, a red-blooded male with an insatiable hunger for same, is the perfect antidote to the effete malcontents haunting bookstores today. *Diary of a Vampire* marks the emergence of a bold and brilliant vision, firmly rooted in past *and* present. $6.95/331-7

RENE MAIZEROY

FLESHLY ATTRACTIONS
Lucien Hardanges was the son of the wantonly beautiful actress, Marie-Rose Hardanges. When she decides to let a "friend" introduce her son to the pleasures of love, Marie-Rose could not have foretold the erotic excesses that would lead to her own ruin and that of her cherished son. $6.95/299-X

EDITED BY LAURA ANTONIOU

NO OTHER TRIBUTE
A collection of stories sure to challenge Political Correctness in a way few have before, with tales of women kept in bondage to their lovers by their deepest passions. Love pushes these women beyond acceptable limits, rendering them helpless to deny the men and women they adore. A companion volume to *By Her Subdued*. $6.95/294-9

SOME WOMEN
Over forty essays written by women actively involved in consensual dominance and submission. Professional mistresses, lifestyle leatherdykes, whipmakers, titleholders—women from every conceivable walk of life lay bare their true feelings about about issues as explosive as feminism, abuse, pleasures and public image. $6.95/300-7

RHINOCEROS BOOKS

BY HER SUBDUED
Stories of women who get what they want. The tales in this collection all involve women in control—of their lives, their loves, their men. So much in control, in fact, that they can remorselessly break rules to become the powerful goddesses of the men who sacrifice all to worship at their feet. Woman Power with a vengeance! $6.95/**281-7**

JEAN STINE

SEASON OF THE WITCH
"A future in which it is technically possible to transfer the total mind... of a rapist killer into the brain dead but physically living body of his female victim. Remarkable for intense psychological technique. There is eroticism but it is necessary to mark the differences between the sexes and the subtle altering of a man into a woman." —*The Science Fiction Critic* $6.95/**268-X**

JOHN WARREN

THE TORQUEMADA KILLER
Detective Eva Hernandez has finally gotten her first "big case": a string of vicious murders taking place within New York's SM community. Piece by piece, Eva assembles the evidence, revealing a picture of a world misunderstood and under attack—and gradually comes to understand her own place within it. A hot, edge-of-the-seat thriller from the author of *The Loving Dominant*—and an exciting insider's perspective on "the scene." $6.95/**367-8**

THE LOVING DOMINANT
Everything you need to know about an infamous sexual variation—and an unspoken type of love. Mentor—a longtime player in the dominance/submission scene—guides readers through this world and reveals the too-often hidden basis of the D/S relationship: care, trust and love. $6.95/**218-3**

GRANT ANTREWS

SUBMISSIONS
Once again, Antrews portrays the very special elements of the dominant/submissive relationship...with restraint—this time with the story of a lonely man, a winning lottery ticket, and a demanding dominatrix. One of erotica's most discerning writers. $6.95/**207-8**

MY DARLING DOMINATRIX
When a man and a woman fall in love it's supposed to be simple, uncomplicated, easy—unless that woman happens to be a dominatrix. Curiosity gives way to unblushing desire in this story of one man's awakening to the joys to be experienced as the willing slave of a powerful woman. $6.95/**3055-5**

LAURA ANTONIOU WRITING AS "SARA ADAMSON"

THE TRAINER
The long-awaited conclusion of Adamson's stunning Marketplace Trilogy! The ultimate underground sexual realm includes not only willing slaves, but the exquisite trainers who take submissives firmly in hand. And it is now the time for these mentors to divulge their own secrets—the desires that led them to become the ultimate figures of authority. $6.95/**249-3**

THE SLAVE
The second volume in the "Marketplace" trilogy. *The Slave* covers the experience of one exceptionally talented submissive who longs to join the ranks of those who have proven themselves worthy of entry into the Marketplace. But the price, while delicious, is staggeringly high.... Adamson's plot thickens, as her trilogy moves to a conclusion in *The Trainer*. $6.95/**173-X**

RHINOCEROS BOOKS

THE MARKETPLACE

"Merchandise does not come easily to the Marketplace.... They haunt the clubs and the organizations.... Some of them are so ripe that they intimidate the poseurs, the weekend sadists and the furtive dilettantes who are so endemic to that world. And they never stop asking where we may be found...." $6.95/3096-2

THE CATALYST

After viewing a controversial, explicitly kinky film full of images of bondage and submission, several audience members find themselves deeply moved by the erotic suggestions they've seen on the screen. "Sara Adamson"'s sensational debut volume! $5.95/328-7

DAVID AARON CLARK

SISTER RADIANCE

A chronicle of obsession, rife with Clark's trademark vivisections of contemporary desires, sacred and profane. The vicissitudes of lust and romance are examined against a backdrop of urban decay and shallow fashionability in this testament to the allure—and inevitability—of the forbidden. $6.95/215-9

THE WET FOREVER

The story of Janus and Madchen, a small-time hood and a beautiful sex worker, *The Wet Forever* examines themes of loyalty, sacrifice, redemption and obsession amidst Manhattan's sex parlors and underground S/M clubs. Its combination of sex and suspense led Terence Sellers to proclaim it "evocative and poetic." $6.95/117-9

ALICE JOANOU

BLACK TONGUE

"Joanou has created a series of sumptuous, brooding, dark visions of sexual obsession and is undoubtedly a name to look out for in the future."
—*Redeemer*

Another seductive book of dreams from the author of the acclaimed *Tourniquet*. Exploring lust at its most florid and unsparing, *Black Tongue* is a trove of baroque fantasies—each redolent of the forbidden. Joanou creates some of erotica's most mesmerizing and unforgettable characters. A critical favorite. $6.95/258-2

TOURNIQUET

A heady collection of stories and effusions from the pen of one our most dazzling young writers. Strange tales abound, from the story of the mysterious and cruel Cybele, to an encounter with the sadistic entertainment of a bizarre after-hours cafe. A sumptuous feast for all the senses.. $6.95/3060-1

CANNIBAL FLOWER

"She is waiting in her darkened bedroom, as she has waited throughout history, to seduce the men who are foolish enough to be blinded by her irresistible charms....She is the goddess of sexuality, and *Cannibal Flower* is her haunting siren song."—Michael Perkins $4.95/72-6

MICHAEL PERKINS

EVIL COMPANIONS

Set in New York City during the tumultuous waning years of the Sixties, *Evil Companions* has been hailed as "a frightening classic." A young couple explores the nether reaches of the erotic unconscious in a shocking confrontation with the extremes of passion. With a new introduction by science fiction legend Samuel R. Delany. $6.95/3067-9

RHINOCEROS BOOKS

AN ANTHOLOGY OF CLASSIC ANONYMOUS EROTIC WRITING

Michael Perkins, acclaimed authority on erotic literature, has collected the very best passages from the world's erotic writing—especially for Rhino*ceros* readers. "Anonymous" is one of the most infamous bylines in publishing history—and these steamy excerpts show why! $6.95/140-3

THE SECRET RECORD: Modern Erotic Literature

Michael Perkins, a renowned author and critic of sexually explicit fiction, surveys the field with authority and unique insight. Updated and revised to include the latest trends, tastes, and developments in this misunderstood and maligned genre. An important volume for every erotic reader and fan of high quality adult fiction. $6.95/3039-3

HELEN HENLEY

ENTER WITH TRUMPETS

Helen Henley was told that woman just don't write about sex—much less the taboos she was so interested in exploring. So Henley did it alone, flying in the face of "tradition" by producing *Enter With Trumpets*, a touching tale of arousal and devotion in one couple's kinky relationship. $6.95/197-7

PHILIP JOSE FARMER

FLESH

Space Commander Stagg explored the galaxies for 800 years. Upon his return, the hero Stagg is made the centerpiece of an incredible public ritual—one that will repeatedly take him to the heights of ecstasy, and inexorably drag him toward the depths of hell. $6.95/303-1

A FEAST UNKNOWN

"Sprawling, brawling, shocking, suspenseful, hilarious…"
—Theodore Sturgeon

Farmer's supreme anti-hero returns. *A Feast Unknown* begins in 1968, with Lord Grandrith's stunning statement: "I was conceived and born in 1888." Slowly, Lord Grandrith—armed with the belief that he is the son of Jack the Ripper—tells the story of his remarkable and unbridled life. Beginning with his discovery of the secret of immortality, Grandrith's tale proves him no raving lunatic—but something far more bizarre…. $6.95/276-0

THE IMAGE OF THE BEAST

Herald Childe has seen Hell, glimpsed its horror in an act of sexual mutilation. Childe must now find and destroy an inhuman predator through the streets of a polluted and decadent Los Angeles of the future. One clue after another leads Childe to an inescapable realization about the nature of sex and evil…. $6.95/166-7

SAMUEL R. DELANY

EQUINOX

The *Scorpion* has sailed the seas in a quest for every possible pleasure. Her crew is a collection of the young, the twisted, the insatiable. A drifter comes into their midst, and is taken on a fantastic journey to the darkest, most dangerous sexual extremes—until he is finally a victim to their boundless appetites. $6.95/157-8

DANIEL VIAN

ILLUSIONS

Two tales of danger and desire in Berlin on the eve of WWII. From private homes to lurid cafés, passion is exposed and explored in stark contrast to the brutal violence of the time. A singularly arousing volume. $6.95/3074-1

RHINOCEROS BOOKS

PERSUASIONS

"The stockings are drawn tight by the suspender belt, tight enough to be stretched to the limit just above the middle part of her thighs..." A double novel, including the classics *Adagio* and *Gabriela and the General*, this volume traces desire around the globe. International lust! $6.95/183-7

ANDREI CODRESCU

THE REPENTANCE OF LORRAINE

"One of our most prodigiously talented and magical writers."
—*NYT Book Review*

An aspiring writer, a professor's wife, a secretary, gold anklets, Maoists, Roman harlots—and more—swirl through this spicy tale of a harried quest for a mythic artifact. Written when the author was a young man, this lusty yarn was inspired by the heady days of the Sixties. Includes a new Introduction by the author, painting a portrait of *Lorraine*'s creation. $6.95/329-5

LEOPOLD VON SACHER-MASOCH

VENUS IN FURS

This classic 19th century novel is the first uncompromising exploration of the dominant/submissive relationship in literature. The alliance of Severin and Wanda epitomizes Sacher-Masoch's dark obsession with a cruel, controlling goddess and the urges that drive the man held in her thrall. Includes the letters exchanged between Sacher-Masoch and Emilie Mataja—an aspiring writer he sought as the avatar of his forbidden desires. $6.95/3089-X

SOPHIE GALLEYMORE BIRD

MANEATER

Through a bizarre act of creation, a man attains the "perfect" lover—by all appearances a beautiful, sensuous woman but in reality something far darker. Once brought to life she will accept no mate, seeking instead the prey that will sate her hunger for vengeance. A biting take on the war of the sexes, this debut goes for the jugular of the "perfect woman" myth. $6.95/103-9

TUPPY OWENS

SENSATIONS

A piece of porn history. Tuppy Owens tells the unexpurgated story of the making of *Sensations*—the first big-budget sex flick. Originally commissioned to appear in book form after the release of the film in 1975, *Sensations* is finally released under Masquerade's stylish Rhino*ceros* imprint. $6.95/3081-4

LIESEL KULIG

LOVE IN WARTIME

An uncompromising look at the politics, perils and pleasures of sexual power. Madeleine knew that the handsome SS officer was a dangerous man. But she was just a cabaret singer in Nazi-occupied Paris, trying to survive in a perilous time. When Josef fell in love with her, he discovered that a beautiful and amoral woman can sometimes be wildly dangerous. $6.95/3044-X

MASQUERADE BOOKS

THE MISTRESS OF CASTLE ROHMENSTADT
Olivia M. Ravensworth
Lovely Katherine inherits a secluded European castle from a mysterious relative. Upon arrival, she discovers, much to her delight, that the castle is a haven of sensual pleasure. Katherine learns to shed her inhibitions and enjoy her new home's many delights—and is drawn deeper into the mystery surrounding the secret chamber far below ground.... $5.95/372-4

THE GUARDIAN *Lyn Davenport*
Felicia grew up under the tutelage of the lash—and she learned her lessons well. Sir Rodney Wentworth has long searched for a woman capable of fulfilling his cruel desires, and after learning of Felicia's talents, sends for her. Upon arrival in his home, Felicia discovers that the "position" offered her is delightfully different than anything she could have expected! $5.95/371-6

TENDER BUNS *P.N. Dedeaux*
Meet Marc Merlin, the wizard of discipline! In a fashionable Canadian suburb, Merlin indulges his yen for punishment with an assortment of the town's most desirable and willing women. Things come to a rousing climax at a party planned to cater to just those whims Marc is most interested and able to satisfy....
$5.95/396-1

COMPLIANCE *N. Whallen*
Fourteen stories exploring the pleasures of release. Characters from many walks of life learn to trust in the skills of others, only to experience the thrilling liberation of submission. Here are the real joys to be found in some of the most forbidden sexual practices around.... $5.95/356-2

LA DOMME: A DOMINATRIX ANTHOLOGY *Edited by Claire Baeder*
A steamy smorgasbord of female domination! Erotic literature has long been filled with heartstopping portraits of domineering women, and now the most memorable come together in one beautifully brutal volume. No fan of real woman power can afford to miss this ultimate compendium. $5.95/366-X

THE GEEK *Tiny Alice*
"An adventure novel told by a sex-bent male mini-pygmy. This is an accomplishment of which anybody may be proud."—Philip José Farmer
The Geek is told from the point of view of, well, a chicken who reports on the various perversities he witnesses as part of a traveling carnival. When a gang of renegade lesbians kidnaps Chicken and his geek, all hell breaks loose. A strange tale, filled with outrageous erotic oddities. $5.95/341-4

SEX ON THE NET *Charisse van der Lyn*
Electrifying erotica from one of the Internet's hottest and most widely read authors. Encounters of all kinds—straight, lesbian, dominant/submissive and all sorts of extreme passions—are explored in thrilling detail. Discover what's turning on hackers from coast to coast! $5.95/399-6

BEAUTY OF THE BEAST *Carole Remy*
A shocking tell-all, written from the point-of-view of a prize-winning reporter. And what reporting she does! All the secrets of an uninhibited life are revealed, and each lusty tableau is painted in glowing colors. Join in on her scandalous adventures—and reap the rewards of her extensive background in Erotic Affairs! $5.95/332-5

NAUGHTY MESSAGE *Stanley Carten*
Wesley Arthur, a withdrawn computer engineer, discovers a lascivious message on his answering machine. Aroused beyond his wildest dreams by the unmentionable acts described, Wesley becomes obsessed with tracking down the woman behind the seductive voice. His search takes him through strip clubs and no-tell motels—and finally to his randy reward.... $5.95/333-3

MASQUERADE BOOKS

The Marquis de Sade's JULIETTE *David Aaron Clark*
The Marquis de Sade's infamous Juliette returns—and at the hand of David Aaron Clark, she emerges as the most powerful, perverse and destructive nightstalker modern New York will ever know. Under this domina's tutelage, two women come to know torture's bizarre attractions, as they grapple with the price of Juliette's promise of immortality.
Praise for Dave Clark:
"David Aaron Clark has delved into one of the most sensationalistically taboo aspects of eros, sadomasochism, and produced a novel of unmistakable literary imagination and artistic value." —Carlo McCormick, *Paper*
$5.95/240-X

THE PARLOR *N.T. Morley*
Lovely Kathryn gives in to the ultimate temptation. The mysterious John and Sarah ask her to be her slave—an idea that turns Kathryn on so much that she can't refuse! But who are these two mysterious strangers? Little by little, Kathryn comes to know the inner secrets of her stunning keepers. Soon, all is revealed—to the delight of everyone involved! $5.95/291-4

NADIA *Anonymous*
"Nadia married General the Count Gregorio Stenoff—a gentleman of noble pedigree it is true, but one of the most reckless dissipated rascals in Russia..." Follow the delicious but neglected Nadia as she works to wring every drop of pleasure out of life—despite an unhappy marriage. A classic story providing a peek into the secret sexual lives of another time and place. $5.95/267-1

THE STORY OF A VICTORIAN MAID *Nigel McParr*
What were the Victorians really like? Chances are, no one believes they were as stuffy as their Queen, but who would have imagined such unbridled libertines! One maid is followed from exploit to smutty exploit, and all secrets are revealed! $5.95/241-8

CARRIE'S STORY *Molly Weatherfield*
"I had been Jonathan's slave for about a year when he told me he wanted to sell me at an auction. I wasn't in any condition to respond when he told me this..." Desire and depravity run rampant in this story of uncompromising mastery and irrevocable submission. $5.95/228-0

CHARLY'S GAME *Bren Flemming*
A rich woman's gullible daughter has run off with one of the toughest leather dykes in town—and sexy P.I. Charly's hired to lure the girl back. One by one, wise and wicked women ensnare one another in their lusty nets! $4.95/221-3

ANDREA AT THE CENTER *J.P. Kansas*
Lithe and lovely young Andrea is, without warning, whisked away to a distant retreat. There she is introduced to the ways of the Center, and soon becomes quite friendly with its other inhabitants—all of whom are learning to abandon restraint in their pursuit of the deepest sexual satisfaction. $5.95/324-4

ASK ISADORA *Isadora Alman*
An essential volume, collecting six years' worth of Isadora Alman's syndicated columns on sex and relationships. Alman's been called a "hip Dr. Ruth," and a "sexy Dear Abby," based upon the wit and pertinence of her advice. Today's world is more perplexing than ever—and Isadora Alman is just the expert to help untangle the most personal of knots. $4.95/61-0

THE SLAVES OF SHOANNA *Mercedes Kelly*
Shoanna, the cruel and magnificent, takes four maidens under her wing—and teaches them the ins and outs of pleasure and discipline. Trained in every imaginable perversion, from simple fleshly joys to advanced techniques, these students go to the head of the class! $4.95/164-0

MASQUERADE BOOKS

LOVE & SURRENDER — *Marlene Darcy*
"Madeline saw Harry looking at her legs and she blushed as she remembered what he wanted to do.... She casually pulled the skirt of her dress back to uncover her knees and the lower part of her thighs. What did he want now? Did he want more? She tugged at her skirt again, pulled it back far enough so almost all of her thighs were exposed...." $4.95/3082-2

THE COMPLETE *PLAYGIRL* FANTASIES — *Editors of Playgirl*
The best women's fantasies are collected here, fresh from the pages of *Playgirl*. These knockouts from the infamous "Reader's Fantasy Forum" prove, once again, that truth can indeed be hotter, wilder, and *better* than fiction. $4.95/3075-X

STASI SLUT — *Anthony Bobarzynski*
Need we say more? Adina lives in East Germany, far from the sexually liberated, uninhibited debauchery of the West. She meets a group of ruthless and corrupt STASI agents who use her as a pawn in their political chess game as well as for their own perverse gratification— until she uses her talents and attractions in a final bid for total freedom! $4.95/3050-4

BLUE TANGO — *Hilary Manning*
Ripe and tempting Julie is haunted by the sounds of extraordinary passion beyond her bedroom wall. Alone, she fantasizes about taking part in the amorous dramas of her hosts, Claire and Edward. When she finds a way to watch the nightly debauch, her curiosity turns to full-blown lust—and soon Julie's eager to join in! $4.95/3037-7

LOUISE BELHAVEL

FRAGRANT ABUSES
The saga of Clara and Iris continues as the now-experienced girls enjoy themselves with a new circle of worldly friends whose imaginations match their own. Perversity follows the lusty ladies around the globe! $4.95/88-2

DEPRAVED ANGELS
The final installment in the incredible adventures of Clara and Iris. Together with their friends, lovers, and worldly acquaintances, Clara and Iris explore the frontiers of depravity at home and abroad. $4.95/92-0

TITIAN BERESFORD

THE WICKED HAND
With a special Introduction by *Leg Show*'s Dian Hanson. A collection of fanciful fetishistic tales featuring the absolute subjugation of men by lovely, domineering women. From Japan and Germany to the American heartland—these stories uncover the other side of the "weaker sex." $5.95/343-0

CINDERELLA
Beresford triumphs again with this intoxicating tale, filled with castle dungeons and tightly corseted ladies-in-waiting, naughty viscounts and impossibly cruel masturbatrixes—nearly every conceivable method of erotic torture is explored and described in lush, vivid detail. $4.95/305-8

JUDITH BOSTON
Young Edward would have been lucky to get the stodgy old companion he thought his parents had hired for him. Instead, an exquisite woman arrives at his door, and Edward finds his compulsively lewd behavior never goes unpunished by the unflinchingly severe Judith Boston! $4.95/273-6

NINA FOXTON
An aristocrat finds herself bored by run-of-the-mill amusements for "ladies of good breeding." Instead of taking tea with proper gentlemen, naughty Nina invents a contraption to "milk" them of their most private essences. No man ever says "No" to Nina! $4.95/145-4

MASQUERADE BOOKS

A TITIAN BERESFORD READER

Wild dominatrixes, perverse masochists, and mesmerizing detail are the hallmarks of the Beresford tale—and encountered here in abundance. The very best scenarios from all of Beresford's bestsellers make this a must-have for the Compleat Fetishist. $4.95/114-4

CHINA BLUE

KUNG FU NUNS

"When I could stand the pleasure no longer, she lifted me out of the chair and sat me down on top of the table. She then lifted her skirt. The sight of her perfect legs clad in white stockings and a petite garter belt further mesmerized me. I lean particularly towards white garter belts." China Blue returns! $4.95/3031-8

HARRIET DAIMLER

DARLING • INNOCENCE

In *Darling*, a virgin is raped by a mugger. Driven by her urge for revenge, she searches New York in a furious sexual hunt that leads to rape and murder. In *Innocence*, a young invalid determines to experience sex through her voluptuous nurse. Two critically acclaimed novels. $4.95/3047-4

AKBAR DEL PIOMBO

SKIRTS

Randy Mr. Edward Champdick enters high society—and a whole lot more—in his quest for ultimate satisfaction. For it seems that once Mr. Champdick rises to the occasion, nothing can bring him down. $4.95/115-2

DUKE COSIMO

A kinky romp played out against the boudoirs, bathrooms and ballrooms of the European nobility, who seem to do nothing all day except each other. The lifestyles of the rich and licentious are revealed in all their glory. $4.95/3052-0

A CRUMBLING FAÇADE

The return of that incorrigible rogue, Henry Pike, who continues his pursuit of sex, fair or otherwise, in the most elegant homes of the most debauched aristocrats. No one can resist the irrepressible Pike! $4.95/3043-1

PAULA

"How bad do you want me?" she asked, her voice husky, breathy. I shrank back, for my desire for her was swelling to unspeakable proportions. "Turn around," she said, and I obeyed....This canny seductress tests the mettle of every man who comes under her spell—and every man does! $4.95/3036-9

ROBERT DESMOND

PROFESSIONAL CHARMER

A gigolo lives a parasitical life of luxury by providing his sexual services to the rich and bored. Traveling in the most exclusive circles, this gun-for-hire will gratify the lewdest and most vulgar sexual cravings! This dedicated pro leaves no one unsatisfied. $4.95/3003-2

THE SWEETEST FRUIT

Connie is determined to seduce and destroy Father Chadcroft. She corrupts the unsuspecting priest into forsaking all that he holds sacred, destroys his parish, and slyly manipulates him with her smoldering looks and hypnotic aura. $4.95/95-5

MICHAEL DRAX

SILK AND STEEL

"He let his robe fall to the floor. She could offer no resistance as the shadowy figure knelt before her, gazing down upon her. Why would she resist? This was what she wanted all along...." $4.95/3032-6

MASQUERADE BOOKS

OBSESSIONS
Victoria is determined to become a model by sexually ensnaring the powerful people who control the fashion industry: Paige, who finds herself compelled to watch Victoria's conquests; and Pietro and Alex, who take turns and then join in for a sizzling threesome. $4.95/3012-1

LIZBETH DUSSEAU

TRINKETS
"Her bottom danced on the air, pert and fully round. It would take punishment well, he thought." A luscious woman submits to an artist's every whim—becoming the sexual trinket he had always desired. $5.95/246-9

THE APPLICANT
"Adventuresome young woman who enjoys being submissive sought by married couple in early forties. Expect no limits." Hilary answers an ad, hoping to find someone who can meet her needs. Beautiful Liza turns out to be a flawless mistress; with her husband Oliver, she trains Hilary to be submissive. $4.95/306-6

SPANISH HOLIDAY
She didn't know what to make of Sam Jacobs. He was undoubtedly the most remarkable man she'd ever met.... Lauren didn't mean to fall in love with the enigmatic Sam, but a once-in-a-lifetime European vacation gives her all the evidence she needs that this hot man might be the one for her.... A tale of romance and insatiable desires, this is one holiday that may never end! $4.95/185-3

CAROLINE'S CONTRACT
After a life of repression, Caroline goes out on a limb. On the advice of a friend, she meets with the alluring Max Burton—a man more than willing to indulge her fantasies of domination and discipline. Caroline soon learns to love his ministrations—and agrees to a very *special* arrangement.... $4.95/122-5

MEMBER OF THE CLUB
"I wondered what would excite me.... And deep down inside, I had the most submissive thoughts: I imagined myself … under the grip of men I hardly knew. If there were a club to join, it could take my deepest dreams and make them real. My only question was how far I'd really go?" A woman finally goes all the way in a quest to satisfy her hungers, joining a club where she *really* pays her dues—with any one of the many men who desire her! $4.95/3079-2

SARA H. FRENCH

MASTER OF TIMBERLAND
"Welcome to Timberland Resort," he began. "We are delighted that you have come to serve us. And...be assured that we will require service of you in the strictest sense. Our discipline is the most demanding in the world. You will be trained here by the best. And now your new Masters will make their choices." A tale of sexual slavery at the ultimate paradise resort. $5.95/327-9

RETURN TO TIMBERLAND
It's time for a trip back to Timberland, the world's most frenzied sexual resort! Prepare for a vacation filled with delicious decadence, as each and every visitor is serviced by unimaginably talented submissives. These nubile maidens are determined to make this the raunchiest camp-out ever! $5.95/257-4

SARAH JACKSON

SANCTUARY
Tales from the Middle Ages. *Sanctuary* explores both the unspeakable debauchery of court life and the unimaginable privations of monastic solitude, leading the voracious and the virtuous on a collision course that brings history to throbbing life. $5.95/318-X

MASQUERADE BOOKS

HELOISE
A panoply of sensual tales harkening back to the golden age of Victorian erotica. Desire is examined in all its intricacy, as fantasies are explored and urges explode. Innocence meets experience time and again. $4.95/3073-3

JOYCELYN JOYCE

PRIVATE LIVES
The lecherous habits of the illustrious make for a sizzling tale of French erotic life. A widow has a craving for a young busboy; he's sleeping with a rich businessman's wife; her husband is minding his sex business elsewhere! Mind boggling sexual entanglements! $4.95/309-0

CANDY LIPS
The world of publishing serves as the backdrop for one woman's pursuit of sexual satisfaction. From a fiery femme fatale to a voracious Valentino, she takes her pleasure where she can find it. Luckily for her, it's most often found between the legs of the most licentious lovers! $4.95/182-9

KIM'S PASSION
The life of a beautiful English seductress. Kim leaves India for London, where she quickly takes upon herself the task of bedding every woman in sight! One by one, the lovely Kim's conquests accumulate, until she finds herself in the arms of gentry and commoners alike. $4.95/162-4

CAROUSEL
A young American woman leaves her husband when she discovers he is having an affair with their maid. She then becomes the sexual plaything of various Parisian voluptuaries. Wild sex, low morals, and ultimate decadence in the flamboyant years before the European collapse. $4.95/3051-2

SABINE
There is no one who can refuse her once she casts her spell; no lover can do anything less than give up his whole life for her. Great men and empires fall at her feet; but she is haughty, distracted, impervious. It is the eve of WW II, and Sabine must find a new lover equal to her talents. $4.95/3046-6

THE WILD HEART
A luxury hotel is the setting for this artful web of sex, desire, and love. A newlywed sees sex as a duty, while her hungry husband tries to awaken her to its tender joys. A Parisian entertains wealthy guests for the love of money. Each episode provides a new variation in this lusty Grand Hotel! $4.95/3007-5

JADE EAST
Laura, passive and passionate, follows her husband Emilio to Hong Kong. He gives her to Wu Li, a connoisseur of sexual perversions, who passes her on to Madeleine, a flamboyant lesbian. Madeleine's friends make Laura the centerpiece in Hong Kong's infamous underground orgies. Slowly, Laura descends into the depths of depravity, where she becomes just another steamy slave—for sale! $4.95/60-2

RAWHIDE LUST
Diana Beaumont, the young wife of a U.S. Marshal, is kidnapped as an act of vengeance against her husband. Jack Beaumont sets out on a long journey to get his wife back, but finally catches up with her trail only to learn that she's been sold into white slavery in Mexico. $4.95/55-6

THE JAZZ AGE
The time: the Roaring Twenties. A young attorney becomes suspicious of his mistress while his wife has an fling with a lesbian lover. *The Jazz Age* is a romp of erotic realism from the heyday of the speakeasy—when all pleasures were taken in private. $4.95/48-3

MASQUERADE BOOKS

AMARANTHA KNIGHT

THE DARKER PASSIONS: *THE FALL OF THE HOUSE OF USHER*
The Master and Mistress of the house of Usher indulge in every form of decadence, and are intent on initiating their guests into the many pleasures to be found in utter submission. But something is not quite right in the House of Usher, and the foundation of its dynasty begins to crack.... $5.95/313-9

THE DARKER PASSIONS: *FRANKENSTEIN*
What if you could create a living, breathing human? What shocking acts could it be taught to perform, to desire, to love? Find out what pleasures await those who play God.... $5.95/248-5

THE DARKER PASSIONS: *DR. JEKYLL AND MR. HYDE*
It is an old story, one of incredible, frightening transformations achieved through mysterious experiments. Now, Amarantha Knight explores the steamy possibilities of a tale where no one is quite who—or what—they seem. Victorian bedrooms explode with hidden demons. $4.95/227-2

THE DARKER PASSIONS: *DRACULA*
"Well-written and imaginative, Amarantha Knight gives fresh impetus to this myth, taking us through the sexual and sadistic scenes with details that keep us reading.... This author shows superb control. A classic in itself has been added to the shelves." —*Divinity* $5.95/326-0

ALIZARIN LAKE

THE EROTIC ADVENTURES OF HARRY TEMPLE
Harry Temple's memoirs chronicle his amorous adventures from his initiation at the hands of insatiable sirens, through his stay at a house of hot repute, to his encounters with a chastity-belted nympho! $4.95/127-6

MORE EROTIC ADVENTURES OF HARRY TEMPLE
Harry Temple's lustful adventures continue. this time he begins his amorous pursuits by deflowering the ample and eager Aurora. harry soon discovers that his little protégée is more than able to match him at every lascivious game and very willing to display her own talents. An education in sensuality that only Harry Temple can provide! $4.95/67-X

CLARA
The mysterious death of a beautiful, aristocratic woman leads her old boyfriend on a harrowing journey of discovery. His search uncovers a woman on a quest for deeper and more unusual sensations, each more shocking than the one before. $4.95/80-7

DIARY OF AN ANGEL
A long-forgotten diary tells the story of angelic Victoria, lured into a secret life of unimaginable depravity. "I am like a fly caught in a spider's web, a helpless and voiceless victim of their every whim." $4.95/71-8

EROTOMANIA
The bible of female sexual perversion! It's all here, everything you ever wanted to know about kinky women past and present. From simple nymphomania to the most outrageous fetishism, all secrets are revealed in this look into the forbidden rooms of feminine desire. $4.95/128-4

AN ALIZARIN LAKE READER
A selection of wicked musings from the pen of Masquerade's perennially popular author. It's all here: *Business as Usual, The Erotic Adventures of Harry Temple, Festival of Venus,* the mysterious *Instruments of the Passion,* the devilish *Miss High Heels*—and more. $4.95/106-3

MASQUERADE BOOKS

MISS HIGH HEELS
It was a delightful punishment few men dared to dream of. Who could have predicted how far it would go? Forced by his sisters to dress and behave like a proper lady, Dennis finds he enjoys life as Denise much more! $4.95/3066-0

THE INSTRUMENTS OF THE PASSION
All that remains is the diary of a young initiate, detailing the twisted rituals of a mysterious cult institution known only as "Rossiter." Behind sinister walls, a beautiful young woman performs an unending drama of pain and humiliation. Will she ever have her fill of utter degradation? $4.95/3010-5

FESTIVAL OF VENUS
Brigeen Mooney fled her home in the west of Ireland to avoid being forced into a nunnery. But the refuge she found in the city turned out to be dedicated to a very different religion. The women she met there belonged to the Old Religion, devoted to the ways of sex and sacrifices. $4.95/37-8

PAUL LITTLE

THE DISCIPLINE OF ODETTE
Odette's family was harsh, but not even public humiliation could keep her from Jacques. She was sure marriage would rescue her from her family's "corrections." To her horror, she discovers that Jacques, too, has been raised on discipline. A shocking erotic coupling! $5.95/334-1

THE PRISONER
Judge Black has built a secret room below a penitentiary, where he sentences the prisoners to hours of exhibition and torment while his friends watch. Judge Black's House of Corrections is equipped with one purpose in mind: to administer his own brand of rough justice! $5.95/330-9

TUTORED IN LUST
This tale of the initiation and instruction of a carnal college co-ed and her fellow students unlocks the sex secrets of the classroom. Books take a back seat to secret societies and their bizarre ceremonies in this story of students with an unquenchable thirst for knowledge! $4.95/78-5

DANGEROUS LESSONS
Incredibly arousing morsels of Paul Little classics: *Tears of the Inquisition, Lust of the Cossacks, Poor Darlings, Captive Maidens, Slave Island*, even the scandalous *The Metamorphosis of Lisette Joyaux*. $4.95/32-7

THE LUSTFUL TURK
The majestic ruler of Algiers and a modest English virgin face off—to their mutual delight. Emily Bartow is initially horrified by the unrelenting sexual tortures to be endured under the powerful Turk's hand. But soon she comes to crave her debasement—no matter what the cost! $4.95/163-2

TEARS OF THE INQUISITION
The incomparable Paul Little delivers a staggering account of pleasure and punishment. *"There was a tickling inside her as her nervous system reminded her she was ready for sex. But before her was...the Inquisitor!"* $4.95/146-2

DOUBLE NOVEL
Two of Paul Little's bestselling novels in one spellbinding volume! *The Metamorphosis of Lisette Joyaux* tells the story of an innocent young woman initiated into a new world of lesbian lusts. *The Story of Monique* reveals the sexual rituals that beckon the ripe and willing Monique. $4.95/86-6

CHINESE JUSTICE AND OTHER STORIES
The story of the excruciating pleasures and delicious punishments inflicted on foreigners under the leaders of the Boxer Rebellion. Each foreign woman is brought before the authorities and grilled. Scandalous tortures are inflicted upon the helpless females by their relentless, merciless captors. $4.95/153-5

MASQUERADE BOOKS

SLAVES OF CAMEROON
This sordid tale is about the women who were used by German officers for salacious profit. These women were forced to become whores for the German army in this African colony. The most perverse forms of erotic gratification are depicted in this unsavory tale of women exploited in every way possible. One of Paul Little's most infamous titles. $4.95/3026-1

ALL THE WAY
Two excruciating novels from Paul Little in one hot volume! *Going All the Way* features an unhappy man who tries to purge himself of the memory of his lover with a series of quirky and uninhibited women. *Pushover* tells the story of a serial spanker and his celebrated exploits in California. $4.95/3023-7

CAPTIVE MAIDENS
Three beautiful young women find themselves powerless against the wealthy, debauched landowners of 1824 England. They are banished to a sexual slave colony, and corrupted by every imaginable perversion. $4.95/3014-8

SLAVE ISLAND
A leisure cruise is waylaid, finding itself in the domain of Lord Henry Philbrock, a sadistic genius, who has built a hidden paradise where captive females are forced into slavery. The ship's passengers are kidnapped and spirited to his island prison, where the women are trained to accommodate the most bizarre sexual cravings of the rich, the famous, the pampered and the perverted. $4.95/3006-7

MARY LOVE

MASTERING MARY SUE
Mary Sue is a rich nymphomaniac whose husband is determined to pervert her, declare her mentally incompetent, and gain control of her fortune. He brings her to a castle where, to Mary Sue's delight, she is unleashed for a veritable sex-fest! $5.95/351-1

THE BEST OF MARY LOVE
Mary Love leaves no coupling untried and no extreme unexplored in these scandalous selections from *Mastering Mary Sue, Ecstasy on Fire, Vice Park Place, Wanda,* and *Naughtier at Night*. $4.95/3099-7

ECSTASY ON FIRE
The inexperienced young Steven is initiated into the intense, throbbing pleasures of manhood by the worldly Melissa Staunton, a well-qualified teacher of the sensual arts. Soon he's in a position—or two—to give lessons of his own! Innocence and experience in an erotic explosion! $4.95/3080-6

NAUGHTIER AT NIGHT
"He wanted to seize her. Her buttocks under the tight suede material were absolutely succulent—carved and molded. What on earth had he done to deserve a morsel of a girl like this?" $4.95/3030-X

RACHEL PEREZ

ODD WOMEN
These women are lots of things: sexy, smart, innocent, tough—some even say odd. But who cares, when their combined ass-ettes are so sweet! There's not a moral in sight as an assortment of Sapphic sirens proves once and for all that comely ladies come best in pairs. $4.95/123-3

AFFINITIES
"Kelsy had a liking for cool upper-class blondes, the long-legged girls from Lake Forest and Winnetka who came into the city to cruise the lesbian bars on Halsted, looking for breathless ecstasies...." A scorching tale of lesbian libidos unleashed, from an uncommonly vivid writer. $4.95/113-6

MASQUERADE BOOKS

CHARLOTTE ROSE

A DANGEROUS DAY
A new volume from the best-selling author who brought you the sensational *Women at Work* and *The Doctor Is In*. And if you thought the high-powered entanglements of her previous books were risky, wait until Rose takes you on a journey through the thrills of one dangerous day! $5.95/293-0

WOMEN AT WORK
Hot, uninhibited stories devoted to the working woman! From a lonesome cowgirl to a supercharged public relations exec, these women know how to let off steam after a tough day on the job. Includes "A Cowgirl's Passion," ranked #1 on Dr. Ruth's list of favorite erotic stories for women! $4.95/3088-1

THE DOCTOR IS IN
"Finally, a book of erotic writing by a woman who isn't afraid to get down—and with deliciously lavish details that open out floodgates of lust and desire. Read it alone ... or with somebody you really like!"
—Candida Royalle

A delectable trio of fantasies inspired by one of life's most intimate relationships. Charlotte Rose once again writes about women's forbidden desires, this time from the patient's point of view. $4.95/195-0

SYDNEY ST. JAMES

RIVE GAUCHE
Decadence and debauchery among the doomed artists in the Latin Quarter, Paris circa 1920. Expatriate bohemians couple with abandon—before eventually abandoning their ambitions amidst the intoxicating temptations waiting to be indulged in every bedroom. $5.95/317-1

THE HIGHWAYWOMAN
A young filmmaker making a documentary about the life of the notorious English highwaywoman, Bess Ambrose, becomes obsessed with her mysterious subject. It seems that Bess touched more than hearts—and plundered the treasures of every man and maiden she met on the way. $4.95/174-8

GARDEN OF DELIGHT
A vivid account of sexual awakening that follows an innocent but insatiably curious young woman's journey from the furtive, forbidden joys of dormitory life to the unabashed carnality of the wild world. Pretty Pauline blossoms with each new experiment in the sensual arts. $4.95/3058-X

ALEXANDER TROCCHI

THONGS
"...In Spain, life is cheap, from that glittering tragedy in the bullring to the quick thrust of the stiletto in a narrow street in a Barcelona slum. No, this death would not have called for further comment had it not been for one striking fact. The naked woman had met her end in a way he had never seen before—a way that had enormous sexual significance. My God, she had been..." $4.95/217-5

HELEN AND DESIRE
Helen Seferis' flight from the oppressive village of her birth became a sexual tour of a harsh world. From brothels in Sydney to harems in Algiers, Helen chronicles her adventures fully in her diary. Each encounter is examined in the scorching and uncensored diary of the sensual Helen! $4.95/3093-8

THE CARNAL DAYS OF HELEN SEFERIS
P.I. Anthony Harvest is assigned to save Helen Seferis, a beautiful Australian who has been abducted. Following clues in her explicit diary of adventures, he pursues the lovely, doomed Helen, the ultimate sexual prize. $4.95/3086-5

MASQUERADE BOOKS

WHITE THIGHS
A fantasy of obsession from a modern erotic master. This is the story of Saul and his sexual fixation on the beautiful, tormented Anna. Their scorching passion leads to murder and madness every time. $4.95/3009-1

SCHOOL FOR SIN
When Peggy leaves her country home behind for the bright lights of Dublin, her sensuous nature leads to her seduction by a stranger. He recruits her into a training school where no one knows what awaits them at graduation, but each student is sure to be well schooled in sex! $4.95/ 89-0

MY LIFE AND LOVES (THE 'LOST' VOLUME)
What happens when you try to fake a sequel to the most scandalous autobiography of the 20th century? If the "forgers" are two of the most important figures in modern erotica, you get a masterpiece, and THIS IS IT! One of the most thrilling forgeries in literature. $4.95/52-1

MARCUS VAN HELLER

TERROR
Another shocking exploration of lust by the author of the ever-popular *Adam & Eve*. Set in Paris during the Algerian War, *Terror* explores the place of sexual passion in a world drunk on violence. $5.95/247-7

KIDNAP
Private Investigator Harding is called in to investigate a mysterious kidnapping case involving the rich and powerful. Along the way he has the pleasure of "interrogating" an exotic dancer named Jeanne and a beautiful English reporter, as he finds himself enmeshed in the crime underworld. $4.95/90-4

LUSCIDIA WALLACE

KATY'S AWAKENING
Katy thinks she's been rescued after a terrible car wreck. Little does she suspect that she's been ensnared by a ring of swingers whose tastes run to domination and unimaginably depraved sex parties. With no means of escape, Katy becomes the newest initiate into this sick private club—much to her pleasure! $4.95/308-2

FOR SALE BY OWNER
Susie was overwhelmed by the lavishness of the yacht, the glamour of the guests. But she didn't know the plans they had for her: Sexual torture, training and sale into slavery! How many maids had been lured onto this floating prison? And how many gave as much pleasure as the newly wicked Susie? $4.95/3064-4

THE ICE MAIDEN
Edward Canton has ruthlessly seized everything he wants in life, with one exception: Rebecca Esterbrook. Frustrated by his inability to seduce her with money, he kidnaps her and whisks her away to his remote island compound, where she emerges as a writhing, red-hot love slave! $4.95/3001-6

DON WINSLOW

THE MANY PLEASURES OF IRONWOOD
Seven lovely young women are employed by The Ironwood Sportsmen's club for the entertainment of gentlemen. A small and exclusive club with seven carefully selected sexual connoisseurs, Ironwood is dedicated to the relentless pursuit of sensual pleasure. $5.95/310-4

CLAIRE'S GIRLS
You knew when she walked by that she was something special. She was one of Claire's girls, a woman carefully dressed and groomed to fill a role, to capture a look, to fit an image crafted by the sophisticated proprietress of an exclusive escort agency. High-class whores blow the roof off! $4.95/108-X

MASQUERADE BOOKS

GLORIA'S INDISCRETION
"He looked up at her. Gloria stood passively, her hands loosely at her sides, her eyes still closed, a dreamy expression on her face ... She sensed his hungry eyes on her, could almost feel his burning gaze on her body...." $4.95/3094-6

THE MASQUERADE READERS

THE COMPLETE EROTIC READER
The very best in erotic writing together in a wicked collection sure to stimulate even the most jaded and "sophisticated" palates. $4.95/3063-6

INTIMATE PLEASURES
Forbidden liaisons, bizarre public displays of carnality and insatiable cravings abound in these excerpts from six bestsellers. $4.95/38-6

THE VELVET TONGUE
An orgy of oral gratification! *The Velvet Tongue* celebrates the most mouthwatering, lip-smacking, tongue-twisting action. A feast of fellatio and *soixante-neuf* awaits readers of excellent taste at this steamy suck-fest. $4.95/3029-6

A MASQUERADE READER
Strict lessons are learned at the hand of *The English Governess*. Scandalous confessions are found in *The Diary of an Angel*, and the story of a woman whose desires drove her to the ultimate sacrifice in *Thongs* completes the collection. $4.95/84-X

THE CLASSIC COLLECTION

SCHOOL DAYS IN PARIS
The rapturous chronicles of a well-spent youth! Few Universities provide the profound and pleasurable lessons one learns in after-hours study—particularly if one is young and available, and lucky enough to have Paris as a playground. A stimulating look at the pursuits of young adulthood. $5.95/325-2

MAN WITH A MAID
The adventures of Jack and Alice have delighted readers for eight decades! A classic of its genre, *Man with a Maid* tells an outrageous tale of desire, revenge, and submission. Over 200,000 copies in print! $4.95/307-4

MAN WITH A MAID II
Jack's back! With the assistance of the perverse Alice, he embarks again on a trip through every erotic extreme. Jack leaves no one unsatisfied—least of all, himself, and Alice is always certain to outdo herself in her capacity to corrupt and control. An incendiary sequel! $4.95/3071-7

MAN WITH A MAID: The Conclusion
The final chapter in the epic saga of lust that has thrilled readers for decades. The adulterous woman who is corrected with enthusiasm and the maid who receives grueling guidance are just two who benefit from these lessons! Don't miss this conclusion to erotica's most famous tale. $4.95/3013-X

CONFESSIONS OF A CONCUBINE III: PLEASURE'S PRISONER
Filled with pulse-pounding excitement—including a daring escape from the harem and an encounter with an unspeakable sadist—*Pleasure's Prisoner* adds an unforgettable chapter to this thrilling confessional. $5.95/357-0

CONFESSIONS OF A CONCUBINE II: HAREM SLAVE
The concubinage continues, as the true pleasures and privileges of the harem are revealed. For the first time, readers are invited behind the veils that hide uninhibited, unimaginable pleasures from the world.... $4.95/226-4

CONFESSIONS OF A CONCUBINE
What *really* happens behind the plush walls of the harem? An inexperienced woman, captured and sentenced to service the royal pleasure, tells all in an outrageously unrestrained memoir. No affairs of state could match the passions of a young woman learning to relish a life of ceaseless sexual servitude. $4.95/154-3

MASQUERADE BOOKS

INITIATION RITES
Every naughty detail of a young woman's breaking in! Under the thorough tutelage of the perverse Miss Clara Birchem, Julia learns her wicked lessons well. During the course of her amorous studies, the resourceful young lady is joined by an assortment of lewd characters who contribute to her carnal education in unspeakable ways.... $4.95/120-9

TABLEAUX VIVANTS
Fifteen breathtaking tales of erotic passion. Upstanding ladies and gents soon adopt more comfortable positions, as wicked thoughts explode into sinfully scrumptious acts. $4.95/121-7

LADY F.
An uncensored tale of Victorian passions. Master Kidrodstock suffers deliciously at the hands of the stunningly cruel and sensuous Lady Flayskin—the only woman capable of taming his wayward impulses. $4.95/102-0

SACRED PASSIONS
Young Augustus comes into the heavenly sanctuary seeking protection from the enemies of his debt-ridden father. Within these walls he learns lessons he could never have imagined and soon concludes that the joys of the body far surpass those of the spirit. $4.95/21-1

PROTESTS, PLEASURES AND RAPTURES
Invited for an allegedly quiet weekend at a country Vicarage, a young woman is stunned to find herself surrounded by shocking acts of sexual sadism. Soon her curiosity is piqued, and she begins to explore her own capacities for cruelty—leading to an all-out search for an appropriately punishable partner. Latent depravity explodes! $4.95/204-3

CLASSIC EROTIC BIOGRAPHIES

JENNIFER III
The further adventures of erotica's most daring heroine. Jennifer, the quintessential beautiful blonde, has a photographer's eye for detail—particularly details of the masculine variety! A raging nymphomaniac! $5.95/292-2

JENNIFER AGAIN
One of contemporary erotica's hottest characters returns, in a sequel sure to blow you away. Once again, the insatiable Jennifer seizes the day—and extracts from it every last drop of sensual pleasure! $4.95/220-5

JENNIFER
From the bedroom of an internationally famous—and notoriously insatiable—dancer to an uninhibited ashram, *Jennifer* traces the exploits of one thoroughly modern woman. $4.95/107-1

ROSEMARY LANE *J.D. Hall*
The ups, downs, ins and outs of Rosemary Lane. Raised as the ward of Lord and Lady D'Arcy, after coming of age she discovers that her guardians' generosity is boundless—as they contribute to her carnal education! $4.95/3078-4

THE ROMANCES OF BLANCHE LA MARE
When Blanche loses her husband, it becomes clear she'll need a job. She sets her sights on the stage—and soon encounters a cast of lecherous characters intent on making her path to sucksess as hot and hard as possible! $4.95/101-2

THE FURTHER ADVENTURES OF MADELEINE
"What mortal pen can describe these driven orgasmic transports?" writes Madeleine as she explores Paris' sexual underground. She discovers that the finest clothes may cover the most twisted personalities of all—especially of mad monk Rasputin, whose sexual desires match even those of the wicked Madeleine! $4.95/04-1

MASQUERADE BOOKS

KATE PERCIVAL
Kate, the "Belle of Delaware," divulges the secrets of her scandalous life, from her earliest sexual experiments to the deviations she learns to love. Nothing is secret, and no holes barred in this titilating tell-all. $4.95/3072-5

THE AMERICAN COLLECTION

LUST *Palmiro Vicarion*
A wealthy and powerful man of leisure recounts his rise up the corporate ladder and his corresponding descent into debauchery. A tale of a classic scoundrel with an uncurbed appetite for sexual power! $4.95/82-3

WAYWARD *Peter Jason*
A mysterious countess hires a tour bus for an unusual vacation. Traveling through Europe's most notorious cities, she picks up friends, lovers, and acquaintances from every walk of life in pursuit of pleasure. $4.95/3004-0

LOVE'S ILLUSION
Elizabeth Renard yearned for the body of Dan Harrington. Then she discovers Harrington's secret weakness: a need to be humiliated and punished. She makes him her slave, and together they commence a journey into depravity that leaves nothing to the imagination—*nothing!* These two are a scandalously perfect match! $4.95/100-4

DANCE HALL GIRLS
The dance hall in Modesto was a ruthless trap for women of all ages. They learned to dance under the tutelage of sexual professionals. So grateful were they for the attention, they opened their hearts and their legs! Scandalous sexual slavery! $4.95/44-0

THE RELUCTANT CAPTIVE
Kidnapped by ruthless outlaws who kill her husband and burn their prosperous ranch, Sarah's journey takes her from the bordellos of the Wild West to the bedrooms of Boston, where she's bought by a stranger from her past. The ultimate eroticroad novel! $4.95/3022-9

A RICHARD KASAK BOOK

EDITED BY MICHAEL PERKINS

COMING UP: THE WORLD'S BEST EROTIC WRITING 1995
Author and critic Michael Perkins (*The Secret Record: Modern Erotic Literature, Evil Companions*) has scoured the field of erotic writing to produce this anthology sure to challenge the limits of even the most seasoned reader. Using the same sharp eye and transgressive instinct that have established him as America's leading commentator on sexually explicit fiction, Perkins here presents the cream of the current crop: a trend-setting, boundary-crashing bunch including such talents as Carol Queen, Samuel R. Delany, Maxim Jakubowski, and Lucy Taylor among many others. $12.95/370-8

CECILIA TAN, EDITOR

SM VISIONS
"Fabulous books! There's nothing else like them."
—Susie Bright, *Best American Erotica* and *Herotica 3*.
A volume of the very best speculative erotica available today. Circlet Press, the first publishing house to devote itself exclusively to the erotic science fiction and fantasy genre, is now represented by the best of its very best: *SM Visions*—sure to be one of the most thrilling and eye-opening rides through the erotic imagination ever published. $12.95/339-2

A RICHARD KASAK BOOK

FELICE PICANO
DRYLAND'S END
Set five thousand years in the future, *Dryland's End* takes place in a fabulous techno-empire ruled by intelligent, powerful women. While the Matriarchy has ruled for over two thousand years, and altered human language, thought and society, it is now unraveling. Military rivalries, religious fanaticism and economic competition threaten to destroy the empire from within—just as a rebellion also threatens human existence throughout the galaxy. $12.95/279-5

EDITED BY RANDY TUROFF
LESBIAN WORDS: State of the Art
One of the widest assortments of lesbian nonfiction writing in one revealing volume. Dorothy Allison, Jewelle Gomez, Judy Grahn, Eileen Myles, Robin Podolsky and many others are represented by some of their best work, looking at not only the current fashionability the media has brought to the lesbian "image," but important considerations of the lesbian past via historical inquiry and personal recollections. A fascinating, provocative volume, *Lesbian Words* is a virtual primer to contemporary trends in lesbian thought. $10.95/340-6

MICHAEL ROWE
WRITING BELOW THE BELT: Conversations with Erotic Authors
Journalist Michael Rowe interviewed the best erotic writers—both those well-known for their work in the field and those just starting out—and presents the collected wisdom in *Writing Below the Belt*. Rowe speaks frankly with cult favorites such as Pat Califia, crossover success stories like John Preston, and up-and-comers Michael Lowenthal and Will Leber. $19.95/363-5

EURYDICE
f/32
"Its wonderful to see a woman...celebrating her body and her sexuality by creating a fabulous and funny tale." —Kathy Acker

With the story of Ela (whose name is a pseudonym for orgasm), Eurydice won the National Fiction competition sponsored by Fiction Collective Two and Illinois State University. A funny, disturbing quest for unity, *f/32* prompted Frederic Tuten to proclaim "almost any page ... redeems us from the anemic writing and banalities we have endured in the past decade..." $10.95/350-3

LARRY TOWNSEND
ASK LARRY
Starting just before the onslaught of AIDS, Townsend wrote the "Leather Notebook" column for *Drummer* magazine. Now, readers can avail themselves of Townsend's collected wisdom as well as the author's contemporary commentary—a careful consideration of the way life has changed in the AIDS era. $12.95/289-2

RUSS KICK
OUTPOSTS:
A Catalog of Rare and Disturbing Alternative Information
A huge, authoritative guide to some of the most offbeat and bizarre publications available today! Rather than simply summarize the plethora of controversial opinions crowding the American scene, Kick has tracked down and compiledreviews of work penned by political extremists, conspiracy theorists, hallucinogenic pathfinders, sexual explorers, religious iconoclasts and social malcontents. Each review is followed by ordering information for the many readers sure to want these publications for themselves. $18.95/0202-8

A RICHARD KASAK BOOK

WILLIAM CARNEY
THE REAL THING

Carney gives us a good look at the mores and lifestyle of the first generation of gay leathermen. A chilling mystery/romance novel as well. —Pat Califia

With a new introduction by Michael Bronski. Out of print for years, *The Real Thing* has long served as a touchstone in any consideration of gay "edge fiction." First published in 1968, this uncompromising story of New York leathermen received instant acclaim. Out of print for years, *The Real Thing* returns, ready to thrill a new generation. $10.95/280-9

MICHAEL LASSELL
THE HARD WAY

Lassell is a master of the necessary word. In an age of tepid and whining verse, his bawdy and bittersweet songs are like a plunge in cold champagne. —Paul Monette

The first collection of renowned gay writer Michael Lassell's poetry, fiction and essays. As much a chronicle of post-Stonewall gay life as a compendium of a remarkable writer's work. $12.95/231-0

AMARANTHA KNIGHT, EDITOR
LOVE BITES

A volume of tales dedicated to legend's sexiest demon—the Vampire. Including such names as Ron Dee, Nancy A. Collins, Nancy Kilpatrick, Lois Tilton and David Aaron Clark, *Love Bites* is not only the finest collection of erotic horror available—but a virtual who's who of promising new talent. $12.95/234-5

LOOKING FOR MR. PRESTON

Edited by Laura Antoniou, *Looking for Mr. Preston* includes work by Lars Eighner, Pat Califia, Michael Bronski, Joan Nestle, and others who contributed interviews, essays and personal reminiscences of John Preston—a man whose career spanned the industry. Preston was the author of over twenty books, including *Franny, the Queen of Provincetown*, and *Mr. Benson*. He also edited the noted *Flesh and the Word* erotic anthologies, *Personal Dispatches: Writers Confront AIDS*, and *Hometowns*. Ten percent of the proceeds from sale of the book will go to the AIDS Project of Southern Maine. $23.95/288-4

MICHAEL LOWENTHAL, EDITOR
THE BEST OF THE BADBOYS

A collection of the best of Masquerade Books' phenomenally popular Badboy line of gay erotic writing. The very best of the leading Badboys is collected here, in this testament to the artistry that has catapulted these "outlaw" authors to bestselling status. John Preston, Aaron Travis, Larry Townsend, John Rowberry, Clay Caldwell and Lars Eighner are here represented by their most provocative writing. Michael Lowenthal both edited this remarkable collection and provides the Introduction. $12.95/233-7

GUILLERMO BOSCH
RAIN

An adult fairy tale, *Rain* takes place in a time when the mysteries of Eros are played out against a background of uncommon deprivation. The tale begins on the 1,537th day of drought—when one man comes to know the true depths of thirst. In a quest to sate his hunger for some knowledge of the wide world, he is taken through a series of extraordinary, unearthly encounters that promise to change not only his life, but the course of civilization around him. $12.95/232-9

A RICHARD KASAK BOOK

LUCY TAYLOR
UNNATURAL ACTS
"*A topnotch collection...*" —Science Fiction Chronicle

A remarkable debut volume from a provocative writer. **Unnatural Acts** plunges deep into the dark side of the psyche, far past all pleasantries and prohibitions, and brings to life a disturbing vision of erotic horror. Unrelenting angels and hungry gods play with souls and bodies in Taylor's murky cosmos: where heaven and hell are merely differences of perspective; where redemption and damnation lie behind the same shocking acts. $12.95/181-0

SAMUEL R. DELANY
THE MAD MAN
For his thesis, graduate student John Marr researches the life and work of the brilliant Timothy Hasler: a philosopher whose career was cut tragically short over a decade earlier. Marr encounters numerous obstacles, as other researchers turn up evidence of Hasler's personal life that is deemed simply too unpleasant. Marr soon begins to believe that Hasler's death might hold some key to his own life as a gay man in the age of AIDS.

What Delany has done here is take the ideas of Marquis de Sade one step further, by filtering extreme and obsessive sexual behavior through the sieve of post-modern experience....
—Lambda Book Report

Delany develops an insightful dichotomy between [his protagonist]'s two worlds: the one of cerebral philosophy and dry academia, the other of heedless, 'impersonal' obsessive sexual extremism. When these worlds finally collide ... the novel achieves a surprisingly satisfying resolution....
—Publishers Weekly $23.95/193-4

THE MOTION OF LIGHT IN WATER
"*A very moving, intensely fascinating literary biography from an extraordinary writer. Thoroughly admirable candor and luminous stylistic precision; the artist as a young man and a memorable picture of an age.*"   —William Gibson

Award-winning author Samuel R. Delany's riveting autobiography covers the early years of one of science fiction's most important voices. Delany paints a vivid and compelling picture of New York's East Village in the early '60s—a time of unprecedented social transformation. **The Motion of Light in Water** traces the roots of one of America's most innovative writers. $12.95/133-0

KATHLEEN K.
SWEET TALKERS
Kathleen K. opens up her diary for a rare peek at the day-to-day life of a phone sex operator—and reveals a number of secrets and surprises. Because far from being a sleazy, underground scam, the service Kathleen provides often speaks to the lives of its customers with a directness and compassion they receive nowhere else. $12.95/192-6

ROBERT PATRICK
TEMPLE SLAVE
...you must read this book.
—Quentin Crisp

This is nothing less than the secret history of the most theatrical of theaters, the most bohemian of Americans and the most knowing of queens. Patrick writes with a lush and witty abandon, as if this departure from the crafting of plays has energized him. **Temple Slave** *is also one of the best ways to learn what it was like to be fabulous, gay, theatrical and loved in a time at once more and less dangerous to gay life than our own.* —Genre

Temple Slave tells the story of the Espresso Buono—the archetypal alternative performance space—and the talents who called it home. $12.95/191-8

A RICHARD KASAK BOOK

DAVID MELTZER

THE AGENCY TRILOGY

...'The Agency' is clearly Meltzer's paradigm of society; a mindless machine of which we are all 'agents' including those whom the machine supposedly serves.... —Norman Spinrad

With the Essex House edition of *The Agency* in 1968, the highly regarded poet David Meltzer took America on a trip into a hell of unbridled sexuality. The story of a supersecret, Orwellian sexual network, *The Agency* explored issues of erotic dominance and submission with an immediacy and frankness previously unheard of in American literature, as well as presented a vision of an America consumed and dehumanized by a lust for power. $12.95/216-7

SKIN TWO

THE BEST OF *SKIN TWO* Edited by Tim Woodward

For over a decade, *Skin Two* has served the international fetish community as a groundbreaking journal from the crossroads of sexuality, fashion, and art, *Skin Two* specializes in provocative, challenging essays by the finest writers working in the "radical sex" scene. Collected here are the articles and interviews that established the magazine's reputation. Including interviews with cult figures Tim Burton, Clive Barker and Jean Paul Gaultier. $12.95/130-6

CARO SOLES

MELTDOWN!
An Anthology of Erotic Science Fiction and Dark Fantasy for Gay Men

Editor Caro Soles has put together one of the most explosive collections of gay erotic writing ever published. *Meltdown!* contains the very best examples of this increasingly popular sub-genre: stories meant to shock and delight, to send a shiver down the spine and start a fire down below. An extraordinary volume, *Meltdown!* presents both new voices and provocative pieces by world-famous writers Edmund White and Samuel R. Delany. $12.95/203-5

JOHN PRESTON

MY LIFE AS A PORNOGRAPHER
And Other Indecent Acts

...essential and enlightening...His sex-positive stand on safer-sex education as the only truly effective AIDS-prevention strategy will certainly not win him any conservative converts, but AIDS activists will be shouting their assent.... [My Life as a Pornographer] is a bridge from the sexually liberated 1970s to the more cautious 1990s, and Preston has walked much of that way as a standard-bearer to the cause for equal rights.... —*Library Journal*

My Life as a Pornographer...*is not pornography, but rather reflections upon the writing and production of it. In a deeply sex-phobic world, Preston has never shied away from a vision of the redemptive potential of the erotic drive. Better than perhaps anyone in our community, Preston knows how physical joy can bridge differences and make us well.*
—*Lambda Book Report* $12.95/135-7

HUSTLING:
A Gentleman's Guide to the Fine Art of Homosexual Prostitution

John Preston solicited the advice of "working boys" from across the country in his effort to produce the ultimate guide to the hustler's world.

...fun and highly literary. What more could you expect from such an accomplished activist, author and editor? —*Drummer* $12.95/137-3

A RICHARD KASAK BOOK

BIZARRE SEX

BIZARRE SEX AND OTHER CRIMES OF PASSION
Edited by Stan Tal

From the pages of *Bizarre Sex*: Over twenty small masterpieces of erotic shock make this one of the year's most unexpectedly alluring anthologies. This incredible volume, edited by Stan Tal, including such masters of erotic horror and fantasy as Edward Lee, Lucy Taylor and Nancy Kilpatrick, ***Bizarre Sex and Other Crimes of Passion***, is a treasure-trove of arousing chills. The perfect accompaniment for a dark and stormy night. $12.95/213-2

PAT CALIFIA

SENSUOUS MAGIC

A new classic, destined to grace the shelves of anyone interested in contemporary sexuality.

Sensuous Magic is clear, succinct and engaging even for the reader for whom S/M isn't the sexual behavior of choice.... Califia's prose is soothing, informative and non-judgmental—she both instructs her reader and explores the territory for them.... When she is writing about the dynamics of sex and the technical aspects of it, Califia is the Dr. Ruth of the alternative sexuality set.... —Lambda Book Report

Don't take a dangerous trip into the unknown—buy this book and know where you're going! —SKIN TWO $12.95/131-4

LARS EIGHNER

ELEMENTS OF AROUSAL

Acclaimed gay writer Lars Eighner develops a guideline for success with one of publishing's best kept secrets: the novice-friendly field of gay erotic writing. In *Elements of Arousal*, Eighner details his craft, providing the reader with sure advice. Because *Elements of Arousal* is about the application and honing of the writer's craft, which brought Eighner fame with not only the steamy *Bayou Boy*, but the illuminating *Travels with Lizbeth*. $12.95/230-2

MICHAEL PERKINS

THE GOOD PARTS: An Uncensored Guide to Literary Sexuality

Michael Perkins, one of America's only critics to regularly scrutinize sexual literature, presents sex as seen in the pages of over 100 major volumes from the past twenty years. *The Good Parts* takes an uncensored look at the complex issues of sexuality investigated by so much modern literature. $12.95/186-1

GAUNTLET

THE BEST OF *GAUNTLET* Edited by Barry Hoffman

Gauntlet has, with its semi-annual issues, taken on such explosive topics as race, pornography, political correctness, and media manipulation—always publishing the widest possible range of opinions. Only in *Gauntlet* might one expect to encounter Phyllis Schlafley *and* Annie Sprinkle, Stephen King *and* Madonna—often within pages of one another. The most provocative articles have been gathered by editor-in-chief Barry Hoffman, to make *The Best of Gauntlet* a riveting exploration of American society's limits. $12.95/202-7

MARCO VASSI

THE STONED APOCALYPSE

"...Marco Vassi is our champion sexual energist."—VLS

During his lifetime, Marco Vassi was hailed as America's premier erotic writer. His reputation was worldwide. *The Stoned Apocalypse* is Vassi's autobiography, financed by his other groundbreaking erotic writing. $12.95/132-2

A RICHARD KASAK BOOK

A DRIVING PASSION
While the late Marco Vassi was primarily known and respected as a novelist, he was also an effective and compelling speaker. *A Driving Passion* collects the wit and insight Vassi brought to his lectures, and distills the philosophy—including the concept of Metasex—that made him an underground sensation. $12.95/134-9

THE EROTIC COMEDIES
A collection of stories from America's premier erotic philosopher. Marco Vassi was a dedicated iconoclast, and *The Erotic Comedies* marked a high point in his literary career. Also includes his groundbreaking writings on the Erotic Experience, including the concept of Metasex—the premises of which were derived from the author's own unbelievable experiences. $12.95/136-5

THE SALINE SOLUTION
During the Sexual Revolution, Marco Vassi established himself as an intrepid explorer of an uncharted sexual landscape. During this time he also distinguished himself as a novelist, producing *The Saline Solution* to great acclaim. Vassi examines the dangers of intimacy in an age of freedom. $12.95/180-2

CHEA VILLANUEVA

JESSIE'S SONG
"It conjures up the strobe-light confusion and excitement of urban dyke life, moving fast and all over the place, from NYC to Tucson to Miami to the Philippines; and from true love to wild orgies to swearing eternal celibacy and back. Told in letters, mainly about the wandering heart (and tongue) of writer and free spirit Pearly Does; written mainly by Mae-Mae Might, a sharp, down-to-earth but innocent-hearted Black Femme. Read about these dykes and you'll love them." —Rebecca Ripley
Based largely upon her own experience, Villanueva's work is remarkable for its frankness, and delightful in its iconoclasm. Widely published in the alternative press, Villanueva is a writer to watch. Toeing no line, *Jessie's Song* is certain to redefine all notions of "mainstream" lesbian writing, and provide a reading experience quite unlike any other this year. $9.95/235-3

SHAR REDNOUR, EDITOR

VIRGIN TERRITORY
An anthology of writing by women about their first-time erotic experiences with other women. From the longings and ecstasies of awakening dykes to the sometimes awkward pleasures of sexual experimentation on the edge, each of these true stories reveals a different, radical perspective on one of the most traditional subjects around: virginity. Included in this daring volume are such cult favorites as Susie Bright, Shannon Bell, Bayla Travis, Carol Queen, Lisa Palac and others. $12.95/238-8

BADBOY BOOKS

FRINGE BENEFITS Bert McKenzie
From the pen of a widely published short story writer comes a volume of highly immodest tales. Not afraid of getting down and dirty, McKenzie produces some of today's most visceral sextales. Learn the real benefits of working long and hard.... $5.95/354-6

FLEDERFICTION: Stories of Men and Torture Fledermaus
Fifteen blistering paeans to men and their suffering. Notorious for his unrelenting tales of lust and its consequences, Fledermaus unleashes his most thrilling tales of punishment in this special volume designed with Badboy readers in mind. No less an authority than Larry Townsend introduces this volume of Fledermaus' best work. $5.95/355-4

BADBOY BOOKS

CABIN FEVER and Other Stories *Donald Vining*
Eighteen blistering stories in celebration of the most intimate of male bonding. From Native Americans to Buckingham Palace sentries, suburban husbands to kickass bikers, *Cabin Fever* shows the many faces of male desire. Time after time, Donald Vining's men succumb to nature, and reaffirm both love and lust in modern gay life. $5.95/338-4

THE JOY SPOT *Phil Andros*
"Andros gives to the gay mind what Tom of Finland gives the gay eye—this is archetypal stuff. There's none better." —**John F. Karr, Manifest Reader**
A classic from one of the founding fathers of gay porn. *The Joy Spot* looks at some of Andros' favorite types—cops, servicemen, truck drivers—and the sleaze they love. Nothing's too rough, and these men are always ready. So get ready to give it up—or have it taken by force! $5.95/301-5

THE ROPE ABOVE, THE BED BELOW *Jason Fury*
The irresistible Jason Fury returns! Once again, our built, blond hero finds himself in the oddest—and most compromising—positions imaginable. And his combination of heat and heart has made him one of gay erotica's most distinctive voices. $4.95/269-8

SUBMISSION HOLDS *Key Lincoln*
A bright talent unleashes his first collection of gay erotica. From tough to tender, the men between these covers stop at nothing to get what they want. These sweat-soaked tales show just how bad boys can get.... $4.95/266-3

SKIN DEEP *Bob Vickery*
Skin Deep contains so many varied beauties no one will go away unsatisfied. From Daddy's Boys to horny go-go studs, no tantalizing morsel of manflesh is overlooked—or left unexplored! Beauty may be only skin deep, but a handful of beautiful skin is a tempting proposition. $4.95/265-5

ANIMAL HANDLERS *Jay Shaffer*
Hot on the tails of the bestselling *Wet Dreams*, *Full Service* and *Shooters* comes another volume from a master of scorching fiction. In Shaffer's world, each and every man finally succumbs to the animal urges deep inside. And if there's any creature that promises a wild time, it's a beast who's been caged for far too long.... $4.95/264-7

RAHM *Tom Bacchus*
A volume spanning the many ages of hardcore queer lust—from Creation to the modern day. The overheated imagination of Tom Bacchus brings to life an extraordinary assortment of characters, from the Father of Us All to the cowpoke next door, the early gay literati to rude, queercore mosh rats. No one is better than Bacchus at staking out sexual territory with a swagger and a sly grin. $5.95/315-5

REVOLT OF THE NAKED *D. V. Sadero*
In a distant galaxy, there are two classes of humans: Freemen and Nakeds. Freemen are full citizens in this system, which allows for the buying and selling of Nakeds at whim. Nakeds live only to serve their Masters, and obey every sexual order with haste and devotion. Until the day of revolution—when an army of sex toys rises in anger.... $4.95/261-2

WHiPs *Victor Terry*
Connoisseurs of gay writing have known Victor Terry's work for some time. With *WHiPs*, Terry joins Badboy's roster at last. Cruising for a hot man? You'd better be, because one way or another, these WHiPs—officers of the Wyoming Highway Patrol—are gonna pull you over for a little impromptu interrogation.... $4.95/254-X

BADBOY BOOKS

PRISONERS OF TORQUEMADA *Torsten Barring*
The infamously unsparing Torsten Barring (*The Switch, Peter Thornwell, Shadowman*) weighs in with another volume sure to push you over the edge. How cruel *is* the "therapy" practiced at Casa Torquemada? Rest assured that Barring is just the writer to evoke such steamy malevolence. $4.95/252-3

SORRY I ASKED *Dave Kinnick*
The gay world's favorite working boys—up close and very personal! Unexpurgated interviews with gay porn's rank and file. Haven't you wondered what it's like to be in porn pictures? Kinnick, video reviewer for *Advocate Men*, gets personal with the guys behind (and under) the "stars," and reveals the dirt and details of the porn business. A must-read, from a writer and journalist more than qualified to get beneath the skin of today's busiest badboys.
$4.95/3090-3

THE SEXPERT *Edited by Pat Califia*
For many years now, the sophisticated gay man has known that he can turn to one authority for answers to virtually any question on the subject of man-to-man intimacy and sexual performance. Straight from the pages of *Advocate Men* comes The Sexpert! From penis size to toy care, bar behavior to AIDS awareness, The Sexpert responds to real concerns with uncanny wisdom and a razor wit. $4.95/3034-2

ERIC BOYD

MIKE AND ME
Mike joined the college gym squad to bulk up on muscle and enjoy the competition. Little did he know he'd be turning on every muscle jock in southern Minnesota! Hard bodies collide in a series of workouts designed to generate a lot more than rips and cuts. $5.95/419-4

MIKE AND THE MARINES
At long last—the further adventures of muscular Mike! *Mike and Me* was one of Badboy's earliest hits, and now the many readers who devoured Mike's college exploits can revel in another sexy extravaganza. This time, Mike takes on America's most elite corps of studs—running into more than a few good men!
$5.95/347-3

DEREK ADAMS

MY DOUBLE LIFE
Every man leads a double life, dividing his hours between the mundanities of the day and the outrageous pursuits of the night. In this, his second collection of stories, the author of *Boy Toy* and creator of sexy P.I. Miles Diamond shines a little light on what men do when no one's looking. Derek Adams proves, once again, that he's the ultimate chronicler of our wicked ways. $5.95/314-7

BOY TOY
Poor Brendan Callan—sent to the Brentwood Academy against his will, he soon finds himself the guinea pig of a crazed geneticist. Brendan becomes irresistibly alluring—a talent designed for endless pleasure, but coveted by others with the most unsavory motives.... $4.95/260-4

CLAY CALDWELL

ASK OL' BUDDY
One of this legendary author's most popular titles. Set in the underground SM world, Caldwell takes you on a journey of discovery—where men initiate one another into the secrets of the rawest sex of all. And when each stud's initiation is complete, he takes his places among the masters—eager to take part in the training of another hungry soul... $5.95/346-5

BADBOY BOOKS

SERVICE, STUD
The setting is the Los Angeles of a distant future. Here the all-male populace is divided between the served and the servants—an arrangement guaranteeing the erotic satisfaction of all involved.. $5.95/336-8

STUD SHORTS
"If anything, Caldwell's charm is more powerful, his nostalgia more poignant, the horniness he captures more sweetly, achingly acute than ever."
—*Aaron Travis*

A new collection of this legendary writer's latest sex-fiction. With his customary candor, Caldwell tells all about cops, cadets, truckers, farmboys (and many more) in these dirty jewels. $5.95/320-1

QUEERS LIKE US
A very special delivery from one of gay erotica's premier talents. For years the name Clay Caldwell has been synonymous with the hottest, most finely crafted gay tales available. *Queers Like Us* is one of his best: the story of a randy mailman's trek through a landscape of willing, available studs. $4.95/262-0

CLAY CALDWELL/LARS EIGHNER

QSFx2
A volume of the wickedest, wildest, other-worldliest yarns from two master storytellers. Caldwell and Eighner take a trip to the furthest reaches of the sexual imagination, sending back stories proving that as much as things change, one thing will always remain the same.... $5.95/278-7

LARS EIGHNER

WHISPERED IN THE DARK
Hailed by critics, Eighner continues to produce gay fiction whose quality rivals the best in the genre. *Whispered in the Dark* demonstrates Eighner's unique combination of strengths: poetic descriptive power, an unfailing ear for dialogue, and a finely tuned feeling for the nuances of male passion. $5.95/286-8

AMERICAN PRELUDE
Praised by the *New York Times*, Eighner is widely recognized as one of our best, most exciting gay writers. What the *Times* won't admit, however, is that he is also one of gay erotica's true masters. Scalding heat blends with wry emotion in this red-blooded bedside volume. $4.95/170-5

DAVID LAURENTS, EDITOR

WANDERLUST: HOMOEROTIC TALES OF TRAVEL
A volume dedicated to the special pleasures of faraway places. Gay men have always had a special interest in travel—and not only for the scenic vistas. *Wanderlust* celebrates the freedom of the open road, and the allure of men who stray from the path.... $5.95/395-3

THE BADBOY BOOK OF EROTIC POETRY
Over fifty of gay literature's biggest talents are here represented by their hottest verse. Erotic poetry has long been considered the *enfant terrible* of serious literature. *The Badboy Book of Erotic Poetry* aims at rectifying this situation; both learned and stimulating, it restores eros to its rightful place of honor in contemporary gay writing. $5.95/382-1

LARRY TOWNSEND

BEWARE THE GOD WHO SMILES
A torrid time-travel tale from one of gay erotica's most notorious writers. Two lusty young Americans are transported to ancient Egypt—where they are taken as slaves by marauding barbarians. $5.95/321-X

ORDERING IS EASY!

MC/VISA orders can be placed by calling our toll-free number
PHONE 800-375-2356 / FAX 212 986-7355
or mail this coupon to:
MASQUERADE BOOKS
DEPT. W74A, 801 2ND AVE., NY, NY 10017

BUY ANY FOUR BOOKS AND CHOOSE ONE ADDITIONAL BOOK, OF EQUAL OR LESSER VALUE, AS YOUR FREE GIFT.

QTY.	TITLE	NO.	PRICE
			FREE
			FREE

W74A

SUBTOTAL

POSTAGE and HANDLING

We Never Sell, Give or Trade Any Customer's Name. **TOTAL**

In the U.S., please add $1.50 for the first book and 75¢ for each additional book; in Canada, add $2.00 for the first book and $1.25 for each additional book. Foreign countries: add $4.00 for the first book and $2.00 for each additional book. No C.O.D. orders. Please make all checks payable to Masquerade Books. Payable in U.S. currency only. New York state residents add 8¼% sales tax. Please allow 4-6 weeks delivery.

NAME _____

ADDRESS _____

CITY _____ STATE _____ ZIP _____

TEL ( ) _____

PAYMENT: ☐ CHECK ☐ MONEY ORDER ☐ VISA ☐ MC

CARD NO. _____ EXP. DATE _____

BADBOY BOOKS

RUN, LITTLE LEATHER BOY
The classic story of one man's sexual awakening. A chronic underachiever, Wayne seems to be going nowhere. When he is sent abroad, Wayne soon finds himself bored with the everyday and increasingly drawn to the masculine intensity of a dark sexual underground. $4.95/143-8

SEXUAL ADV. OF SHERLOCK HOLMES
What Conan Doyle didn't know about the legendary sleuth. Holmes's most satisfying adventures, from the unexpurgated memoirs of the faithful Mr. Watson. "A Study in Scarlet" is transformed to expose Mrs. Hudson as a man in drag, the Diogenes Club as an S/M arena, and clues only Sherlock Holmes could piece together. $4.95/3097-0

AARON TRAVIS

BIG SHOTS
Two fierce tales in one electrifying volume. In *Beirut*, Travis tells the story of ultimate military power and erotic subjugation; *Kip*, Travis' hypersexed and sinister take on film noir, appears in unexpurgated form for the first time. $4.95/112-8

SLAVES OF THE EMPIRE
"[A] wonderful mythic tale. Set against the backdrop of the exotic and powerful Roman Empire, this wonderfully written novel explores the timeless questions of light and dark in male sexuality. Travis has shown himself expert in manipulating the most primal themes and images. The locale may be the ancient world, but these are the slaves and masters of our time...."
—John Preston $4.95/3054-7

JOHN PRESTON

TALES FROM THE DARK LORD
Twelve stunning works from the man called "the Dark Lord of gay erotica." The ritual of lust and surrender is explored in all its manifestations in this triumph of authority and vision from the Dark Lord! $5.95/323-6

MR. BENSON
A classic novel from a time when there was no limit to what a man could dream of doing. Jamie is led down the path of erotic enlightenment by the magnificent Mr. Benson, learning to accept cruelty as love, anguish as affection, and this man as his master. $4.95/3041-5

MAX EXANDER

DEEDS OF THE NIGHT: Tales of Eros and Passion
From the man behind *Mansex* and *Leathersex*—two whirlwind tours of the hypermasculine libido—comes another unrestrained volume of sweat-soaked fantasies. $5.95/348-1

HARD CANDY

RED JORDAN AROBATEAU

DIRTY PICTURES
"[Arobateau]'s a natural—raw talent that is seething, passionate, hard, remarkable." —Lillian Faderman, editor of *Chloe Plus Olivia: An Anthology of Lesbian Literature from the 17th Century to the Present*
Another red-hot tale from lesbian sensation Red Jordan Arobateau. *Dirty Pictures* tells the story of a lonely butch tending bar—and the femme she finally calls her own. With the same precision that made *Lucy and Mickey* a breakout debut, Arobateau tells a love story that's the flip-side of "lesbian chic." Not to be missed. $5.95/345-7